F ar, far, away, although not altogether over the rainbow), a picture book bl surely be a glorious day. Beautifully ir the ether, drifting endlessly on a faint L_____.

It was absolutely the last place that one might expect to see the soaring, silent shape of a pirate galleon, and yet there one floated, bold as brass. Or more specifically, bold as wood and brass. It hung in the air, like a resounding punch in the face of gravity, and carved wispy swathes through the cumulonimbii which surrounded it.

Though the sun shone large and bright in the heavens, the deck sat in shadow. A large, bird shaped shadow to be exact. Small forms scurried from port to starboard beneath the mighty sails, and high above them in the rigging, the caster of the shadow gripped the central mast in massive claws. The giant metallic bird hovered in mid-air, holding the ship in its grasp.

One of the diminutive figures below stood at the ship's bow, peering through a small, brass telescope at something off in the distance beneath them. This was not your standard, common or garden, run of the mill something, however. It was large, had no discernable shape, and gave off a bright orange glow. Given that it was the most unusual thing in a skyline already populated by a massive floating pirate ship, it certainly merited closer inspection.

The galleon shifted, angling towards the twinkling anomaly and descending out of the sky. The light expanded, bursting outwards and filling the horizon up ahead, and the telescope wielder on deck whistled excitedly.

"What is it?" A voice from the deck behind him asked.

Lowering the telescope from his one good eye, Timbers, captain of the Flying Fathom, shook his head, a mischievous grin spreading across his face. "I have no idea, but it's shiny. Let's go take a looksee."

THE FATHOM FLIES AGAIN

by JAMES WALLEY

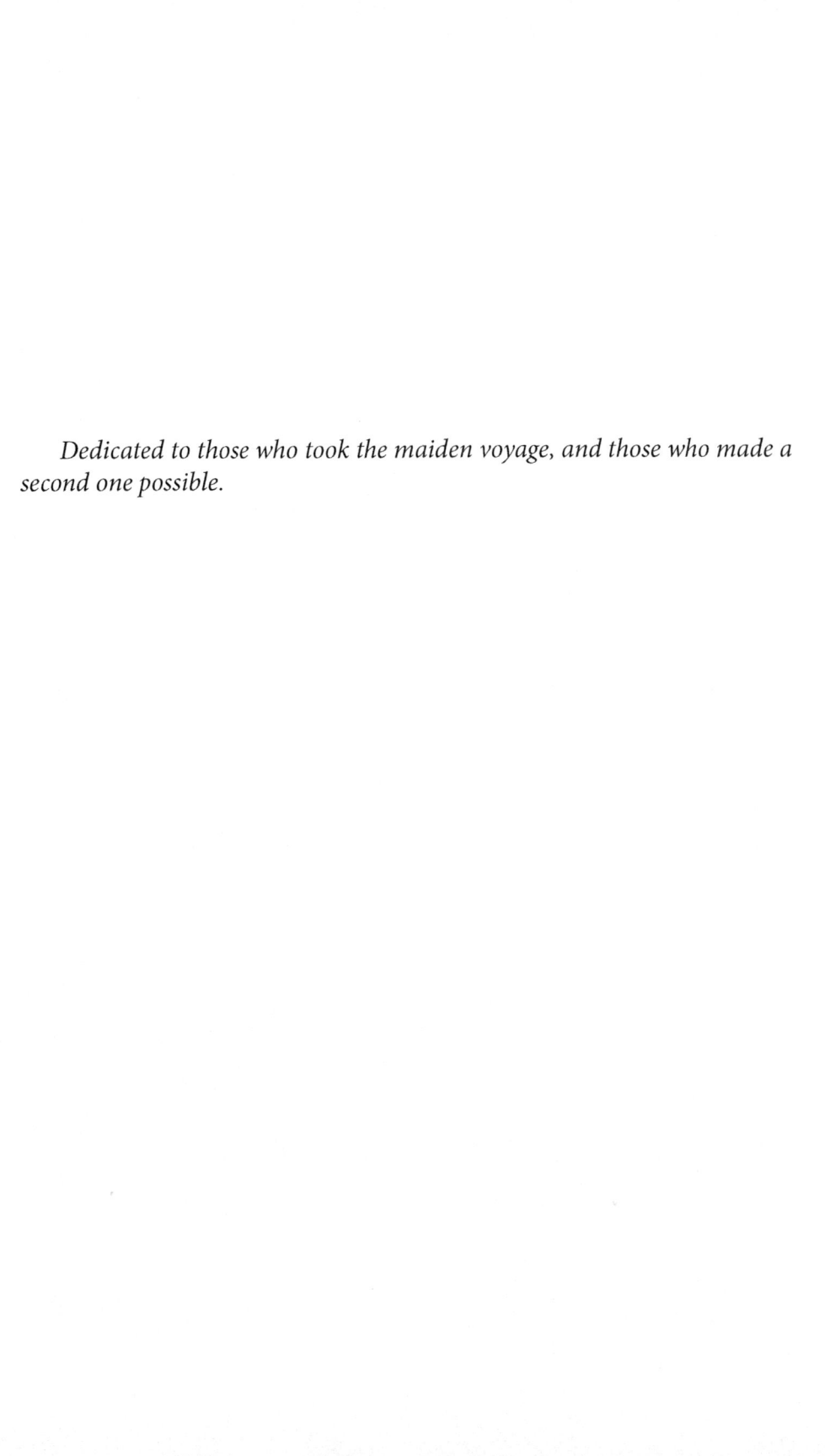

Dedicated to those who took the maiden voyage, and those who made a second one possible.

Chapter One

Oddly enough, it wasn't a dark and stormy night, as may have been befitting of a tiny figure's midnight scuttle across the gloomy landing to his parents' room.

Only two things were likely to prompt a seven year-old to make the ominous journey out of his bedroom and into the night: either too much juice before bed had led to an urgent visit to the bathroom, or there was a monster under the bed.

Worryingly for little Terence, it had been the latter.

He tried to convince himself it had been a trick of the light, which probably would have carried some weight, had there *been* any light. He had awoken to a soft click, as the dim glow from the nightlight at his bedside extinguished, and the goblins in his head came out to play. Except they weren't in his head. He could hear them, skulking beneath his bed, scurrying, even whispering? Maybe he hadn't needed to go to the bathroom, but this new, alien sound beneath him had certainly given his bladder a little squeeze.

He cast a nervous glance back towards his bedroom door. It was ajar, but thankfully absent of boogeymen. He rapped softly on his parents' door.

"There's a monster under my bed." He quivered as his dad appeared, disheveled and half asleep before him. Dad rubbed his eyes, focusing on the meek figure before him, and put a hand on Terence's head. "It's just a nightmare, buddy. Go back to sleep." He smiled and yawned, already heading back to bed, almost oblivious to his son's protests.

Why does nobody listen to the kid? Terence wondered, realizing that he now had to go back into that dark room and battle the monster alone. Battle, of course being little boy code for 'leap onto your bed and hide beneath the covers', and in three skipping steps, Terence landed on his mattress, throwing the protective blankety shield up for protection. Clutching his teddy bear in the darkness, he wished that the little toy would somehow come to life, protecting him and standing up to the unseen bully beneath. "Stupid," he whispered. "Toys can't do that." He shifted under his flannel barrier. "It was just a dream," he chided, clutching Captain Fluffbags tighter anyway.

There was a faint hiss from under the bed, almost inaudible, and for a moment, Terence thought it was his own fear, flatulently getting the better of him. He sat upright, the covers sliding from him. He hadn't had nachos for supper, so the phantom chuckle couldn't have been his own doing. Again, it gurgled, almost contentedly, smugly, from below. Thrusting Captain Fluffbags out in self-defense, Terence closed his eyes tightly against what was now definitely not a gaseous intruder.

"You moved." A voice churned out from beneath the bed, like steam escaping from some kind of despicable kettle. "That means you're it," it rasped, the words arriving like intangible vapors on the night air. Clenched eyelids popped open as a decidedly real looking shadow fell over Terence. There was an instant flurry of activity, masked by the midnight gloom, followed by an instant stillness. There was nothing more to mask, but the gloom remained, probably wishing that it had been a dark and stormy night, to enhance the atmosphere.

Captain Fluffbags stared cheerfully up at the ceiling, as the room fell into an eerie silence. An empty, Terence-less silence.

Joe was drunk. Not the kind of drunk where one might proposition a long-suffering bar maid or commandeer a traffic cone for one's own nefarious purposes, but blind, can't-find-your-own-face, hammered. He stumbled out of the dingy bar, struggling to remember how many feet he had. An imminent, onrushing hangover was heading straight for him, and it tasted like the bottom of a garbage can in an alley, possibly because he had just fallen *into* a garbage can in an alley. Hangovers have such a way of finding the wayward over-indulger.

The ground, and how to operate it, was becoming rapidly more alien with each lurching step. Joe hunched over. Hands on thighs, he waiting for the world to stop wobbling. "Ugh," he managed, gagging as his stomach threatened to mutiny. "There'll be beer monkeys in the morning."

Realizing that morning was already fast approaching, he breathed a silent prayer and began the long stagger home. The first order of business would have to be negotiating the alleyway, into which he had arrived through no conscious thought or intent. Perhaps the grinning figure who peered out from behind a pile of stacked beer crates would be gracious enough to help. Of course, Joe wasn't about to question what a leering stranger was doing here in the middle of the night or why he was all painted up like a mime from hell.

The mystery alley-dweller stepped forward, and Joe almost laughed out loud. It was a clown. The laugh may have upgraded from surprised to amused, had the thing standing before him not been so utterly horrendous. It seemed contorted and unnatural, and worse, it was approaching. Two more garish figures appeared behind the ghastly joker, filing in and making their way towards the puzzled drunkard. Rooted to the spot, Joe made a stab at convincing himself that he was seeing double, or in this case, triple. Even if that were the case, it didn't belie the fact that he faced something he didn't even want to see one of. He tried to move, somehow lurch back the way he had come, but his legs were full of beer and sloshed uncooperatively, skewing him sideways. With no other option available, Joe landed in a boozy heap, staring blearily up as white gloved hands grasped for him.

As the hellish circus troupe dragged him slowly back into the darkness of the alley, two thoughts occurred to Joe. His dear old mum had been right, the sauce was going to be the death of him, and for once, the beer monkeys didn't seem such a bad option.

Far, far, away, although not altogether that far really (certainly not over the rainbow), a picture book blue sky heralded what would surely be a glorious day. Beautifully intricate clouds hung high in the ether, drifting endlessly on a faint breeze.

It was absolutely the last place that one might expect to see the soaring, silent shape of a pirate galleon, and yet there one floated, bold as brass. Or more specifically, bold as wood and brass. It hung in the air, like a resounding punch in the face of gravity, and carved wispy swathes through the cumulonimbii which surrounded it. Though the sun shone large and bright in the heavens, the deck sat in shadow. A large, bird shaped shadow to be exact. Small forms scurried from port to starboard beneath the mighty sails, and high above them in the rigging, the caster of the shadow gripped the central mast in massive claws. The giant metallic bird hovered in mid-air, holding the ship in its grasp.

One of the diminutive figures below stood at the ship's bow, peering through a small, brass telescope at something off in the distance beneath them. This was not your standard, common or garden, run of the mill something, however. It was large, had no discernable shape, and gave off a bright orange glow. Given that it was the most unusual thing in a skyline already populated by a massive floating pirate ship, it certainly merited closer inspection.

The galleon shifted, angling towards the twinkling anomaly and descending out of the sky. The light expanded, bursting outwards and filling the horizon up ahead, and the telescope wielder on deck whistled excitedly.

"What is it?" A voice from the deck behind him asked.

Lowering the telescope from his one good eye, Timbers, captain of the Flying *Fathom*, shook his head, a mischievous grin spreading across his face. "I have no idea, but it's shiny. Let's go take a looksee."

Heaving forward, they vaulted recklessly into the center of the sparkling vortex. High up in the rigging, the huge steel bird shot out a robotic squawk as the *Fathom* disappeared into the blinding light, plunging through, but not out, the other side.

Mysterious portals tend to be funny like that.

Chapter Two

Harvey the Space Beagle nonchalantly reached up and yanked his own head off. Sprouting out from beneath, a Marty-shaped face sighed as it was reintroduced to the night air. Bringing joy, and occasionally confused terror to hundreds of children was decidedly stuffy, and lacked adequate toilet facilities.

Marty pulled the cord attached to the zipper on his back, and the oversized space suit fell to the ground, delivering yet more relief. It wasn't compulsory to wear clothes under the giant fluffy suits that paraded around Stellar Island all day, but Marty felt that some dignity needed to be upheld. What if he got into an accident, and was forced to evacuate the suit in a hurry? "Hi, kids, behold Harvey's tighty whities!" No, it just wouldn't do, and so he suffered for his art.

The dim light in the changing rooms was still bright enough to cause him to squint, having been behelmeted all day, and it took a moment for his eyes to adjust. This was the unseen backstage of Stellar Island. Metal lockers spanned the walls, and low wooden benches gave the pretense that management gave a damn about the monkeys in their employ. High up in one of the halogen light fittings, a moth decided to grace Marty with its presence and flitted redundantly, casting shadows into the stark, paltry chamber. Disneyland, this was not.

Flitting less airily, but no less annoyingly, Geoffrey entered the room. He was the guy that crops up in every office, who one has to converse with out of necessity, but probably wouldn't be top of anyone's list of people to save from a burning building. Geoffrey shrugged off the Cosmo Badger suit he was wearing, and sidled over to Marty, who was doing his best 'not here' impression in an attempt to avoid detection.

"Marty!" He yelled, way too loudly. "You're pulling the graveyard shift too, huh?"

Marty nodded, not wishing to add fuel to a conversation which was already threatening to become a fire hazard, although in truth, nothing had come close to setting off the sprinklers lately. When you've spent time sailing through the skies with miniature buccaneers, battled freaks on pogo sticks and rubbed shoulders with superheroes, everyday life seemed to range from gray, to slightly less gray.

"You should have been down at the Zero G Funhouse earlier," Geoffrey continued, oblivious to Marty's apathy. "I scared a bunch of pre-schoolers, chased 'em round for ages, it was hilarious!"

Marty raised an eyebrow, suddenly glad he'd been at the other end of the park that day. He made for the door, vaguely aware that Geoffrey was continuing his one-man crusade against decency. Marty had no problem with people in general, just those people who abused their oxygen privileges.

The door opened and shut quietly, and his escape was complete. Sadly, no giant galleon sat waiting to whisk him away to some ludicrous adventure. No whirling chambers of chaos from which to implausibly escape. Marty was trapped in reality, and it was boring the hell out of him.

Stellar Island's concourse was shrouded in darkness, and bereft of frantic merrymakers. Even though all lights had gone out as the last of the patrons left, Marty knew his way out only too well. The cable car which led back into town was the only structure which still sparkled, almost beacon like, for the late leavers and night shifters. Not wishing to dawdle, lest he learn more of the hilarious misadventures of Geoffrey, Marty made for the light, already halfway home in his head.

As he reached the cable car station, doors sprung to life automatically, and the nearest car opened, chirping a cheery autonomous response as it did so. *Thank you for visiting Stellar Island, please come again soon, we miss your face already!*

"Thanks, man!" Marty replied, almost wishing for something more. "I had fun. The costume itches a little, maybe don't wash it in asbestos tonight, eh?"

Thank you for visiting Stellar Island, please come again soon, we miss your face already!

Clearly the cable car was lacking in the humor department, not to mention a lousy conversationalist. If he'd been dreaming right now, the thing would most likely have given him a lecture on how hard it was being a cable car, and how it wasn't easy washing clothes, you know, without arms and such. Oh, to be dreaming again.

Marty boarded and stared blankly out the window as the car jolted onto its short journey back to civilization. At least if Kate had been here, he'd have gotten a human response.

Since that fateful call, on *that* morning after, things had gone well. Not fireworks, champagne, standing at the bow of a cruise ship in each other's arms well, but when does that ever happen? A few dates down the line and things were progressing at a decent pace. Sure, some might call it a snail's pace, but how many heartbroken snails were there? Not many, and that was surely a good sign.

So wrapped up was Marty in this bizarre line of reasoning, that he barely heard the human response he'd been craving. "Good evening to you, Marty," the labored, gentle voice greeted from behind him. Immediately, Marty remembered that Cabbie was on duty tonight. So called because his sole job, and apparent *raison d'etre*, was to man the cable car station which linked Stellar Island to the town. What he was doing surfing the cables at this hour was a mystery, and Marty's expression seemed to beg the question.

"I'm getting out of the office for a while. It's just me down there, so it gets a little boring," the old gent offered. He stared at his feet forlornly. "You get to my age, and a trip on the cars is like a day out."

Marty's expression softened. Cabbie was a nice old guy, older than God's dog it seemed, and almost as hairy. He saw something of himself in that tired face, wistful of adventures past, and seeking some small crumb of excitement through a ride in a rickety old carriage. "Hey, Cabbie" he mumbled, "I know what you mean, sometimes life needs a kick in the pants eh?"

Cabbie continued to ramble on throughout Marty's reply, misty-eyed, oblivious, and mid-sentence. "...back when I was working for the British Secret Service. They were more exciting times, make no mistake..."

Marty, still lost in his own thoughts, offered a stray one into the mix. "Do you ever feel like you're missing out, Cabbie? Like there's so much more out there that puts reality in a headlock and makes it cry?"

"…I had no idea why he needed so many watermelons, but I was under orders…" Cabbie yapped on, unabated.

"I mean, things could be worse, don't get me wrong." Marty pressed on with his train of thought, talking over the old man's meandering mine cart. "I've got a steady job, a nice girl, occasionally all the ingredients for a hangover in the fridge…"

"…of course, that sort of thing should never happen, I don't care if he was a licensed tree surgeon…" The babbling was getting worse, and simultaneously more intriguing, had Marty been listening.

"…I guess I just miss the pirate life." Marty blurted, immediately realizing he had said too much. He glanced furtively over at the aged cable car operator.

Cabbie gazed longingly out of the window, lost in his own memories. "…I managed to smuggle all the llamas out of the building before the bomb went off. I was a hero." He sighed, returning his attention to his bewildered passenger. "Happier times, eh?"

A knowing smile crept awkwardly across Marty's face. In truth, he had no clue what the old geezer had been going on about, but the closing sentiment rang true, and he nodded a half-hearted agreement.

Cabbie opened his mouth, no doubt to regale Marty with more intrepid and befuddling tales of his younger days, when a blinding flash of light shook them almost out of their respective seats and back into the here and now. Outside, daylight took hold for a brief moment, ejecting *something* into the world before darkness presided once more. Whatever it was cannoned past Marty's cable car like a bull piloting a juggernaut, that china shop firmly in its sights. Through the deafening roar and whoosh of an object suddenly deposited into this world, Marty thought he heard shrieking voices. Complaining voices. Shrill pirate voices, grumbling loudly about something shiny?

As quickly as it had appeared, the calamitous din subsided, trailing into the darkness behind the now swaying cable car, like unexpected thunder on a calm summer's evening. Cabbie *whooped* tamely, like a hamster who'd overdone it slightly in its wheel, and was once again swimming in his own nostalgia. "That was rather fun, wasn't it? It reminds me of the time..." he trailed off again, embarking on a story which seemed to involve saving the world in some unfeasible way, again.

Marty was again lost in his own thoughts. They hadn't been pirate voices. Had they? Wishful thinking, or some kind of delayed insanity, a reaction to Marty's recent sojourn into his own dreamspace? Whatever it was, it was gone now. Probably something easily explainable, like a meteor crashing into Stellar Island. Something boring like that. Whatever it had been, the cable car seemed unaffected, and unlikely to plummet horrendously into the depths below at least. It continued on its squeaky course, reaching the terminus as Cabbie continued his stories of averting several potentially world exploding incidents. The car shuddered to a halt, and Marty sidled out through the silently opening doors. Cabbie was, in all likelihood, a crayon chewing lunatic, but Marty almost turned as he left, suppressing the urge to thank the old man for repeatedly saving the world. And a herd of innocent llamas, apparently.

The bottom of the cable car station was steeped in darkness, and Marty wasted no time in locating the bicycle that he had left moored in the parking zone that morning. Just a normal, everyday bicycle that didn't fly, didn't talk, and served only to transport Marty from his dull home to his dull place of work. Odd then, that a koala should be sat upon its saddle, a faint blue light emanating from it.

The koala started, clearly surprised at Marty's approach, before impossibly clearing its throat and speaking. "Pardon me, sir. Could I trouble you for a ride? I appear to be lost."

Marty froze. Not only did koalas not speak, but to the best of his knowledge, they didn't stray far from their native Australia. Also, the ones he had seen on nature programs weren't prone to glowing. The little marsupial held out its hands and hopped down from the bicycle seat. "I didn't mean to startle you," it said. "I'm a little startled myself. Is there any chance of a ride?"

In the weeks that had passed after Marty's dreamtime encounter, life had seemed annoyingly real, and yet now, it seemed alarmingly unusual. This wasn't supposed to happen, not here anyway. Throwing caution and his lunchbox to the wind, Marty leapt towards his bicycle and stamped on the pedals with all his might. The bike launched from its station and careened at speed off into the night.

The luminous koala looked on forlornly, rummaging in his pouch and producing a sprig of eucalyptus.

"Not cool, sir." it mumbled, munching on the leafy stem. He was glowing bluer than ever.

Chapter Three

"If you're not in costume, you can't come in." A rather bed-sheeted Julius Caesar stood, hands on hips in the doorway, chastising a bunch of party latecomers who had apparently not realized there was a dress code. "That's kinda the point of fancy dress costume parties."

One of the revelers raised a hand in protest. "But we brought a keg."

Mighty Caesar sighed, plunging a hand through his laureled hair. "Is it part of your costume?"

The wannabee gatecrashers blinked at one another, no doubt trying to think of a character who would wield a barrel of alcohol that they could pass themselves off as. "Well, no."

The blanket-covered Emperor of Rome solemnly raised a hand, flipping out his thumb, and plunged it dramatically downwards. Just as emphatically, he stepped back inside the house, and slammed the door.

Party etiquette must be observed, Caesar mused as he returned to the very un-Roman disco in full swing in the living room. Especially costume party etiquette. He smiled as he viewed the various heroes, villains, and randoms from history, who were mingling and getting along quite nicely. This was particularly noteworthy since Hitler appeared to be leading a conga line, Frankenstein's monster crooned out a soulful karaoke number, and a gang of zombies picked gingerly through the buffet table. Julius squinted through the low hanging streamers and bobbling balloons at the group of surly flesh eaters. He didn't recognize a single one of them, which could of, course, be down to the meticulous nature of their costumes. They were certainly very believable as a small legion of undead, right down to the torn clothing, blood splattered faces, and gray, ashen skin. One even carried a severed arm, which trailed messily behind him. They were a little *too* realistic, and not unlike the horde which had consistently haunted his recurring dreams as a child. Another sported a red baseball cap, with a peak that hung raggedly unstitched at one end. They turned as one to regard Caesar, as though they had realized that their cover was blown, and shambled away from the smartly cut sandwiches and helpfully labelled dips. Caesar's eyes widened as they moved closer. He had seen these shuffling ghouls before, many times. He had awoken to the sound of his own screams on several occasions as these moaning nasties had cornered him in his dreams, wailing and sizing up his particularly chewable parts. How was this possible? One thought rushed into Caesar's head as the lead zombie dropped his spare arm and reached for the white linen hem of the Emperor's robe, an insane thought, an impossible thought, but one which took hold and refused to budge.

Those aren't costumes.

Flapping sheets signaled Caesar's rapid departure into the kitchen, and as he turned mid-flee, he caught sight of various partygoers queueing up to provide munchable proof to his hypothesis.

Six of the seven dwarves, George Washington and a purple dinosaur became the new buffet table for the insatiable people snackers as they made their way towards the retreating Roman.

As he attempted to somehow fit into a cupboard that was not built for hiding cowering dignitaries, many thoughts should have crossed Caesar's mind. As the zombie horde filed clumsily into the kitchen, he should have been wondering how this had happened, how a bunch of flesh-eating dream corpses had somehow turned up at his costume bash, and were eating their way through his guests. He should have been pondering what force had made his nightmares into flakey, unpleasant flesh, and why on earth this was happening.

As the undead closed on his wholly impractical hiding place, only one thought, comprising three helpless words prevailed. Julius Caesar turned to face his uninvited guests and mumbled them, almost automatically.

"*Et tu*, zombie."

As last words went, they were plagiarized, but not half bad.

The little college on the outskirts of town was not known for being a party hub. And yet several gallons of something approaching alcoholic had been consumed in what had been imaginatively named 'Dorm A.'

No-one had known where the giant white rabbits that had stampeded through the campus had come from, but they had left in their wake a single shivering student, clutching an empty beer bottle and peeking out from beneath his bed.

Without fully realizing the truth of his thoughts, his mind raced at what he could only rationalize as the stuff of nightmares, which had hopped bewilderingly through the college grounds only moments earlier. They had trampled everything in their path: goths, preppies, and jocks. There had been no discrimination. And now only he was left, perhaps in the whole town, hell, maybe in the whole world. Who knew that the apocalypse would come on the vaulting heels of gargantuan carrot nibblers?

Above him, the lights flickered and winked black, no doubt snuffed out by the cute, fluffy onslaught which had gone before. In the darkness, he wished that better grades had taken him to a better school, one with less reality defying fauna, and certainly one with better nightlife. He shifted, allowing the empty bottle to roll out from under the bed and clatter noisily against something unseen in the darkness.

Behind the hapless student, something stirred, delivering a throaty chuckle.

"School's out, forever." A voice slithered out from somewhere beside him.

In an evening where commendable last words were being handed out like candy, the sadly nameless student lamented the fact that right here, right now, it was the bad guy that had stolen his, as something formless dragged him away.

Across town, past the leafy suburbs, heroism was flexing its considerable muscles in the dark recesses of a forgotten cave. A band of impressively armored do-gooders stood in a circle, pondering their next move, yet unaware of the rampant naughtiness spawning hither and thither in their neighborhood. Their leader, a tall, reedy knight decked out in leather and sporting a gleaming steel helm, leaned forward. Long had he wished his name to be uttered in hushed, reverent tones by the townsfolk, and even longer had he gathered here with his allies to prove his worth. Someday, people would sing songs of his deeds. They would talk of his exploits in taverns far and wide, and he would be known as a vanquisher of evil, and a paragon of light. For now, he was simply Geoff the Avenger, and he rolled two shiny silver dice to see if he could get out of paying for the pizza.

The group had been gathering on a weekly basis in Geoff's garage to play *Basements and Broadswords*, and whilst costumes were mandatory, any knowledge of how to actually play the game was apparently not.

"That's a five." A wizardly looking figure next to him chanted. "A five's not enough, you have to pay."

Geoff tapped his hip smugly. "You forget, I'm wearing my Plus Seven Belt of Excuses, so my check hasn't cleared yet, from when I slayed the ravenous beast of Angenthorstenfeld...mere...shire." He scanned his head shaking brethren. "Sorry guys, someone else is going to have to pay the piper tonight."

Almost on cue, the doorbell rang upstairs, and a jaunty member of the group, resplendent in brightly colored finery and matching lute, sang out. "Hark! Tis the conveyor of cheese and pepperoni. He doth wait at our gates, demanding entrance!" He spread his arms wide, bowing theatrically, provoking much sighing and eye rolling. Frank the Bard was an English major, and didn't really get involved in much fighting. He was a dab hand with a sonnet, though, and pitched in with something florid at any given opportunity.

"All right, Frank. You just volunteered to usher in the mighty pizza dude. Go forth and fetch the sacred munchies."

Frank sagged. "You guys do this every time. I'm not made of money. This lute was expensive, you know." His protests fell on deaf ears, and he trapesed up the stairs to the hallway, where his solo quest to answer the door and bring pizza awaited.

The hallway was dimly lit, giving the mission a suitable air of danger, as Frank fumbled with the latch, eventually swinging the door open to herald the arrival of dinner.

"Hold on a sec," Frank mumbled, sadly forgetting to add a 'Prithee' as he wrestled with his Purse of Thriftiness (Plus Four!)

A shadow fell across the distracted bard, and he glanced up to regard its owner. Standing before Frank on the porch was a hefty, drooling cave troll, not here to deliver pizza, it seemed, but to dispense whoop ass. Several cans thereof.

Hunkered in the garage, Frank's hungry companions' only hint at his crashing arrival came with a high pitched, preceding squeal, as the unfortunate poet took the stairs roughly none at a time and landed in a heap in front of them.

"Dude, where's the pizza?" A young elf archer who in real life may or may not have been Geoff's younger brother, cried. Several disapproving glances forced him to restate his query. "I mean, well met, stout bard. Where art the glorious feast of cheese, and buffalo wings…and such." He flushed and shrugged at his fellow dungeon dwellers, who had apparently decided to focus their attention on the monster in the doorway.

"It's a monster. A real one!" Brian the Berserker shrieked, dutifully going berserk, to ill effect as the troll swatted him aside, mid charge. Flanking Geoff, a duo of wizards stepped up to deliver magical defense to their fallen comrade. "Fireball!" They chimed as one, casting their arcane enchantments at the advancing creature. The fiery balls of fury flew through the air and bounced harmlessly off the troll's chest, like the painted tennis balls that they actually were. Their unstoppable foe continued to advance upon them, just like the creatures they had all fought, talked of, and dreamed about so many times. With party members falling left and right, Geoff turned to the gaming table, the only rational thing to do in a totally irrational situation.

Skillfully, and with all the knowledge, experience, and bravery that he had amassed over dozens of dangerous skirmishes in times past, Geoff the Avenger summoned all of his might and rolled a double six.

He didn't need to check the rule book. Tonight, double six meant run away.

Chapter Four

Marty pedaled as though all the hounds of hell were behind him, and not in fact a small, glowing koala. In fairness, a small glowing anything would probably have prompted a certain amount of eyebrow raising from the average bystander, even before it had started talking.

The old clock in the center of town clanged out a midnight declaration as Marty sped on. The streets were empty and quiet, making the hollow *bongs* seem even louder, but it was the same old, dull, uninspiring town that he had seen a million times before.

A few wholly unremarkable cars trundled past him as he sped on. None of them hopped on pogo sticks, and there was no evidence of sinister painted faces behind their windscreens. In fact, nothing at all seemed any more unusual than one was likely to see on a typical Friday night. There were people here and there, but they were acting, rather perplexingly like people. Walking, chatting, peeing up against lampposts, pretty much how people normally acted on a Friday night. Things that really had no business talking, or flying, or doing anything vaguely untoward were behaving just as they should. Sure, there was a man dressed as a chicken, carrying a traffic cone, but in all honesty, who hasn't spent a normal, hum-drum Friday night involved in such an activity?

Marty scanned the street before him, searching for something downright odd, almost craving it. Was he still dreaming? It seemed highly unlikely. Anyone who can dream up flying pirate galleons, whirling bouncy castles of death, and roller coaster trains would surely not have cooked up the two hour staff meeting he'd suffered that very morning. And yet, something odd *had* happened. Granted, Marty had never been an enthusiast of biology, preferring instead to spend his half-remembered science lessons working out what was flammable, edible, or throwable. Nonetheless, he was fairly certain that the cute little teddy bear things from Australia that he'd once seen at the zoo weren't prone to glowing, and were even less likely to ask for a lift home.

Lost in his thoughts, Marty barely noticed as he passed his favorite night spot, The Pickled Judge. A band called Kinky Ninja had advertised their musical stylings on several shoddily made posters out front, and by the sounds of it, weren't going down too well inside. It was a raucous den of untold shenanigans at the best of times, but tonight's injection of dubious culture had seemingly angered the natives. Having long since ditched the age-old *boo* in favor of simply throwing things, the patrons of The Judge appeared to have shown their opinion of the band's musical prowess by relocating much of the pub to the street, amid much swearing and smashing of whatever wasn't indestructible.

Marty smiled, for a moment removed from his existential debate about whether any of this was real. He swerved to avoid a clutch of chairs which had formed a huddle of their own in the center of the road, possibly debating themselves how the hell they had come to be there in the first place. Stray bottles whizzed through the air, and his swerve became a slalom. This town was quaint, it was dull. These days it was infuriatingly realistic, but by God, if you were a dodgy band who didn't play *Stairway to Heaven*, it could be savage.

Had Marty taken a moment to properly survey the carnage, the extent of the savagery might have caused him to topple, however. In the alleyway beside The Judge, a host of figures huddled in the shadows. They chuckled quietly as a slumped, drunken form in their midst was dragged into the darkness of the alley. Two of the figures looked up as Marty rocketed past, already impossibly huge eyes widening still. Their painted red grins drew back even further, displaying yellow, broken, and jagged teeth. The two onlookers skulked away from their brethren, and peered out into the bedlam of the street, and the departing Marty. His rate of knots had carried him into the thankfully unviolated street beyond, and he had turned the corner out of sight in an instant. The huge pairs of eyes remained fixed however, and a look of gleeful excitement spread across the demented faces. There was something else in those eyes, too. As they stared out into the night, they twinkled with demonic intent. A shrill whooping sound filled the air.

Those dark eyes clearly liked what they'd seen as it sped silently past and into the distance. They recognized the departing cyclist.

Marty recognized nothing, pedaling on into the night with his head full of thoughts. He was far more preoccupied with the fact that none of the buses seemed to be floating, and that all the birds seemed to be doing was tweeting, and occasionally aiming feces in his direction. As he rumbled onwards, passing another three silent streets and dodging sticky avian artillery, he realized that he actually hoped for something out of the ordinary. Whether it was to rationalize the bizarre marsupial encounter he'd had, or to stave off the spectacular non-event his waking life now presented, he wasn't sure. One thing was clear, though. When you've chowed down on a deep fried unicorn sandwich, switching to a plain old bacon double boredom burger just didn't quite cut the mustard anymore. Even if you added mustard.

More streets came and went, and before he could snap out of the sudden desire for some kind of unicorn based deli snack, Marty arrowed past familiar houses, and turned into the street that contained his humble abode.

Food would have to wait. It was late, and another shift sat ominously on the horizon, waiting to ride the sunrise and bully Marty awake in the morning. He pulled into the small driveway and fished around in the semi-darkness for his door key. Taking one last look out into the street behind him, Marty sighed as precisely nothing bounded out of the serene twilight to tickle his sanity.

Maybe tomorrow would be different, he thought, opening the door and jostling the bike into the hallways beyond. He closed the door and peered suspiciously into the mirror that hung on the wall beside him. His reflection gazed suspiciously back at him, but said nothing. Tomorrow would definitely be better. Kate was working tomorrow, and Marty brightened at the thought, taking it with him as he headed for the comforting embrace of his pillow.

When it came right down to it, things weren't really that bad. He had a relatively decent job, and some of his co-workers were almost bearable. He'd even started drawing again, perhaps fueled by lofty dreams and crazy nightmares that had seemed real not so long ago. And he had Kate. Not too shabby, all things considered. Marty smiled in the dim glow of his bedside lamp. He didn't need all that bizarre absurdity, life was ticking along just fine, and when push came to shove, anyone who went out looking for clowns was just looking for trouble. He turned onto his side and reached over to the flip the light switch. *Tomorrow will be as crazy as I make it,* he thought, plunging the room into silent blackness.

Amongst the empty shoeboxes, lost coins, and dust bunnies beneath Marty's bed, something stirred in the dark. Something that had no business being under his bed, and in truth, had no business *being* at all. Marty had never been a fan of the phrase 'be careful what you wish for.' If you're wishing for something, chances are it's going to be shiny, expensive, or strawberry flavored. The something under his bed was none of these things, and it chuckled ever so softly as it began to shuffle out from its hiding place.

Chapter Five

Things were not going well at The Pickled Judge. Kinky Ninja were finishing up a rather disastrous set, and Kate shrank further into the little alcove in the corner, sipping on something not dissimilar to paint thinner.

The drinks menu wasn't what you might call cosmopolitan, a decision backed up by the surly, furniture chewing clientele, but it was the closest watering hole to Stellar Island, and many of the park's staff braved the dubious establishment as a result.

Kate had finished her shift, and decided that an evening of culture from a local band might be a distraction from the trials of the dreaded day job. It surely would have been a good idea, had culture featured at all in the discordant twanging of the hapless four piece. She had even considered calling Marty, who was due for release from employed bondage any time now, but three 'dates' in, they weren't living in each other's pockets just yet. Besides, she would be seeing him in a few hours, and as well as things appeared to be going, she didn't want to rock the boat.

How she dearly wished that boat sported a Jolly Roger.

Kate scanned the pub, almost enjoying the bedlam that Kinky Ninja were causing with their peculiar brand of music. At the bar, two gruff looking gents argued over who's turn it was to throw bottles at the stage. Beside the jukebox, a gang of amazingly hairstyled teens competed with the noise by pumping coins into the blinking machine. And still Kinky Ninja played on, possibly assessing potential escape routes rather than encores.

As was the tradition on Friday nights, the evening's shenanigans appeared to have tumbled out into the street beyond, and Kate turned to watch as a fight erupted, sending its participants churning through the front doors into the darkness outside. She squinted through the musty, expletive filled atmosphere of The Judge, attempting to pick out the contestants of this boozy joust. Aside from random limbs which jabbed out here and there, nothing betrayed who was fighting, or indeed why. Nothing except the faint flash of a bright orange, outrageously fluffy wig. Kate strained in her seat, craning for a better view of the melee. She could almost hear giggling amidst the poignant second verse of '*I left my spleen in San Francisco*'. She'd heard that laughter before, recently, and for a moment, Kate felt her own spleen make a bolt for sunnier climes.

Just as her mind started issuing assurances that this was reality, and nothing grinning and murderous tended to frequent these parts, she spied two faces peering in through the front windows. They seemed transfixed, leering and illuminated by the streetlights outside. Kate had seen some strange things whilst on a night out in town before. This town was no stranger to sombrero wearing penguins, or the odd gorilla in a tutu. Such was the uniform of the drunken merry maker. And yet, the sight of two grease-painted faces, noses as red as traffic signals, atop grins more befitting your average crocodile, stirred shrieking alarm bells in her brain.

Almost instinctively, Kate moved further back into the darkness of the corner, edging towards the back door of The Judge, and away from the mystery spectators at the window.

"There you are." A guttural voice rumbled at Kate's side. "I've been looking for you."

Sudden panic shook Kate from her clown induced hypnosis. She whirled, eyes darting for possible escape routes, her hands outstretched to fend off whatever had apparently found her. The back door was indeed her best hope, but it stood beyond the still caterwauling band, who had launched into an ear defiling rendition of '*Fridge Over Troubled Water*. Even more unsettling, the imminent arrival of grasping hands seemed to be somewhat lacking in the 'imminent' department.

Kate turned to where the mystery hide-and-seek enthusiast had last spoken. Standing over her, a look of vague confusion chiseled onto his granite face, was Old Mad Bill, the hulking bartender of The Pickled Judge. Bizarrely, he was neither old, nor particularly mad. Kate wasn't even sure if his name was Bill, but it seemed the most plausible part of the extravagant moniker. Oldish, slightly mad, possibly Bill cracked a smile that was simultaneously endearing and terrifying, like a golem in a bonnet. "How come you're hiding way over here?" he boomed, holding up a beaming, bright pink teddy bear. "You won the raffle. Here." Bill handed over the bear grudgingly, "His name is Sir Reginald." The look on the bartender's weathered face suggested that he would have quite liked to have won it himself. Kate wasn't sure what was stranger. Bill's apparent disappointment, or the fact that such a rampant den of iniquity gave out cuddly toys as prizes.

"Bill, what's going on outside?" She ventured, "There seems to be a lot of...clowns." Kate eyed the windows warily as she spoke, but there were no gaunt, white faces staring back this time. Bill rubbed his craggy jaw thoughtfully. "Clowns? I didn't see any clowns. Just the standard, run of the mill, Friday night bloodshed." He smiled warmly, as though this routine of carnage was in some way reassuring to him.

Behind them, Kinky Ninja had launched into a new song. Kate had no idea what this one was, but it was no improvement on their earlier offerings. Suffice to say, if howler monkeys could sing, they'd have hated it too.

"Things do seem to be getting pretty animated out there, though," Bill added. "A little too punchy and bitey for a girly like yourself." He was attempting to inject a soothing tone into his voice, but it still sounded like a Panzer tank in a blender. "D'you want me to call you a cab?"

As ear shattering as Bill's voice was, he probably meant to use the telephone to order a taxi. And yet even before he'd finished speaking, the interior of The Judge was bathed in dazzling light as headlights loomed at the windows, and a veering yellow cab exploded through the wall, adding a splintery new layer of carnage to proceedings. The patrons who were still not fighting with each other scattered as it came to rest, dented and battered, atop The Judge's already dented and battered pool table. For a moment, nothing stirred. A taxi cab through the window will often have that kind of awe inspiring effect on a crowd. Just as abruptly, however, all the noise and movement in the world seemed to arrive in the shattered bar of The Pickled Judge.

Scrambling from his stricken vessel, the cab driver hit the ground at a stumbling gallop, glancing behind him feverishly as he did so. Thankfully some way away from all the destruction, Kate could clearly see what leapt out after the cabbie, grabbing at his fleeing heels and cackling manically. Huge flapping feet hit the deck, and the giggling harlequin straightened itself, seemingly aware that it was now standing in a room full of things it could chase.

Kate had seen enough, which was unfortunate, as four or five more things that she didn't want to see poured into The Judge from the cab shaped hole in the wall. They gibbered, hooted, and jerkily scuttled at anyone who hadn't realized that discretion was the better part of valor. Clutching Sir Reginald under her arm, Kate made a dash for the back door, past the band, who were still obliviously attempting to coax music out of their instruments. She hit the door at a rate of knots and barreled gracelessly into the dingy alley beyond. There were two ways out of the narrow passage, although one of them seemed to be blocked by a silhouetted figure, standing silently in the darkness. The frizzy hair and billowing pantaloons were something of a giveaway, and Kate instinctively backed away towards the far exit of the alleyway. The frizzy shadow advanced, far more rapidly than seemed possible in those trousers, and before she realized it, Kate frantically pitched Sir Reginald in the direction of the onrushing fiend. The hapless bear tumbled end over end towards its fate, finally plucked out of the air by the clown who had now reached a pool of dim streetlight. It paused, eyeing the toy curiously. The eyes shifted to Kate, still retreating steadily, and then returned to the smiling bear. Like some kind of grease-painted boa constrictor, its grinning jaw dropped, unhinged and gaped. Kate could swear it was still laughing manically as poor Sir Reginald was deposited swiftly into the circus freak's dreadful maw. Its jaw reset and chewed sickeningly, before the monstrous jester resumed his advance.

Clowns eat teddy bears? Kate mused as she turned tail and bolted for the end of the alley.

Chalk that one up as another reason to never sleep again.

Chapter Six

It's a well-known fact that most of your garden variety horrors tend to favor darkness. Vampires, ghouls, zombies, they all seem to favor the spooky shimmer of moonlight. Darting unseen through alleys, deserted streets and equally unpleasant places. They skulk, unknown to those asleep in their beds, and carry out their nefarious business in secret, sinister ways.

That said, this is also the remit of Santa Claus, so it was anyone's guess what was lurking beneath Marty's bed, as he began to slip into slumber. Whatever it was lay formless in the darkness. Had anyone taken the time to flip on the light, no slavering, growling monster would have shrunk back into the shadows from whence it came. The boogeyman that would doubtless cause even clowns to fill their baggy trousers was made of far less tangible stuff. The monster who lives under your bed *is* the shadows.

Marty shifted slightly, still dancing on the edge of sleep. Dreams of riding in the clouds on a pirate ship, and trying to fit the world's largest marshmallow into his mouth vied for position in his mind. As he moved, his arm dropped over the side of the bed, which is a firm no-no when guarding yourself against the perceived terrors that hide beneath. The shadows eyed the swinging limb, chuckling faintly as it sized up its target, and Marty stirred at the sound which pierced the darkness. The chuckle became a voice, raspy and unnatural, issued from under the bed like a squeaky wheel on Satan's own tricycle. "You moved, you moved!" it whispered. "Mine now."

In a flurry of movement, Marty was wrenched awake as something grasped his hand and pulled. All thoughts of marshmallows and pirate ships flew from his mind as he tumbled off the bed towards his mystery assailant. Although Marty couldn't feel anything solid holding him, his jerky descent to the floor continued, and threatened to yank him underneath the bed. For a moment, he thought he must be dreaming, but surely his bedroom floor would be cleaner, or at least covered in less socks were that the case. Still the living shadow reeled him in, drawing him closer to what was almost certainly not adventures and fun times under his bed. His arm disappeared into the blackness, and Marty's stomach lurched as he realized this was not a fight he was likely to win. In truth, he was not a fighter, haphazard clown skirmishes aside, and no amount of kicking and struggling seemed to be doing much good.

Ironically, at that moment, an amount of kicking seemed to do a great deal of good at his bedroom door, as it exploded inwards, casting in blessed beams from the landing light. Two figures leapt through, tiny voices raised in a squeaky, gravelly battle cry that Marty had heard before.

"Arrrrrr!"

As light tumbled into the room, so did the two miniature pirates, one catching Marty in the ribs, the other sending his bedside lamp crashing to the floor. In terms of graceful entrances, it fell somewhere between drunk uncle at a wedding and human cannonball, and yet it seemed to have the desired effect.

The inhuman grip around Marty's hand vanished as light invaded the room. All that remained were several flailing limbs, some human, some sack cloth and pirate shaped.

Timbers sprang to his feet on Marty's chest, cutlass already drawn. "Front and center bad guys, the cavalry's here!"

From amongst a tangle of wires and broken lamp, Whipstaff emerged, grimacing and clearly displeased that he'd missed his target. "Captain, we can't be the cavalry. We don't have horses."

The mini buccaneer shot an irritated glance at his first mate. "Shh. I've told you before about stepping on my one liners," he growled.

Staring blearily up at his pint-sized rescuers, Marty quickly retrieved his hand from beneath the bed and sat up, sending Timbers sliding to the floor. "Timbers?" he managed, still attempting to dispel the sleep which had recently dangled its dreams before him. "What the hell are you doing here?"

The little captain stood defiantly, hands on hips. "Rescuing you, obviously." He was clearly still caught up in mid-swashbuckle.

"Well, yes, but from what?" Marty glanced at the now completely unthreatening looking floor under his bed. Nothing stared back, and various unassuming items of clutter continued with their non-lethal, non-graspy existence beneath.

Timbers shrugged. "Damned if I know, we probably scared it off with that awesome battle cry. Either that or you just fell out of bed."

Whipstaff joined them in peering under the bed. "Always enter a room expecting a fight. If you get one, you're prepared. If you don't, at least you'll look impressive." It was flawless logic, and Timbers seemed to agree, nodding and patting his first mate on the shoulder.

Marty was fully awake now, and wanted answers. This was reality. *His* reality, and as much as he had wanted his tiny allies to be here, their presence was no less mystifying. "How did you get here? This is…my side of the fence," he blurted, forming his pin balling thoughts in the best way he could.

Timbers beamed proudly, "We came in through your cat flap."

Getting to his feet, Marty surveyed the room. Something had grabbed him, and he wasn't entirely convinced that it wasn't still here somewhere. Still, Timbers' reply hadn't answered his question, in more ways than one. "I haven't got a cat."

The little captain deflated slightly. Holding up a ragged piece of wood, he clarified apologetically. "Oh right. Sorry, your new cat flap. Incidentally, your front door might need some attention."

Behind them, Whipstaff had taken to turning over furniture, peeking behind doors, and generally making a complete mess. Marty couldn't decide if the first mate was, like him, not entirely sure that the shadowy assailant had vacated, or whether Whipstaff was just being obtrusively nosey.

"Where's Oaf?" Marty enquired to Timbers, who had hopped up onto the bed beside him.

Timbers' expression soured. He looked down at his gleaming buckled boots and sighed deeply. "He didn't make it."

A silence fell over the room, and even Whipstaff's continued demolition of the place seemed to drop into a muted pause. Marty's eyes widened. "He didn't make it? You mean he's…?"

Something dawned on Timbers' face, and his roguish grin

returned. "No, of course not! I mean through the hole in the door. He didn't fit. He's outside on lookout."

Marty puffed out his cheeks, partly in relief, but also because his question still hadn't been answered. He attempted to maneuver into a different way of asking it. "You're here," he began, hoping that Timbers would fill in the blanks. The little captain stood on one foot, attempting to dislodge a stone from his boot with his cutlass. Clearly, he wasn't listening and the blanks remained unfilled. "You're here in my reality. How?" Marty spelled out as his distracted comrade finally ousted the stone and got with the program.

The program, it seemed, was no more enlightening. "Funny thing, that." Timbers shrugged. "We were sailing the seven skies and happened upon this swirly, shiny thing."

Whipstaff joined his captain and chimed in with his two pence worth. "We like shiny things. We've got chests full of shiny things. It's kind of in the job description." He beamed.

Timbers shot his first mate another glance. A pirate's booty was not to be openly discussed, and certainly not before it had been suitably deposited beneath an 'X' somewhere. "Anyway" he cut in, before Whipstaff could give away any more piratey secrets. "We swooped in to investigate, and sort of fell through into…this place." He glanced around at the dimly lit room, kicking a random sock which had landed beside him amid Whipstaff's ransacking. "It's altogether less exciting than I expected, I'll be honest. Massive invisible monster fighting aside."

Marty shuffled the sporadic deck of thoughts in his mind. "What? You landed here? I don't recall seeing a pirate galleon outside my house when I got here."

"No, no, not here." Timbers explained, sheathing his blade and trotting over to Marty. "We set down in that big theme park. We arrived almost on top of it, and I wasn't about to fly around a new plane of existence without getting my bearings first." He headed towards the door, leading from the front as any pirate captain worth his buckles should. "We took the lifeboat and came to find you."

Falling in behind him, Whipstaff peered over his shoulder at Marty, clearly expecting him to follow them. "All stealthy-like, y'know?" He tapped his nose and smirked.

Marty was already donning the clothes he had carefully flung by his bedside, and attempted to bring up the rear. It was no mean feat in the dingy glow of the landing light. "Okay, so where are we going now?" he gasped, almost toppling as two legs went down one trouser hole.

Timbers ceased his purposeful advancing at the door. He turned, a familiar glint in his eye. "There's shenanigans afoot, matey," he declared excitedly. "What pirate in good conscience could sit idly by as the possibility for reckless adventure wiggled its cheeky backside in his face?" He beamed, fixing Marty with his one good eye. "Do I really need to ask if you are in?"

Marty could find no flaw in his miniature friend's logic. Something was most assuredly going on, and what was the alternative? Slinking off back to sleep to wait for the invisible man eating dust bunny to crawl out from under his bed again? He was still not altogether sure what had attacked him, but he was fairly sure it hadn't been a clown. There was no smell of greasepaint and candy coated fear in the air, and anyway, clowns don't just vanish. Do they? Whatever it was, further theorizing would have to wait for a more opportune moment, which, given Marty's track record for spectacularly winging it, would probably be the next time whatever it was happened to be breathing down his neck again.

He shrugged, finally placing the correct limbs into the proper items of clothing. Even in the face of impending monster breath, and the almost certain hijinks which were waiting mischievously somewhere out there in the night, he felt suddenly refreshed by the rampant madness wantonly reintroduced to his life.

"And besides," Whipstaff chipped in, obviously caught up in the moment, "if we came through, you can bet that there's a clown or two in need of some serious keelhauling."

It wasn't the best caveat to what had been a rousing call to arms. Marty shuddered at the thought, but still fell in line with the departing pirates. They had resoundingly, if somewhat fortuitously, kicked clown bottom before, and it had been kind of fun, hideously terrifying near misses aside.

A gruff shriek called a halt to the merriment, and a muffled voice rang out from the darkness on the other side of the landing. "It's coming! It's after me!" it bellowed, causing Timbers to once again draw his sword. Two pirates and one almost dressed human barreled towards the cry for help, which grew louder and more high pitched as they approached the front door.

A blonde, thatched sack cloth head poked awkwardly through a freshly wrought hole in Marty's front door. It was Oaf shaped, and the source of the squealing. As they approached, Oaf seemed to calm down, his eyes still darting here and there, presumably for signs of his assailant.

"Where is he, Oaf?" Timbers barked, his trusty cutlass waving dramatically. "And what exactly are you doing?"

The tiny giant flushed, still trying to dislodge himself from the hole. "I was trying to get in, and I got stuck," he mumbled sheepishly. "And then it came for me. There it is!" He resumed his squirming as the smallest spider in the world trundled past him.

Timbers rolled his good eye and again sheathed his blade. Whether his frustration was with his lily livered crewmate, or due to the fact that he still hadn't had the chance to buckle his swash wasn't clear, but he took the bull by the horns—or more specifically the Oaf by the head—and delivered an unceremonious push. Like a cork from a bottle, Oaf was freed from his bonds, and Marty swung the door open to reunite the crew on his front doorstep. Mere steps away stood the lifeboat, sitting proudly if implausibly on his front lawn, and within seconds it was heavy four crew. Marty sat back in the stern, feeling simultaneously confused and elated. He had gotten his wish, and reality had veered sharply into crazy town. Muttering about spiders, Oaf took up his position behind the large, boat propelling bellows and hefted a mighty gust into the sails. "Let's be off," Timbers crowed, already caught up in a new, maniacally enthusiastic moment. "Back to the *Fathom*, and ales all round!"

Marty coughed and tapped the little captain on the shoulder. There was an agenda that needed to be addressed here, and a huge, apparently shiny elephant in the room that they needed to investigate. "And we'll get to the bottom of this, yes?"

"Of course, yes, that too," Timbers assured, his grin wider and more gleeful than ever.

"But ales first?" Whipstaff whispered.

Pirates are a simple folk. They will run headlong into danger, laugh in the snarling face of peril, and apparently stow shiny things beneath big sandy X's, but every engine needs fuel, and for the sailors of the seven skies, that fuel came in bottles, and brought with it the possibility of beer monkeys in the morning.

Chapter Seven

Far below the lifeboat, several things that really had no business being anywhere near a normal plane of reality scuttled through the dark, moonlit streets. Unidentifiable in the murky streetlight, they darted in through open windows and unlocked doors, and generally set about looking for something downright naughty to get up to. Some of these things had found their way into the Pickled Judge, which probably looked as lively and murderous as it did every Friday night from where Marty and the pirates sat amongst the clouds. A few of these hellborne things had even chased someone out into the alleyway behind the pub, who had promptly hightailed it into the night, much to the indifference of the crew of the lifeboat, who had spectacularly failed to see any of these events unfold.

As far as hightailing had panned out, Kate had burst out of the alleyway at speed, and reached the other side of the street. A line of shrubs sat, silent and seemingly bedlam free, and far enough away from the decimated pub entrance to pass as a decent enough hiding place. Kate made the decision even as she was in mid-air, ploughing head first into the nearest bush, and bowling over a figure crouched within in the process. Suddenly bathed in bright yellow light, she reeled, expecting a cackle, a chuckle, or a pie to the face. The fate of poor Sir Reginald flashed briefly in her mind, and she lashed out, connecting again with her fellow shrub dweller. Kate squinted as more yellow light pulsed beside her, a startled yelp matching its sudden brilliance and intensity. Just as quickly, it subsided, and Kate found herself staring with some measure of disbelief at a small, glowing koala. The measure immediately became a stiff double, with a chaser of 'what the hell?' as the little creature addressed her.

"Please don't strike me again miss, I haven't done nothin' to you," it whined, still radiating the sort of yellowy iridescence which was not too common for a koala. "Is this your little tree? I only took a few branches."

Kate sat amongst the wreckage of her own rapidly diminishing reality and stared blankly at the babbling marsupial. Why she should be so incredulous after her recent reintroduction to the clowns from nightmare central was unclear. She supposed that, as ghoulish as they were, the clowns were at least grounded somewhat in her version of reality. This little guy, with his own built in nightlight and apologetic ramblings, didn't seem to be part of any sort of reality, and Kate fought to process what was going on.

The koala shifted uncomfortably, aware that questioning eyes were upon him. "Name's Benji." He dropped a half-gnawed twig, wiped his hand against his side and offered a greeting. "I ducked in here when the painted gentlemen arrived. It's quite cozy, so I thought I'd have a bit of a munch." Benji stared down at the small pile of sticks at his feet, a guilty glance quickly returning to Kate. "I'm sorry, I'll be on my way."

Across the street, Alley Clown poked his grinning face out of the shadows and peered around for signs of life that he could potentially murder. Kate's thoughts sprang again to the teddy bear he had effortlessly dispatched moments ago, and she turned quietly back to the now departing Benji. "Wait," she whispered, as gently as she could, given the fraught circumstances. "You don't have to leave. This isn't my tree, and besides, you were here first." She managed a smile, in an attempt to calm the jittery creature. Quite apart from anything else, if he did scramble out of the bush, he would most likely bring every googly eye to bear on their leafy hiding place. The smile, or possibly the kind words seemed to have the desired effect, and Benji stopped in his tracks. Turning to face Kate, his hue changed from faint yellow to glowing pink, and a look of relief fell across his face. At least, she imagined it was relief, having never seen a relieved koala in her life up until now.

"Thank you, miss." Benji beamed, a little too loudly for Kate's liking, and she ventured another glance across the street. Alley Clown loped back towards the entrance of the Pickled Judge, seemingly having spied more poor unfortunates to terrorize.

She let out a sigh which felt as though it had been hiding in her lungs for the past five minutes. Returning her attention to Benji, she realized that he was still babbling. "Truth be told miss, I really don't know what is occurring here. My dream person usually calls me to places that are a lot more colorful than this. Less monsters, too," he whispered, poking his head out of the shrub and eyeing the surrounding carnage worriedly. His pink radiance had receded, and replaced by a bluish tint. "Also, these trees taste awful. And the floor's a bit soggy. I really should find my dream person." He wiped stray leaves from his face and stared up at Kate with wide, sorrowful eyes. "Please miss, can you tell me where I am?"

Kate wasn't sure that any sort of answer would have fit that particular question, and instead replied with one of her own. "How long have you been here? After, you know, arriving. Tell me everything."

Benji seemed to brighten, literally, at the prospect of providing helpful information. "Oh, I've been here quite a while," he chirped. "A big, bright whirly thing opened up, and I went to have a look, but it turned out to be only bright and whirly on my side. Over here, it was dark and damp and made of concrete." He motioned back down the road behind them. "I wandered around for a while, looking for trees, and hiding from more whirly things. There were a fair few cropping up here and there." He rubbed his paws anxiously. "All sorts of strange things came out of them, like the painted men over there, so I decided to hide here. Then you showed up." The little creature paused, seemingly unsure as to whether this was indeed 'everything'. "We started talking, and you shushed me and told me to wait," he added uncertainly.

Kate had no clue who this creature was, where he came from, or in which direction to point him. She had seen the clowns before, though. The same wholly un-common-or-garden circus freaks that she had encountered in Marty's dreamspace. The kind that were likely to make balloon animals out of your insides, or turn a kids' party into a game of *Tag, you're it!* to the death. If they were here, then who knew what else had suddenly arrived on her side of the fence. As if to emphasize this notion, something only a street or two away from them exploded, and not in a good way. "Hold on a second," she whispered to the little koala.

"And we're still talking now," Benji replied, clearly still in 'tell me everything' mode.

"Yes, all right. Thank you, Benji. And it's Kate, by the way."

Benji blinked, absently pulling another twig from the shrub and raising it to his mouth. "Oh, is it? All right then, Miss." His glow changed to a comforting, soft white.

Kate patted at her pockets, almost instantaneously realizing that the phone she was searching for was still in her locker at work. *Ridiculous*, she thought. This sort of thing only happened in cheap horror movies, with heading off to retrieve said phone coming in a close second. Then again, she needed to call Marty, and they were a hell of a lot closer to Stellar Island than they were to his place, so movie clichés be damned.

This was all fine in principle, of course, but the explosion heard moments earlier was unlikely to be fireworks, and there seemed to be more hellish harlequins darting around in the street beyond their hiding place. She couldn't be sure from where she sat, but it seemed as though the whole town was succumbing to some kind of circus Armageddon. And again, this was not the fun kind, where a person would get to wield something sharp or shooty, and fit their car out like a small, economical tank. Kate reminded herself again that this was reality, or had been until very recently.

Caught up in her internal musings and plans of becoming an apocalyptic vigilante, Kate had barely noticed that the clowns seemed to be heading away from them. They appeared to be heading deeper into the town, fanning out in some kind of manic conga line, as though drawn to the explosion that no doubt carried with it the delicious prospect of mayhem. Clearly for them, the explosion had been the good kind.

"This is our chance, Benji." Kate turned towards the marsupial, who was rummaging around his person for something. "It's not safe for you out here, come on, we'll try to figure this whole thing out." She paused as Benji produced a sprig of eucalyptus from his pouch. "Wait, I thought only female koalas had pouches."

Benji was still mumbling about the awfulness of the shrub, and how he would have to use 'his own stash'. "Do they?" He stared down at himself worriedly. "Maybe I should get this looked at, then. How embarrassing."

Kate began to reply but stopped short. Why should this small anatomical inconsistency make any sense at the moment? And besides, their window of escape could be filled by gibbering faces at any moment. Snatching up Benji and diving out of the bushes, she made for the nearest clump of shadows, hopeful that they were not currently occupied.

Thankfully, there were no ghoulish clowns waiting to predictably leap out of the darkness. They had danced, jittered, and flung themselves away into the night. A whole town lay ignorant and unravaged (nearby explosions aside), a twenty block sweet shop just waiting to be plundered by eager, white gloved hands. Kate paused in the shadows to catch her breath and her thoughts. There were going to be serious wrong-doings tonight—the cavorting parade of freaks would see to that—and something had to be done about it. She couldn't do it alone, however. Even with a magical glowing koala at her side, who admittedly didn't seem to know what the hell was going on either. No, she needed backup from someone she trusted, and who knew what was descending upon the town. She needed to make a call, and she dearly hoped that Marty was still awake to answer.

The street ahead looked as though a herd of sumo wrestling elephants had used it for sparring practice, but was mercifully clear. "Sorry, Benji," Kate muttered to the bemused figure in her arms. "But you're not in Kansas anymore."

As they stole past the ruin that was once the Pickled Judge, Benji managed a confused reply as they made stealthily for the lights of Stellar Island. "Miss, what's a Kansas?"

Chapter Eight

All things considered, it was a rather pleasant night to be loop-ing silently through the ether in a flying lifeboat. Even the crisp, whooshing breeze and incessant pirate chatter did little to disturb the calmness of the air, and this in itself was worrying.

Marty had spent the last few weeks berating the unabashed normality of the world that he had re-awoken into, ho-humming at the humdrum, and generally wishing for something ridiculous, absurd and even downright dangerous to gatecrash his life. Now, here he was, reunited with his pint-sized compadres, having narrowly escaped becoming something horrible's bedtime snack, and currently speeding into the gaping jaws of who knows what. His prayers had been answered, his dreams had literally come true, or so it seemed.

It was the quiet that bothered him.

Marty leaned over to where Timbers sat, engaged in a heated game of *Rock, Paper, Scissors* with his first mate, apparently for a handful of shiny buttons. "Timbers, isn't it a little strange that there doesn't seem to be any…bedlam occurring?"

The little captain glanced up with his one good eye, halfway through delivering a devastating paper attack on his opponent.

"I mean, if you're here, it stands to reason something is amiss. Where are the…you know?" Marty reached up to his nose and mimed a honking squeeze, drawing a shiver from the captain.

"Ain't seen any." Timbers shrugged, halting the shudder, mid-shud.

Marty was unconvinced. "They'll be here," he muttered, shaking his head. "If you're here, they'll be around somewhere, lurking, sneaking, cavorting. Where are the screams? The carnage? The explosions?"

Somewhere below them, a rippling boom helpfully answered Marty's query, and four faces peered over the bow. A plume of aforementioned orangey-yellow carnage erupted from one of the streets beneath, drawing gasps from the lifeboat's passengers (even the ones who secretly loved exploding things).

Whipstaff shot a glance at Marty, before drawing his attention skyward. "Where are the pies and buxom ladyfolk?" he shouted, clearly wishing that some magic still hung in the air. Oaf peered hopefully into the heavens, his hands held out in anticipation, but neither pastry nor wench was forthcoming.

Timbers joined Marty, who was already standing, and craning over the side of the lifeboat for a better view. Something had indeed exploded on the ground below, and was now throwing columns of smoke and flame into the air, obscuring whatever had caused it, and whatever was now so much cinder and ash.

A huge gust from the bellows flung the lifeboat into a sweeping upward arc as Oaf set about putting some distance between them and whatever dispensed fiery unpleasantness below. Inside the boat, brows furrowed, nervous glances exchanged, and a tiny voice complained that he'd gone with scissors, and therefore won the buttons.

"They *are* here," Marty finally declared, echoing what the rest of the crew were already thinking.

"Either that, or fireworks in the real world need to carry some serious warnings." Timbers interjected. His one-eyed gaze darted anxiously towards Marty. He desperately wanted to find some mirth in the situation. After all, he was an avid supporter of explosions.

Whilst quite partial to the odd incendiary detonation or two himself, Marty was already thinking two steps ahead. This was a good one and a half steps more than he was used to thinking at, and he fought back the urge to panic. Kate was somewhere down there, possibly completely unaware of the impending unreality which might be sat, giggling on her doorstep even now. He peered out into the darkness behind them. It was a good few miles back into the suburbs, and Stellar Island loomed garishly only a few hundred yards before them. Whatever was down there, it was most likely going to take more than a flying canoe and its passengers to deal with.

Whipstaff clearly caught Marty's train of thought, and poked Oaf urgently with an oar, whilst goading the tiny giant to propel them faster to their destination.

Oaf swatted at his shipmate, protesting as he did so. "Stop it, this is as much wind as I can manage!"

Marty rolled his eyes, expecting the sniggering and wholly inappropriate response that predictably arrived. "C'mon Oaf, I saw what you had for breakfast." Whipstaff chuckled, nearly losing his footing as Timbers fell into him in a fit of spontaneous laughter. The threat of very real peril, and possibly impending doom was still no match for a good fart gag, it seemed.

Blocking out the merriment, Marty squinted into the smothering darkness, for once thankful for the lurid, gaudy lights of Stellar Island as the vast theme park fell into view below them. The sooner they could get there, the sooner they could embark upon a daring rescue, which would no doubt deliver untold boyfriend brownie points, should Kate indeed be in some sort of peril. "Where did you park the *Fathom*?" he called to Timbers, who wiped whatever passed for tears amongst toy pirates from his good eye. Still gasping from the chuckle fit, the little captain rejoined his comrade at the ship's bough, pointing off towards a brightly lit, and bizarrely furnished field before them. "Over yonder, in that big puddle."

Marty immediately caught sight of the mighty vessel, sitting in totally conspicuous splendor in the water hazard of the park's admittedly impressive miniature golf course.

"It's a golf course, isn't it?" Whipstaff had joined them at the ship's bow, and his eyes widened as they descended towards the *Fathom*.

Marty nodded, smiling at the sight before him. "It is indeed. To the power of wow."

Very few people could reasonably describe anything golf related using the word 'wow,' and yet Stellar Island's crazy eighteen-holer was a feat of putting genius. All manner of things rotated, swayed, spun, and twirled amongst the various, space themed greens. The whole course looked as though it had been designed by Albert Einstein on a sugar high.

Marty shot a glance over towards Timbers, who was in a similar state of enthrallment. "I can see why you landed the *Fathom* here."

He could read the glint in his friend's good eye only too well.

"I know, right?" Timbers chattered gleefully. "If there's time, I really want a crack at this little beauty."

"Something tells me that we won't have time," Marty warned, still thinking about the explosion they had passed moments earlier, and more eager than ever to set sail to Kate's place.

Timbers huffed, turning from the cornucopia of fun before him. "Oaf, stow the clubs. We've got work to do." Oaf flinched at hearing his name, peering around for the clubs he was apparently meant to have brought.

They were descending rapidly but gracefully upon the *Fathom* when the latest explosion rang out, much closer than the last. The crew hung on instinctively as their journey came to a skittering halt on the deck of the mighty galleon. Timbers hopped onto the deck as Whipstaff and Oaf secured the lifeboat. "I'd give that an eight for the landing." Whipstaff imparted to his lumbering crewmate.

"Out of what?" Oaf replied.

Whipstaff paused, leaned over the side of the lifeboat and turned back to Oaf. He delivered a non-qualifying shrug before hopping overboard after his captain. Marty found himself doing the same thing as Oaf sought further clarification, hoisting himself onto the deck of the familiar vessel and striding off after his miniature allies. It was exactly as he remembered it, resplendent, and in no way diminished by its arrival in the real world. Marty bristled with gleeful pride as he surveyed what was, in essence, a mighty, majestic product of his own imagination.

The *Fathom* stood silently in the shallow waters, and Marty craned his head upwards as he chased after Timbers and Whipstaff. High up in the rigging, Zephyr sat motionless in the moonlight as a glittering statue with only a faint wisp of steam escaping from his steely beak. The Bobs were nowhere to be seen, although the sounds of hammering, sawing, and general beavering rang out steadily from within the bowels of the *Fathom*.

Catching up with Timbers at the quarterdeck, Marty surveyed the eerily quiet golf course that surrounded them. Not a creature was stirring, not even a clown. "Where are they?" Marty wheezed, rationing his words as he fought to catch his breath.

Timbers whipped out his trust brass telescope from a pocket

in his frock coat. "Probably still down in the town somewhere," he mused, scanning the horizon thoughtfully. "It's Friday night, and they love a good spot of carnage." It was probably not the best attempt at reassurance, and the little captain glanced up sheepishly from his scope. "What I mean to say is, we're probably safe for now."

Marty sighed, feeling no more enlightened than he had when he had toppled out of bed a short while ago. "What exactly is going on?" he mustered. "How are you here, and how are *they* here?"

Timbers looked up from his telescope. "I told you. The SHINY." When presented with something shiny, pirates are about as helpful and specific as magpies. It's pretty, and they want it, and that's as far as it goes. Marty rubbed his face impatiently. "Yes, you said. What about the...shiny?"

Whipstaff trotted down the steps from the quarterdeck. "We've not seen anything like it before. We flew into it, and here we are. Maybe it's a gateway or something."

His captain chimed in. "Yeah, that would explain how they got through as well. It's like a door between here and there. Only there's more than one, and apparently clowns like shiny things too."

Marty held up a steadying hand. "Well we still haven't seen any clowns." He was trying to convince himself as much as offer a note of rationality. "That thing under my bed wasn't a clown. Maybe Peepers' bunch isn't here after all."

The very name caused ripples of repulsion to jar everyone on the deck. Peepers had disappeared, shoeless, over the side of the *Fathom*, with a cannonball to the face, but as every seasoned nightmare sufferer knows, there is never a shortage of clowns in one's own subconscious.

"Well whoever it is, they seem to prefer their Friday nights explosion-flavored," Timbers said, a little too enthusiastically than perhaps intended. Marty couldn't fault the tiny buccaneer, since it was for the most part how he himself liked to start his weekends. Such incendiary musings weren't going to get them anywhere however, and he turned his attention sharply to the deck of the *Fathom*. "Where are the Bobs?" he ventured, the tinkering below deck having subsided upon their arrival.

As if in response to the rollcall, one of the Bobs popped his head out from a small hatchway beneath the central mast. "Hello

Marty," the Bob twin sang cheerfully. "Nice plane of existence you've got here." Immediately, the head vanished below deck, and the hammering continued. Marty leaned closer in an attempt to get a better look into the darkness within the hatch, but whatever the Bobs were messing with down there remained an inky black mystery.

"Nice?" Timber interjected, casting a dubious glance around him. "It's like Disneyland during a power cut." Realizing that Marty was stood next to him, he spluttered an apologetic caveat. "I'm sure it's very nice in the daytime." Marty turned his attention back to the hatch, and the little captain shot a hasty glance at Whipstaff, imparting a distasteful shake of the head.

The miniature first mate chuckled, jabbing at Oaf who was busily paying no attention to the conversation, and fiddling with a button on his waistcoat. "Hoist the anchor, big lad." Whipstaff continued. "We need to be shoving off."

Oaf's single train car of thought returned grudgingly to everything non-button related, and he loped off to where a large iron chain spilled out over the side of the deck.

Marty had given up trying to discern the Bobs' actions, and joined Timbers in peering out across the mighty Stellar Island mini golf course. "Timbers, where are we headed? You're not suggesting that we head into town, cannons blazing, are you?"

The little captain beamed enthusiastically. "Yeah! Well, no. If there's time. We're off to find the shiny." He rubbed his little cloth hands, seeking a similarly hearty response from Marty, which was not forthcoming.

"Look, we need a plan." Marty sighed. "First thing's first. We need to find Kate."

Timbers stifled an urge to go and find some rampantly ablaze thing and toast marshmallows on it, and nodded sharply. "Right you are, matey." Spinning on his heels, the little captain barked out orders to his crew, who were still halfway through his last round of commands. "Bobs! To your stations, and give Zeph a nudge, will you?"

Also Bob retrieved a long, wooden poking device from beside the main sail and sighed forlornly. Clearly the task of giant robot parrot poking was somewhere akin to latrine scrubbing, although the latter was probably less likely to get him hideously lacerated.

Timbers clapped his hands together as Oaf hauled a giant anchor onto the deck behind him. "So, where are we headed?"

Marty glanced at his watch. It was late, and Kate did have to be at work in the morning, so it didn't take much Sherlockian chin rubbing to deduce that her place might be a fairly safe bet. "She doesn't live far from me, so we'll have to head back into town," he began, instantly aware that Timbers was paying absolutely no attention to him whatsoever. The miniature corsair stared up into the rigging, where Also Bob was engaged in a decidedly one sided tug of war bout with Zephyr. Clearly it didn't matter who, or what you were, being rudely awakened by a sharp poke in the ribs doesn't go down all that well. "Come on Also Bob, look lively! We aren't going to find Marty's fine lady sitting in this duck pond, are we?" he bellowed as the grappling twin fought to regain possession of his proddy thing.

"Actually..." Whipstaff chimed in from the edge of the deck. He pointed out past the caddy hut to where two figures were rapidly approaching. Marty followed the cloth finger, his smile almost leaping off his face as he recognized that long blonde hair, with Kate hiding beneath it. He couldn't make out the figure scuttling along next to her, who seemed to be no bigger than his pirate compadres, but lost amid a blurry, red glow. *Did pirates come in neon?* He wondered, realizing how absurd such a thought would have been to him a few months ago. Now, he wouldn't bat an eyelid if he discovered that they came in cereal boxes with a free turnip.

Timbers had joined Marty and Whipstaff at the edge of the deck, and ushered for Oaf to lower a rope ladder over the side. "There! Problem number one solved," he chuckled. "This plan malarky is dead easy! What's next on the list of things requiring zero effort?"

Marty's jaw stiffened, his eyes still firmly fixed on the advancing Kate and her mystery (but seemingly flabouyant) new friend. "Next, we need to go and see who's been painting the town *kaboom*," he muttered, hoping that the hint of reluctance in his voice had been subtle enough to go unnoticed.

Again, Whipstaff's pointing finger was called into action, although shakier and far more ominously than before. A dozen or so new figures emerged from behind the giant rocket ship, which stood proudly over the seventh hole. They were still too far away to see clearly, and yet Marty had seen that stilted, jittering lope before. As bright red noses and ragged, orange hair fell into view, it became clear what was causing Kate and the big red firefly to be steadfastly legging it towards them. Marty glanced down at Timbers, who's good eye would surely have popped out in terror, had it not been a button. In one whirling motion, the little captain darted for the main sail, hurling frantic commands at his navigators in their crows nests. "Bobs, stop messing about with the bird and get us skyward. We've got incoming!"

One Bob peered from his lofty turret worriedly, waving frantically down towards the deck. As Timbers prepared to re-state his order, with added swearing for extra effect, Also Bob planted himself firmly back on deck, causing the planks to shudder and creak. He held in his hand the pokey stick, clearly having won his battle with Zephyr, but not with gravity. The dazed twin shook his head and blinked muddily, no doubt hearing bells or birds or banjos in his be-clattered head.

This was no time to be taking a concussion break, and Timbers hoisted his shipmate to his shaky feet before the poor little guy could remember which Bob he was.

"Clowns! Bird! UP!" Timbers shrieked, clearly under the impression that the situation would not need any further clarification. Whether Also Bob understood what was being barked at him or not, he had one foot on the first rung of the main sail as the *Fathom* took on two boarders. Marty blew out a thankful sigh as Kate scrambled to her feet, hoisting up something small and glowing behind her.

"Hi Kate, no time for pleasantries, hold onto something, we're about to..." Timbers paused, mid-sentence, regarding the luminous creature beside her which pulsed between red and yellow. "Why do you have a badger with you?"

Kate straightened, flashing a smile of relief at Marty. "He's not a badger, he's a..." she began in reply to Timbers, stopping short as the captain waved away the impromptu biology lesson. "Fair enough, he could be a little fluffy mermaid for all I care right now, let's get the hell out of here." The thing that wasn't a badger, or probably a fluffy mermaid, flushed momentarily with a dazzling pink hue, before all eyes returned to the incoming circus goons.

They were whoopingly, gibberingly close to the ship now, and as Also Bob heaved himself back into his crow's nest, they collided heavily with the hull, breaking against it like a shrieking, grease-painted tidal wave.

"Dammit!" Timbers' wailing was almost inaudible as Zephyr finally received the order to take off. "The plan. They're messing with the plan!"

Chapter Nine

The police department phone cackled sharply to life on a desk laden with papers and cold coffee. This would no doubt have caused the lone figure in the office to recoil in surprise, had the damn thing not been doing the same thing for most of the evening. The solitary policeman snatched up the handset testily, and offered a jaded ear to the ranting babble which sprang from it. It seemed that the town had chosen tonight, his turn on the graveyard shift, to turn seven shades of bonkers, and it was about as fun as being the designated driver at an end-of-the-world blowout bash.

Detective Michael O'Riley dropped wearily into his chair, noting down the latest slice of bedlam that was being served by the frantic caller. He was a patient man, a fastidious man, but ultimately just one-man. Hell, he wasn't even a detective, just another blue hatted flatfoot in what had been, until tonight, a reassuringly sleepy town. He liked the term 'detective' though. It carried with it the sort of gravitas and sunglass wielding cool that he had so wanted his job to entail. Had this been one of his beloved cop shows, he would be receiving this news on the police radio in his Lamborghini, as he unsheathed his heavy caliber sidearm and gruffly whispered something immensely slick and quotable to his partner. He grimaced as this glamorous image faded, and his pen ran out of ink, mid-sentence.

He slammed the phone down and leaned back in his chair, casting his eyes over the paperwork-pocalypse of his desk. Attention to detail was all well and good, but this was way too much detail for one night, forming a mountain of misdemeanors before him.

He spied his name plate amongst the pile of scrawled felonies, and his brow furrowed. It seemed that his fellow officers had decided it would be amusing to post-it out Michael O'Riley in favor of the new moniker, 'Crikey O'Blimey'. This made no sense to Michael, since he was neither Irish, nor overly dramatic, and he reached to dispose of the offending jape, simultaneously sending torrents of crime reports cascading to the ground. This was intolerable. Not just the joke, but the whole situation. He was not a man without humor. He tried to be liked and accepted by his fellow officers. *No, that wasn't completely true,* he mused. In fact, he couldn't give a beer monkey's ass about any of them, but here he was, holding down the fort on his own as the town danced the wacky waltz around him. He was a team player, and he cared what happened on his watch. By Crikey O'Blimey, he did give a damn.

O'Riley winced at the realization that his apparent new nickname had already taken root in his mind.

Snatching his keys from the outrageously detailed mayhem on his desk, he made for the door. He was the only one here, and by rights, he shouldn't leave his post, but there were people out there who clearly needed to be protected and served, and what was he doing here? Basically, documenting a riot. The answering machine could quite adequately do that, quickly, efficiently, and with the same amount of usefulness as he was currently providing. As O'Riley punched the blinking red button of the answering machine, another call came squawking into the office.

"Hi! Thank you for calling the police hotline, how may I take your order?" The machine cheerfully enquired. O'Riley shook his head He had no idea who recorded these messages, but since the soup of the day seemed to be carnage noodle, it didn't seem too far out of place.

The door heaved outwards, delivering justice and a small, portly police officer into the night. O'Riley wasted no time leaping into a patrol car and gunning it into the High Street. He had dutifully noted down the technicolor chaos of the evening thus far, so it surely couldn't be long before he happened upon some of this wholesale naughtiness first hand. The thing about wholesale naughtiness, after all, is that it tends not to hide its gleeful, mischievous light under a bushel.

Scarcely ten yards down the High Street, O'Riley's squad car bore him to a screeching halt, as said shenanigans tumbled out from the darkness, cavorted cheekily before him, and scampered disgracefully off into the night.

O'Riley stared after the tumultuous gaggle of mischief, unsure as to what had caused him to slam on the brakes. For all the world, it had seemed like a gang of circus clowns, merry old carnival jesters. Except one had appeared to be carrying a stick of dynamite, its fuse smoldering and fizzing. Another seemed to be actually ablaze, whilst a third had snaked past, dragging a seemingly innocent member of the public behind it. This was probably not good. At the very least, they probably didn't have a permit, if there even was a permit for being on fire.

He watched the chaotic conga line vanish into the next street, unsure of how to proceed. This was not the sort of thing they covered in basic training, or indeed any sort of training. Crowd control, yes. Blazing, explosive wielding clown control, not so much. It wasn't even an image that sat well in one's mind, let alone something that could be effectively dealt with.

The night bellowed into life behind O'Riley, summoning his thoughts back into something resembling order. The back seat of the squad car heaved as someone bundled in through the rear door, slamming it behind them. "Drive!" A thin, reedy voice commanded through the tinted perp shield which separated O'Riley from his new passenger. It was an unexpected entrance, and an even more unexpected order, but given the bizarre scene unfolding in front of him, it seemed not without merit, and the still marginally confused cop stamped a foot down hard on the accelerator pedal, sending the squad car lurching forward.

"Who's back there?" O'Riley enquired weakly, all of his efforts channeled into making the steering wheel behave. Whilst he was committed to protecting and serving, amidst what appeared to be the first and only riot in the town's history, showing and telling was pretty high on the order of business right now, too. The voice, however, seemed far too preoccupied with ranting. As the car veered into a connecting street, the babble from the back seat showed no signs of flirting with coherence. "They're everywhere," it gibbered, as O'Riley plunged the car down a deserted High Street. "The big one, all eyes and teeth," the hysterical passenger continued, shrieking through the glass. "He's around here somewhere, I saw him come this way." The caterwauling was reaching levels that only dogs would be able to hear, and O'Riley suddenly wished that there was some kind of backup that he could call in. "It's all so horrible," the voice wailed. "So heinous," it screamed. "So…much…fun!" it chuckled.

O'Riley glanced into the rearview mirror, realizing too late that victims of wholesale devilry don't usually tend to revel in it, before a pair of white gloved hands smashed through the glass between him and whatever was in the back seat. O'Riley had time to register just how few things actually had been covered in basic training, this being yet another that wasn't, before his foot called an instinctive halt to proceedings, connecting violently with the brake pedal.

The car jolted and skewed crazily to a stop, as the owner of those probing hands shot past O'Riley, and through the windshield in a blurry, brightly colored mass of whooping *Hell No*. Squad car, broken windshield and worryingly mysterious assailant, came to a skittering rest in the middle of the road. O'Riley blinked into the darkness, wondering if post traumatic clown disorder was an actual thing.

Something ragged and jolly rose up into the car's headlights, brushing shards of windshield from a gaudy waistcoat and grinning wickedly at the gawping lawman. *If this was your standard, run of the mill kids' party clown, he had left more than a few popped balloons and a broken piñata in his wake*, O'Riley thought, as the ghastly jester extended white gloved talons and advanced. This kind of carnival carnage was going to require something more than standard police justice. These harlequins from hell were not going to go quietly. No, they were going to go gigglingly, snarlingly, possibly combustibly, and O'Riley couldn't have that. He fought back the urge to heroically growl "Not on my watch!" and slammed a foot on the gas. The demonic prankster let out a toe curling squeal and spread its arms wide, beckoning the oncoming police car with a grand canyon sized grin. All thoughts that this might not be the best plan exploded along with the manic jester, as squad car connected with sparkly pantaloons in an eruptive fountain of brightly colored confetti, and careened off down the street, leaving naught but glittering paper flecks in its path.

Not for the first time that evening, O'Riley attempted to haul sanity back into his mind. Did all clowns do that? In all fairness, he had never mown one down before, so he had no idea, but it didn't seem like a particularly normal occurrence. Reality tapped him on the shoulder as more grease-painted freaks swept into his headlight beams, and he pulled up sharply, his resolve as a keeper of the peace shunning any further need to question his own sanity.

Detective O'Riley darted from the squad car, frankly a few dents south of road worthy, and drew his gun. "Sir!" he barked at the largest of the cavorting jesters. "Sir, I'm going to have to ask you to come with me." He levelled the pistol at the lead clown, who had already turned, and leered silently at him. Placing a trembling finger against the trigger, O'Riley motioned towards the tragically stricken squad car. "Let's go, sir. Don't make me turn you into a pile of party streamers."

The loping clown eyed O'Riley darkly, as two of his sneering lackeys fell in behind him. Their heads pivoted and craned sickeningly, maintaining a mask of glee guaranteed to call a premature halt to any children's party. With jerky, inhuman movements, the clownish trio juddered towards the now rapidly re-evaluating police officer, a mixture of cheerful malevolence and curiosity dancing madly across their ghostly white faces.

O'Riley grimaced. "I'm gonna need a bigger cell," he said as he led the sneering felons away.

Chapter Ten

Even before a gigantic robotic parrot topped pirate galleon had come to rest upon its sweeping turf, Stellar Island's miniature golf course could have feasibly claimed 'Wonder of the World' status. The likes of the Taj Mahal and the great pyramid of Giza were undoubtedly impressive, but it could be argued that they were somewhat lacking in interactivity, and probably had less hot dog stands, so it was safe to make the assumption. It was a hit all year round, and with good reason. From the imposingly centrifugal 'Large Hole-One Collider', to the all-consuming finality of the 'Eighteenth Black Hole', it was a cosmic free-for-all of monoliths, craters, and asteroids. Aside from the occasional floating punter in need of rescue within the zero gravity of Hole Nine, satisfied customers would flock and re-flock to its massive airlocked doors on a daily basis.

The patrons who had chosen this particular evening to do their flocking however, were not here for a spot of planetary pitch and putt. They hadn't even brought clubs with them, and from their appearance were certainly unlikely to have paid any green fees. They seemed totally uninterested in the twirling, strobe casting UFOs which orbited Hole Four, and completely disregarded the friendly looking little green men who stood conspiratorially around the distinctly Roswell-esque Hole Five. All of their attention, and forward momentum was towards the *Flying Fathom* in the center of the course, momentum which didn't cease as they reached it.

Half a dozen hooting clowns barreled into the side of the hull, pounding at it with every available ghastly appendage, and attempting to scramble upwards as the boat rocked at the force of the collision. The crew of the *Fathom*, now heavy a few passengers, clung to whatever they could as the deck creaked and listed to one side. Peering over the edge at the demented broadsiders, Marty dearly wished that his ability to plan was as swift and readily accessible as his ability to panic, and immediately shrank back from the deck rail. Whether the course of action that presented itself to him was borne from fight or from flight wasn't clear, but as he bolted over to the port side of the deck, he barked out an order to the ranting crew, who were pinwheeling in disarray around him.

"Get the *Fathom* airborne, I'll try and lead them away." Even as he finished the sentence, Marty simultaneously questioned his own sanity, inwardly requesting clarification of this supposed plan, and mentally congratulating himself for being such a big damn hero. Even as he dropped in a hopefully unseen, unheroic heap in the shallows of the water hazard, Marty knew that someone would be right behind him, mainly because she had been right beside him ever since he had awoken from *that* dream. Kate landed back on terra-fairway with far more grace than Marty had managed, and shot him a smug, but markedly defiant look.

Women were funny creatures, Marty mused, ignoring the oozing mud filling up his sneakers. Every instinct within him commanded that he valiantly order her back to the relative safety of the *Fathom*, where she could squeal theatrically at his feat of almighty bravery. Women loved being the damsel for their knights in stagnant water, right? Not this one, and Marty immediately revised his concept of chivalry to include ass kicking girlfriends. Beaming with pride and relieved to have the company, Marty motioned towards an oversized effigy of Saturn's rings which circumnavigated Hole Six, and grabbed Kate's hand. That was surely still allowed in the minefield of equal rights chivalry.

They vaulted towards the luminously bathed green, making as much racket as humanly possible in an attempt to make their presence known. "I haven't seen you since this morning," Kate cut in as they ran. "How was your day?"

Marty blinked, almost breaking stride. Amidst all of this other worldly chaos, inviting calamity upon themselves as they were, Kate was as calm and unwavering as ever. Or to put it another way, she was pretty damned spectacular.

The clowns had heard them, and snaked from either side of the

Fathom to give chase. Even so, Marty was now completely caught up in this domestic couple bubble that Kate had flung up around them, and suppressed a smirk as he ran. "Oh, not bad. Ran around the park in a beagle suit, almost got eaten by an invisible monster, met up with the pirates. Pretty standard really. You?" Deep down inside Marty, something cheered. Somewhere amidst the smothering tedium of the day, he had stopped existing, and started living again.

"Pretty humdrum actually." Kate replied, now halfway around Styrofoam Saturn. "Stopped off for a drink at the Judge - awful band. Escaped a bunch of clowns and met up with a glowing koala." She paused, as though searching for something more interesting than this Salvador Dali painting of an evening. "Oh!" she added "And I got my nails done. Nice huh?" She hoisted Marty into the upper atmosphere of the mighty plastic planet and flourished her fingers.

The clowns were getting closer, but Marty felt only a wild exultation, and faint curiosity as to what color Kate's fingernails were now. He barely glanced at them, his eyes instead fixed on hers, which betrayed the same disconnected euphoria that was currently blazing like a tornado through his mind. He nodded his approval, nonetheless.

They were passengers in reality, and they both knew it. This return ticket back into the express lane which should have brought with it confusion and terror seemed instead to carry a sense of familiarity. Marty glanced back at the cavorting, gibbering freaks, barely feet from where they stood. Okay, maybe some terror as well.

Somewhere behind the drooling freaks, Zephyr roared triumphantly. Marty squinted into the darkness, making out the outline of the *Fathom* drifting majestically into the air. Several feet in front of it, something gangly and seemingly made of twisted limbs sprang into hideous clarity. They had stopped moving and the clowns were upon them.

Grabbing Kate's hand again, Marty leapt from the edge of tiny Saturn's rings, dropping to the ground and leaving the rotund platform spinning haphazardly. The two lead clowns sprang into mini-Saturn's orbit, scuttling and stumbling across the rings like devilish DJs on some gigantic, cosmic turntable. It was a short scamper up to Hole Seven-ly Bodies, festooned with mystifyingly mobile meteors and asteroids. Marty had never bothered to enquire as to the mechanics behind some of the physics bending props of the golf course—it was sure to ruin the illusion—and he wasn't sure he wanted to meet the mad genius behind it all. Pursued as they were by grisly carnival hellspawn however, they could not have chosen a better battleground to retreat into. Several smaller portions of space debris floated past, and Marty plucked the nearest one out of the ether, hefting it purposefully in his hand. It was polystyrene, and painfully inadequate, but in the absence of a heavy caliber firearm, it would have to do. He heaved it at the clowns still hopelessly spinning about Saturn, catching the lead giggler square in the bright red hooter. It dropped like a fairground sideshow coconut, although admittedly with more screaming and face clutching, and Marty grinned, spectacularly failing in his attempt to suppress a fist pump. Another, goodly sized meteor hurtled past Marty, and he spun to see Kate winding in her pitching arm. This might have been fun, had their targets not been so intent on grabbing and devouring them. Ducking past another whirling asteroid, Marty sped towards the next hole, motioning for Kate to follow.

Free of the asteroid belt, they skirted the short path down into Hole Cape Canaver-Eight, with its massive space shuttle launch pad. Marty briefly wondered how the guy who had named the holes of this course hadn't been fired yet, before returning his attention to the advancing clown horde. Five of them remained, and they were already negotiating the remaining celestial flotsam of Hole Seven. With unsettlingly jerky movement, and yet also with unerring speed they came, causing Marty to almost stumble as he and Kate clattered into the launch gantry of Hole Eight. Wheezing, he held himself up against the mighty structure. Running had been so much easier in his dream, where gasping lungs and a fervent aversion to exercise had not been a factor. Here, he was at the mercy of his annoyingly real muscles, who were even now crying out for a comfy couch and something deliciously fried. The grotesque carnival procession that hunted them was already past Hole Seven, and chuckling its way down the path they had just traversed. Several hands stretched to almost inhuman lengths, even for killer clowns, and Marty could hear the gnashing of horribly pointed and seldom brushed teeth in their wake. He cursed his love of calories, and attempted to summon a last iota of energy with which to continue his flight. This had clearly been a bad idea, his mind pedantically reminded him as the nearest clown reached neck breathing proximity. Marty winced as familiarly ragged, grasping claws found purchase on his shoulder. Had he been able to summon up any breath, it would most certainly be hurtling out of him on the back of a startled cry as his pursuer cackled in triumph.

With unholy glee hauling Marty backwards, something overhead turned the sky an ear shattering shade of fiery orange, and a huge cloud of confetti erupted, where once a squealing harlequin had stood. Looking up through the festively dissipating clown, Marty spied the broadside of the *Flying Fathom*, Timbers standing defiantly atop a smoking cannon on the ship's quarterdeck.

"Ahahaha!" The little captain spat, hands set firmly on hips. "Hole in one, ya red nosed bilge rat!"

Turning back to the frantically reloading Oaf, Timbers continued his pirate ranting. "Get another one ready to fire, Oaf. I've thought up a bunch of zingers, and I don't want to waste them."

The Fathom veered sideways, blasting off another cannon volley into the onrushing clown phalanx. "Gonna need a sand wedge to pick that one out," Timbers crowed. "Who says golf's boring?"

Caught up in the immensely satisfying clown bashing, Marty hadn't noticed that Kate was making her way up the steel launch gantry. "Are you coming, or waiting for them to play through?" she called, snapping Marty back into the moment. He glanced up at her, one foot already on the steel rig, a smile back on his face, and adrenaline poking his muscles into further action. He tried to tell himself that the head start had carried Kate to the top before he arrived, but his need for breath deprived him of the means to impart the excuse. Still, what mattered was that they were at the apex of the ridiculously high launch pad, and the *Fathom* was sweeping around for another pass.

Three clowns remained below, and were doing their best to join them. Marty held out a hitchhiker thumb, and was already running alongside Kate as the mighty galleon drifted past them. Once again the smile returned, and Marty fought to regain his composure as a familiar song swam through his head.

"Clowns to the left of me, pirates to the right."

"We're going to have to jump," Kate cut in with a dose of good sense and reality as the end of the gantry loomed. The *Fathom* was only a few feet away, and below them, a few dozen feet of unforgiving gravity. How Marty wished that they were on gravity taunting Hole Nine.

The clowns reached the summit behind them, and whooped chaotically as one galloping, biting mass of teeth, claws, and cheerful red noses. With only one course of action left, Kate and Marty reached the end of the launch pad and leapt, screaming at the deck of the *Fathom*.

Had this been a dream, or indeed one of the four million action movies that Marty had seen countless times, this moment would probably have slowed down, to give time for ample reflection, a few explosions, and possibly some soiling of undergarments. Reality however, has a habit of screeching by at the speed of now, and saw both Kate and Marty clatter to a painful rest amongst the rigging of the main sail. Painful, but safe at least. Marty peered up from his haphazardly stuck landing, into the eyes of Kate's new koala friend. Benji blinked, wide eyed at the sudden flurry of things apparently beyond his realm of understanding, and pulsed an alarming shade of bright red. "You nearly landed upon me, sir," he whimpered, casting a worried glace across the deck. Although already unassuming, the tiny marsupial had shrunk back against a clutch of barrels which were tethered to the main sail. Looking up into the rigging, Benju clucked disapprovingly. "This isn't a tree. I can't hide in there. This place is not safe at all."

Of course, Benji was probably right. As was so often the case when attempting to escape murderous clowns, or indeed murderous anything, safe was a precarious and temporary state. One given to collapse into incendiary chunks of unexpected adversity at any given moment, whatever reality you happened to be in at the time. On this occasion, safe lasted approximately five or six seconds, before exploding into brilliant white chaos, and several shrieks of surprise.

From behind the rapidly departing *Fathom*, shards of blinding light erupted, tearing the night sky asunder, and buffeting the fleeing ship violently. From where Marty lay, he could see Timbers, braced against the deck rail, and staring in awe at whatever had been birthed into their sweeping wake. Struggling to his feet, he peered over the side, squinting to see what had momentarily turned the night into day. Whatever it was had engulfed the course, the gantry, and the pursuing clowns. It was vast, shimmering and oh so...

"The shiny!" Whipstaff called out excitedly from somewhere on the quarterdeck. It was, for a moment, an effective description of the oval shaped portal that hung like a tear in the night sky, before something infinitely more animated filled its ragged borders.

Like a torrent of immeasurable wonder, something magnificent poured forth from the portal's blinding depths. It sprayed out like a technicolor geyser, sweeping the *Fathom* up in a wave of reds, yellows, pinks and greens.

Marty glanced down into this tsunami of awesome that was now bearing the *Fathom*, faster than Zephyr could carry them, and it gleamed brilliantly back at him in hues more vibrant than any he had seen before. There were more shades in there, purple and orange and blue.

"It's a rainbow!" Kate exclaimed delightedly as the torrent continued, flinging the *Fathom* out of the golf course, and on a crest of glittering color towards the town. Peering nervously over the side, Benji strobed in a seizure inducing echo of the teeming, multi-hued vortex beneath them.

"Dammit, it is a rainbow," Whipstaff echoed, although markedly less enthusiastically than Kate had pointed out.

"What's the matter?" Kate asked, steadying herself against the rigging as she stretched to get a better view over the side. "It's gorgeous!"

Timbers scuttled down from the quarterdeck, his face more solemn than a toy pirate's had any business being. "You know what's at the end of the rainbow, don't you?" he groaned, cursing under his breath as he joined the others.

"A pot of gold?" Marty offered. Oaf had been untangling his feet from a pile of stray ropes, and brightened at the very mention of every pirate's favorite thing.

Timbers shook his head, waving a cautionary finger, and gripped the railing tighter as the roaring rainbow pulled the boat in a tight, looping arc over the town. "Yeah, and the damned green monster guarding it."

Marty chuckled, half from the implication, and half from the hope that Timbers was telling the truth. "I think we can handle a tiny little leprechaun. We've dealt with worse," he smirked, motioning back at the presumably vanquished clowns behind them, drowned in a myriad of exultant color.

As if to quell what would have been a fairly reasonable boast, a booming voice thunder clapped across the sky, the herald of an equally foreboding shadow which fell like a shroud across the deck of the *Fathom*. All eyes looked up as the bearer of the apocalyptic question, and the all-encompassing shadow spoke again.

"WHO'S AFTER ME GOLD?!"

Chapter Eleven

The three police department cells were gray, sparse, and about the size of your average shoe box. Since the usual criminal mastermind was brought in for disturbing the peace or creatively located public urination, the town had foregone the full maximum security package, and opted for the standard single bunk, single bucket accommodation for its evildoers.

O'Riley shuffled uncomfortably in the narrow corridor spanning the cellblock. He wasn't entirely sure what he was staring at, as the ghoulish occupants of cells one, two and three peered unblinkingly out of the darkness at a spot several thousand yards behind him. At least they had come willingly, if not altogether quietly. His patrol car had been a veritable hell's funhouse of guttural chuckling and clownish shenanigans, as they had made the short journey back to the station. It was like having a car full of drunk, possessed baboons in tow, and it unsettled the bejesus out of him. It had done as they had giggled their way out of the car, and it had done as they had cackled their way into the cells, but now their silence bothered him more. Each gaunt, red nosed face, with its ragged scar mouth and darting eyes, sat deadly silent and watchful as O'Riley paced back and forth, wondering what the hell to do with them. Should he question them? Staring at those eyes, he got the impression that whatever he asked these mystery mannequins, he didn't want to know the answer anyway.

"Well, so much for small talk," O'Riley mumbled, trying to avoid eye contact. He reached the end of the cellblock, surveying the office in its cloak of semi-darkness. If he had known that he would be playing babysitter to a troupe of monstrous mimes, he would not have volunteered for the graveyard shift alone. Suddenly the gun on his belt felt little more effective than a water pistol, and he wondered what kind of mythical weapon would put him at ease in the face of such big top blasphemy. Maybe a huge wooden mallet with a spring-loaded boxing glove. A pie firing rocket launcher. A fearsome cyborg with giant, wobbly, slapping hands.

O'Riley's trip into the realms of cartoon ordnance was cut short by a voice behind him. It issued from one of the dark cells like rancid steam hissing from a storm drain.

"Little pig. Little pig."

O'Riley turned, hoping that his imagination had conjured up those words, and wished he had backup coming, in the form of the T-Wobbly-Slap-1000. A pale, grinning face appeared at the barred door of cell number one, and the voice came again.

"Little pig, let them in."

O'Riley took two steps back into the office, drawing his gun, and training it on the dimly lit corridor of the cell block. If any of his fellow officers weren't face down in their pillows, as beer monkeys hammered pin sharp hangovers into their heads, he would be calling for back up right now. As it was, he settled for inwardly shouting for his mommy, and redundantly shaking his head at the sinister request.

It was surely impossible for the horrendous inmates to see O'Riley's weak protests, and yet the voice continued to taunt him.

"Not by the hair on your chinny chin chin?"

O'Riley mentally slapped himself in the face. Nursery rhymes weren't scary. Kid stories weren't scary. Seven foot tall, bulging-eyed clowns chanting softly in his police cells admittedly were scary, but this was ludicrous. They were messing with him, and it had almost worked. O'Riley allowed himself a half-smile, and took a step towards the cells, as a voice behind him, in the street beyond the locked door of the police station finished the fairy tale monologue.

"Well I'll huff."

O'Riley flinched, the voice carried the same sinister growl as the one that had taunted him from the cells.

"And I'll puff."

It crept through the door, saturated with the same barely contained giggle that he had heard from the back of the squad car as he transported his perps back to the cells.

"And I'll blow your house in!"

Perhaps there were more clowns…

As the door of the police station imploded in a barrage of what could only be described as vanilla cream and pastry mortar fire, a small corner of O'Riley's mind spoke up. The small corner that is left over in all of us from our childhood, that reminds us to look under our beds, check our closets, and keep a nightlight on when we go to sleep. *There are always more clowns* it warned, redundantly, as several snarling, giggling shapes darted in through the custard pie spattered door, and scuttled towards the cowering police officer.

The police issue .45 had felt good on his hip when enlisted in the force. It had been a constant reminder that he was in control, and that any situation could be diffused by a swift draw and point, perhaps with a coolly delivered one-liner, of the sort so ably dished out by steely jawed peacemakers in his beloved cop shows. As O'Riley dove for cover behind the nearest desk, with deliciously baked missiles exploding all around him, it felt more like a lead weight, and he struggled to heave it to bear as the cackling grew louder, and the scampering drew closer. He peered out from behind a stack of unfinished paperwork, not knowing quite what to expect. The station was still dark, although street lights cast an eerie glow through the shattered front doors. Several somethings were in here, no doubt, but he could not see his mystery besiegers, and the room had fallen worryingly silent.

Even the cell dwellers had ceased their yammering as O'Riley crawled out from behind his desk, shakily training his pistol this way and that, but nothing sprang from the dim twilight to visit chuckly death upon him. He straightened, trying to marshal his thoughts into something resembling an escape route, but curiously, only a recipe for vanilla cream pie played through his mind, and refused to budge. Hardly surprising, since the stuff dripped from every drippable surface, and admittedly, smelled delightful.

A clattering, shifting sound jerked O'Riley from his culinary daydream. The darkness parted, filled with something altogether less palatable. Snaking out of the gloom, in a way that no face should, yet in a way that only a ghostly white, fiendishly leering face can, one of Satan's own jesters introduced itself to O'Riley.

"Olly Olly Oxen Free!," the face gibbered, apparently delighted that it had found the cowering police officer, and squealed with completely unconcealed glee. O'Riley yelped, falling backwards into the water cooler which had unbelievably remained untouched throughout the siege. Water and terrified constable slewed across the floor, as the devilish harlequin raised to its full height and crowed manically at the sight of freshly hewn carnage.

Now was a time for action, O'Riley thought, pushing aside the lingering desire for pastry based treats. Now was not the time for loitering in a pool of what was hopefully just cooler water soaking through his trousers. O'Riley levelled his gun at the advancing jester, closed his eyes and pulled the trigger.

Having never actually shot at anything, apart from the helpless hanging targets on the police firing range, O'Riley was unsure how to proceed having sent a bullet racing towards its grease-painted terminus. His experience with the unseatbelted fiend in his car should have given him a clue, however, as brightly colored confetti plumed from where his hideous attacker had been standing. Blinking, O'Riley struggled to his feet as the fronds of cheerful clown-stuff cascaded onto the slick, sodden floor. He almost laughed, nervously at first, and then at the sheer lunacy of the situation. Scratch one killer clown, let's celebrate with a ticker tape parade!

That would, of course, have been a lot funnier, had a single thought not tapped O'Riley on his shoulder, and quietly explained to him that there were probably more denizens of the big top from Hades lurking out there in the darkness. The thought travelled down his arm, into his hand, and yanked at his trigger finger, ploughing several more shots out into the darkness. *This was kind of fun*, he thought, as the bullets momentarily lit up the station. If any of them hit, it wouldn't be so much *Ooh, that's gotta hurt! Let's have a party!* as more confetti shot up out of the dim twilight of the room.

Breathing heavily, O'Riley sank back against the wreckage of the fallen cooler. He had counted a further three confetti geysers, which was surely a good thing, and the office was now reassuringly bereft of hellish giggling.

Still, he wished he felt more like a prime time, cop show badass, and less like a child shooting corks at a fairground attraction, as he rounded the desk, and checked for signs of circus shenanigans. The silence was deafening, and even the chucklers in the cells behind him had fallen in line, possibly to avoid becoming the next party decoration. Moving through the pie blasted office, O'Riley realized his gun hand was no longer shaking. Maybe this was what it felt like to be enforcing the law, to be laying a smack down on the bad guys. It felt like armor, and he straightened to fit properly into it. He had cleared the decks, repelled the boarders, held the fort, and it felt righteous. He scanned the office as bits of glittery paper still wafted hither and thither. There would be no clown invasion tonight. "Not on my watch," he breathed, simultaneously relieved and empowered at having the opportunity to utter the immortal line.

It was perhaps a little rude, then, that a shiny red ball should come bouncing through the front doors and shatter his cop hero scenario. It *boinged* harmlessly to rest at his feet, bringing his internal platitudes screeching to a logic confounding halt. A scrap of paper stuck to its side fluttered in the night air that was now intruding unfettered into the office. O'Riley stooped and plucked it from the ball, craning into the shards of moonlight to read what was written upon it.

There was no need to, as the line of silhouettes suddenly flanking the shrouded windows told O'Riley all he needed to know. There were several figures outside, spanning the length of the far reaching station windows, standing motionless and silent, and far more in number than the remaining bullets in his gun.

O'Riley looked down at the note, as the giggling in the cells behind him returned, and the cartwheeling in his stomach staged an almighty encore. The four words glared back at him, with almost as much malice as the exploding clown had wrought before his impressive exit.

'Give us Mr. Peepers.'

Chapter Twelve

Every child has had the same, awe filled thought process whilst looking up into that magical arcing spectrum in the sky. Whatever they dreamed might be *somewhere over the rainbow*; candy canes, rivers of chocolate, a town full of singing midgets, every wonder struck kid has stared up into a storm cleansed air as color raked the heavens and instantly recalled the old tales of myth and legend.

You didn't even have to live in Ireland to have heard of that most impish of gold hoarders, the eye glinting cheekiest of all fairie folk, the cute little leprechaun. Modern day children might even be forgiven for believing that these diminutive green sprites cared only for the sweet crunch of breakfast cereal, and yet as every good rainbow chaser knows, it is the amassment of cold hard cash that drives these jigging pranksters.

As the *Fathom* soared, hanging ten on the most gnarly of otherworldly technicolor waves, Marty gazed up, blinking in disbelief at the behemoth before them, and couldn't help but wonder how the dreamscape could get something as basic as scale so disastrously wrong.

At his side, Timbers' good eye widened at the sight of the colossal rainbow dweller, taking a step back and making a half motion for his cutlass, as if a toothpick would do any good at all against a thirty story brick wall.

Standing astride the vaulting rainbow, stood a green jacketed skyscraper in a dandy, gold buckled hat. Great tufts of red hair sprouted from beneath the brim, and two angrily glinting eyes regarded what must have seemed like a toy sailboat as the *Fathom* approached. From deep within its thick red beard, the voice spoke again, sending deep but lilting Irish thunder through the rigging of the surfing galleon.

"Keep yer thieving mitts off me gold!" the Gaelic tornado commanded. "And get off me rainbow, you're getting it all dirty!"

A huge, asteroid sized fist swept down on the *Fathom* in an ominous swatting motion. Zephyr, clearly acting more out of self-preservation than Bob-relayed orders, twisted sharply to starboard, flinging the crew of the *Fathom* into varying states of disarray. Still in the lurid grip of the gushing color stream, the ship jack-knifed, pitching wildly to one side as the plunging fist swept past. Marty clung desperately to the deck railing as the world and its contents whistled past him. Behind him, Kate had one arm wrapped around the central mast, and clutched a handful of Benji in the other, the little Koala zipping wildly between shades of yellow and blue.

Marty scanned the deck for the rest of the crew, as another bellowing rebuke blasted through the ether.

"Take your clockwork pigeon, and bugger off!"

Timbers appeared at Marty's side, set defiantly on the deck as though glued to it. Marty had seen the look in his one good eye before. A tiny toy pirate would let a lot of things slide, but nobody, *nobody* mocked his ride. Moments into subconsciously congratulation himself at his unintentional poetry, Marty was snapped back into the here and now by his captain's retort.

"Clear off, you annoying wee giant. We're not after your booty. And the big metal lad up there is no pigeon!"

Whipstaff was similarly adhered to the deck beside him, but evidently had other ideas. "Captain, he's got gold." The first mate cast a glance at the raging monster in their way. "Probably very large gold, or at least a lot of it."

Oaf, who seemingly wasn't wearing his sticky boots today tumbled past, steadying himself against a nearby barrel. Nodding in agreement, he stared imploringly at his captain. It was hard to dissuade a pirate from the pursuit of gold, a task akin to depriving a deep sea diver of oxygen, or taking a cheeseburger away from a starving man.

Timbers, however, was made of sterner stuff. It was probably what had elevated him to the role of captain, that or the fact that he looked the most piratey.

"Lads, you've got enough gold," he offered, diplomatically. "And we've got enough trouble with the clowns. One life threatening situation at a time, eh?"

Lepzilla was loping towards them now, still straddling the rainbow, and close enough to rain down lucky destruction upon them.

"Saints alive, this boy's huge," Timbers remarked, eyeing their lumbering assailant. "Where do you even get that much green felt?"

His words, and everything else audible, were lost as Zephyr pitched again, arrowing the *Fathom* into a nose dive which sent Kate and Benji cartwheeling towards the edge of the deck. Catching his breath, and a pawful of railing, Benji gaped blinkingly at the bedlam surrounding him. "The large gentleman seems quite upset. Should we pull over, or land or something?"

Marty was similarly awe struck, feet now mercifully fixed in place, he gawped up at the massive impish shape which blotted out the moon's dim radiance. "That's the biggest leprechaun I've ever seen," he murmured at nobody in particular.

Timbers smirked beside him, in spite of the newly delivered mighty haymaker which was hurtling towards them. "How many leprechauns have you seen?"

There was no time for a clever reply, as Zephyr changed direction once more. The Bobs flapped frantically in their crow's nests, but to no avail as the mechanical fowl performed a daring loop the loop that would have probably delivered big points from a judging panel, had he not been carrying a hefty-sized galleon in his claws, and had such a panel been present. The *Fathom* crashed back down onto the crest of the rainbow in an uprush of gleaming color, as the leprechaun's upper cut screamed by, inches from the hull.

"We need to get off this rainbow," Kate chipped in, still clutching a flapping, strobing koala in her free hand.

"Couldn't agree more," Timbers replied, "but it's not like they have intersections."

Her brow furrowing at the captain's reply, Kate attempted to continue the debate, but was cut short by another heaving tilt to port, as two gargantuan lepre-hands clapped together, clutching at a stretch of rainbow that had been heavy one pirate ship moments before. The shimmering band of color rippled under the force of the strike, sending it furling backward like some impressively unravelling, but outlandishly over-tye-dyed rug.

Grudgingly, in no small part because nobody had laughed at his clever retort, Timbers conceded to Kate's suggestion. "She's right, we need to depart pronto before Seamus O'Humongous there turns us into kindling." He turned to deliver orders to the crew, just as Whipstaff dashed by, heralded by an impressive, if somewhat unheroic battle cry. "Give us your gold, you massive bearded goblin!" Trotting after him, and somewhat less enthusiastically, Oaf delivered an apologetic half-shrug, as he and the first mate catapulted over the side and directly towards the waiting giant.

Timbers watched, open mouthed as the would-be mutineers sailed through the night sky, landing in a tumbling heap on the shoulders of the enraged leprechaun.

"Gold," he growled, turning with a shake of his head towards Marty. "Always with the gold, those two."

Marty offered what shred of logic he could pick out of this insane situation. "They're pirates, Timbers. Tell me you aren't a little bit tempted."

The little captain paused, reflecting on what was indeed his very job description. He raised his good eye to meet Marty's gaze and beamed. "Marty, I may be a pirate, but I'm not a damn fool." He took a step towards the quarterdeck as Zephyr let fly with a deafening shriek, signaling another jolting change of direction.

"I'll charge into a fight, I'll even start one if it looks like fun." He trotted up the staircase, heading for the aft of the ship. "But I won't stand for mutiny, and the lads aren't getting squished before I get a chance to kick their sorry backsides first."

Benji shrunk back against Kate, shivering slightly. "Sir, that's just reckless." He turned a violent shade of yellow, a color which required no translation. "This is all so very dangerous."

"Hopefully," Timbers shouted, angling an order up to his navigators. "Bobs...dive!"

Chapter Thirteen

Police constable Michael O'Riley was finally living his prime-time TV cop shows. Fire? Check. Explosions? Check. Dastardly wrongdoers? Well, sort of check, if you counted a dozen or so braying, grease-painted demons from a serial killer's birthday party. In truth, he could have done without the latter part of this particular scenario, but one does not choose the hero's trial into which one is flung, even if one protests violently and secretly wishes for a warm bed, or at the very least some kind of SWAT team backup.

The station lay in pregnant silence, punctured only by the incessant and guttural breathing of something outside, waiting to come in. Even the incessant ticking of the large, often over-watched clock atop the front doors seemed to have been muted to the point of sheepishness by the tension in the air. O'Riley wondered, quite justifiably, if he was still breathing, and glanced down to check whether his chest was going through the appropriate motions. A rasping, cautious breath crept out of hiding from somewhere within his ribcage, and huffed under duress from between the officer's quaking lips. Momentarily thankful he hadn't had a heart attack, O'Riley immediately began to curse the feverishly pounding muscle, which was all too obviously belting out a white flag beat in his ears, now that his mind had enquired after its wellbeing. All at once, the other parts of O'Riley's body, hitherto trying to remain unnoticed amid the mounting suspense, formed an orderly queue to lodge complaints to his brain, which began to reel at the sudden onrush of unwanted information. The legs department seemed to be the most insistent, phoning in a mayday, and clearly not too sure whether it was currently dealing with alcohol induced wobbliness, or had recently run a couple of marathons. O'Riley steadied himself against the water cooler next to his desk, inwardly reminding his legs that they belonged to an officer of the law. It was their very duty to be upstanding.

Wiping the slick film of sweat from his palms, he clumsily wrestled the chamber of his pistol open. There were precious few nuggets of bravery remaining nestled within O'Riley, and even fewer nuggets of lead sitting in the gun. If there was a way out of all this, it was unlikely to come from the smoking barrel at the end of it. He had spent around twenty whole minutes practicing on the police firing range, and approximately none of the targets had been clown shaped. What little confetti shaped destruction he'd managed to wreak so far had most certainly been more luck then judgement.

What exactly was going on in his town? Although this was certainly a violently speeding train of thought that was best left for a less life threatening occasion, O'Riley couldn't stop the finger prodding at his mind, enquiring whether this was all some sort of psychotic dream, and if he wouldn't mind awfully waking up, please.

Almost surprising himself, O'Riley heard his own voice speak up shakily in the shattered gloom of the office. "Pardon me," he began, somewhat less authoritatively than he had hoped. "You are interfering with police business, and causing damage to town property. I'm going to have to ask you to disperse, or…" He wasn't exactly sure how to end that sentence. He wasn't even sure where it had come from in the first place. Gritting his teeth, O'Riley summoned up the lingering scraps of heroism in what remained of his train of thought. "…or I'm going to have to write you all up on an 808." It wasn't the most awe inspiring, angry mob quelling command ever uttered, but police protocol was the only thing that presented itself as his mind struggled to remain afloat. "That's disturbing the peace," he added, redundantly, as if clarification would in some way add weight to the limp order that echoed out into the night, and whatever lurked within it.

Still framed against the frosted glass of the front window, the motionless figures struck up a reply, causing O'Riley to tighten his grip on his gun, and loosen his hold on his bowels.

"Police HQ is falling down, falling down, falling down," came the drawling lullaby from outside, altogether less charming than

O'Riley remembered it, and once again, his legs attempted a sit down protest.

"Police HQ is falling down. Give us Peepers!" The song devolved into a mass of chuckling and squealing, and O'Riley did the simple math in his head which pointed out that he was not paid nearly enough to deal with this sort of insanity.

Behind him, and past the cells which housed the object of the mystery intruders' desires, was a back door. Suddenly it was all that O'Riley could think about, and his feet made an executive decision to head for it as the second round of hideous clown karaoke filtered into the room. Clearly feet held precedence over legs, and seemed far more interested in staying attached to their owner.

"Ring a ring o' roses, a pocket full of posies."

It was safe to say that O'Riley's childhood memories of being sung to sleep had been altered forever as he broke into a semi-cowardly gallop towards the back entrance of the station.

"A-tishoo! A-tishoo! Give us the clown."

Scarcely ten feet from the back door, O'Riley risked a glance into the cells that flanked the corridor he was so shamelessly legging it through. Three cold, ghostly faces pressed up against the bars, watching him as he flew past. They grinned, gnashing horribly yellow teeth at him and hopped manically at the prospect of imminent rescue. The end cell housed the largest of the red nosed prisoners, and he glared with impossibly huge eyes which seemed to turn O'Riley's flailing feet into lead weights. There was something deep and devious within that burning stare, that he had not seen in the vacant maniacal faces of the other clowns. It seemed to reach out, calling a whispering halt to the officer's escape, hypnotically beckoning him to the bars of the cell.

O'Riley shifted, acutely aware that there should be a policeman-shaped hole in the back door by now, and yet the tiny voice inside him that wanted answers had seemingly wrestled free of the dogpile of panic in his mind. "Who are you?" he whispered, feeling like a small boy poking at a hornet's nest with a stick. "What is all this madness?"

The hornet's nest stirred, and the gleaming eyes bore down on O'Riley as the giant clown slithered towards the cell door. Two floppy gloved claws grasped at the bars. O'Riley stumbled backwards, inwardly body slamming his troublesome curiosity.

"Madness?" The slimy voice issued from within the cell like a slowly deflating balloon filled with Sulphur and nightmares. "Oh my little friend, this is just the entree." Hot jester breath hit O'Riley like wriggling gummi worms. He glanced over at the back door, wanting to bolt, but needing to hear more. His curiosity, it seemed, could take a kicking and keep on ticking.

"There are worse things than giggly funsters arriving in your little town tonight," the pantalooned fiend continued. "The monster that lives under your bed and only comes out at night, or the teddy bear with something nasty and pointy hidden behind his back." It giggled excitedly. "I'm sure you'll get to meet all my friends in due course. My name is Mr. Peepers, and I'll be here all week."

Mr. Peepers doffed an imaginary cap, and bowed theatrically, emitting a shuddering cackle that seemed to call all the clowns in the world through the main doors of the police station.

Curiosity finally waved a white flag, and allowed bare faced self-preservation sole access to O'Riley's 'run away' switch. As he crashed into the door frame at the back of the office, Mr. Peepers threw a snaking, unsettlingly cheerful farewell from within his cage. "Thank you for the hospitality."

Looking over his shoulder, O'Riley kicked into Olympic sprinter mode, as Peepers waved smugly, and cracked a smile wide enough to play the xylophone on.

Back in the darkness of the office, a crescendo of candy coated chaos whirled jerkily in his direction, all limbs, grins, and bright red noses.

"We'll be seeing you soon." Xylo-clown spat as the shrieking policeman burst out into the night and fled, his clownish tormentors giggling and jeering as he wholeheartedly scarpered.

This was most definitely not how it went down on TV.

Chapter Fourteen

When you're thirty stories above the ground, and watching it rapidly surge up to meet you, it is conceivably quite acceptable to loudly and publicly lose the plot. With the absence of a parachute, or suitable hang gliding equipment, one could be forgiven for misplacing more than a few of one's marbles.

As the *Fathom* hurtled Leprechaun-wards like an oddly shaped, piratey javelin, those spilled marbles would have been lost over the side which Kate and Marty clung to, clattering along the dipping rainbow to be lost along with the last remnants of sanity that had fleetingly inhabited the situation.

From behind him on the quarterdeck, Marty caught a peripheral glance of Timbers, crouched against the gushing wind, and shouting something in his direction. "Marty! I'm just popping out for a bit, the ship's yours 'til I get back. Don't break it." This was the declaration he thought came from the little captain, and of course, with the remaining vestige of reason now sent fluttering to the night sky, it was probably exactly what he'd said. The fact that Timbers proceeded to vault over the side of the quarterdeck also seemed to lend some weight to this possibility, and Marty leapt to the railings to see where the valiant little maniac had disappeared to. He needn't have looked far, as the colossal face of the disgruntled leprechaun filled his line of vision, like a rapidly rising, red-bearded sun. The leprechaun's attention, however, was not focused on the *Fathom*. He flapped and swatted at his splendid green tunic as Whipstaff and Oaf darted from collar to pocket, like scurrying ants looking for sparkly golden sugar. The mighty sprite screamed as another miniscule figure landed in a tumbling heap on his shoulder. It was Timbers, and the little pirate wasted no time in scampering across to the giant lapel that his crewmates were busy rappelling down. He appeared to be shouting at them, and Marty imagined that it was probably not something for young ears, although the bellowing of the leprechaun seemed to be drowning out most of the assumed expletives.

"Are we all going over the side? Because if anyone's interested, I don't want to," Benji babbled nervously from beside Marty. Still holding the little koala tightly, Kate bore the look of someone quite happy to stay on the rainbow coaster, and as acting captain, Marty had no intention of following his cash grabbing comrades into the melee.

The *Fathom* plunged past the crazed face of the leprechaun. Zephyr banked hard to give the towering creature a wide berth, as it threw wildly pinwheeling arms sweeping towards the departing hull of the ship. Mercifully, Seamus O'Gulliver still seemed more preoccupied with his scampering boarders, and crashed heavily into a row of office blocks, which flanked the street below as he attempted to deal with his piratey infestation. Ahead, the rainbow twirled majestically up and sharply right, where it barreled off down Main Street, twisting the *Fathom* over and down to join its gushing resplendent course. Still galloping and cursing alongside them, the leprechaun wove its way along the line of meagre stores and offices, like a huge drunken line dancer. Peering over the side, Marty watched with dismay as a hefty buckled shoe sliced the roof off *Peppe-Ronnie's*, his favorite pizza place. This was definitely the wrong street to be leading an angry, monstrous rainbow dweller down, and he squinted into the murky distance, to where a row of the best fast food joints in town sat, oblivious to their inevitable tramplement. Marty whirled, craning up into the rigging, where the Bobs were being spectacularly ignored by Zephyr. The mighty bird was clearly on auto pilot, and engaging in his own spontaneous evasive maneuvers.

"Kate, we need to get in his face." Marty shouted as the giant beside them ploughed on, taking out the huge decorative zeppelin which hung over *The Hinden-Burger*. Slapping a mortified hand to his forehead, Marty lurched over to where Kate was trying her best to hang on to a mast and a terrifyingly strobing koala. "He's going to mow down the whole of this street if we don't stop him," he ranted.

Kate flashed a wild look, replying in no calmer terms. "How do we do that? He doesn't look in much of a mood to be reasoned with."

Marty glanced feverishly about the deck. "I don't know, we could throw something at him maybe? Do a fly by? Fire a cannon at him?" Something clicked inside Marty's head, and the small boy in him that dealt with such matters turned the question into an exuberant statement. "We should fire a cannon at him!"

Kate's eyes widened, as Marty pin-balled back across the deck to the nearest deck mounted mortar. "Marty, are you sure that's a good idea? I mean, how many cannons have you fired before?"

Marty turned briefly, realizing this was a rational question he could happily brush aside. "Just the one, but I took out a clown at thirty paces with it." He beamed triumphantly. "Besides, they're all pointing outwards, it'll be like shooting fish in a barrel." He gazed up at the enraged behemoth alongside them. "All right, it'll be like shooting huge scary monsters in a barrel." He checked himself, as realization threatened to rob him of what had, moments ago seemed like a brilliant and explosive idea. "Umm, like shooting one huge scary monster, from inside a barrel." The analogy had become less appealing, but Marty was committed, and had reached the nearest cannon. Good sense made one last attempt to interject, but the leprechaun was bearing down on *Unlucky Fried Kitten*. Granted, it wasn't Marty's favorite eatery, but this had to stop, otherwise, who knows how many menus he would have to bin in the morning? Marty yanked the short cord on the back of the cannon, and the world which occupied the ten feet in front him erupted with an immensely satisfying, fiery *boom*. Marty whooped with the unadulterated joy that any man receives from firing anything loud, destructive, and incendiary. A cannonball shrieked from its iron nest towards the unsuspecting pixie.

Thirty or so stories below, the lowly drive thru attendant at *Unlucky Fried Kitten* uttered a silent prayer to his deity as a gargantuan boot plummeted towards the tiny building in which he sat. "Only two more days to retirement as well," he muttered, as the boot closed in.

High above the hapless skivvy however, divine intervention tore through the heavens and found its mark between the eyes of the hulking sprite. "Ahhh, begorrah!" the leprechaun squealed, as the cannonball sent him sprawling sideways, and into a neighboring, and mercifully long derelict shopping mall.

Marty sighed, resting on the still smoking barrel of the cannon. The purveyor of questionable fried meats was safe. For how long, was open for debate, as the vast velvet clad monster struggled back to his feet and loped after the *Fathom*. This was an unexpected turn of events, and Marty hadn't thought as far down the line as reloading, which would have been handy, as their towering pursuer strode ever closer. Further along the deck, another cannon bellowed its cargo at the gaining leprechaun, and Marty turned his attention to Kate, who stood proudly, hand on firing cord, and watched her broadside fly ear-splittingly towards its target. The leprechaun's huge eyes widened. He ducked as the cannonball whistled past his head, carving a scorched black line across his dandy green hat. "Will ye cut that out!" he bellowed, slowing to regain his mighty footing. "For the love of…" The ranting was cut short as movement at his side tore his attention from the annoying little boat with the silver budgie atop it. Scampering, scurrying, pilfering movement, which he had apparently forgotten all about amidst all this gunfire and restaurant squashing.

Turning hard against the tide of the rainbow, the *Fathom* struck back towards the looming giant, and into earshot of the interlopers who were busying themselves about his person. "Lower…lower!" came the cry from the vast green tunic, where Whipstaff hung precariously from a rope at pocket watch height, which in turn was being fed out by Oaf. "He's got a little pursey thing on his belt. I bet it's full of gold." Oaf gazed down at his pickpocketing shipmate and staggered as he realized down was a frighteningly long way off. "Little?" Oaf managed, closing his eyes. "It's huge. You could fit me in there. And I don't want him to fit me in there."

Timbers had apparently taken a wrong turn somewhere around the collar, and sprouted up amongst sprigs of clover which adorned the leprechauns jaunty hat. He ducked back into the lining just as a huge hand gripped the wide brim, pulling it from the thickly thatched red head. A remarkably gleaming bald patch shone out from under the hat, and Marty watched agog as the giant sprite shook his lavish headgear, attempting to wrest Timbers from his hiding place. "Get out of there, you swashbuckling flea. You're unluckifying all me clovers." The green leviathan patted at the hat, crumpling a couple of hundred yards of perfectly good velvet, and peered into it angrily.

The little captain giggled from amongst the unkempt ginger fronds which tufted out of the monster's ear. Dangling from an earlobe, he taunted its owner in a manner not at all befitting of someone in impending danger of being swatted. "Missed me, you potato chewing humpback." He dropped back onto the mighty left shoulder beneath, and doffed his hat, as the now furious leprechaun hastily replaced his.

Marty watched, still gripping the deck railing, as Timbers hopped deftly onto Oaf's shoulders, miraculously dodging a vast Irish paw in the process. Marty wondered how he could hear his battling crewmates through the screeching wind and x-rated Gaelic protests, but pirate rage was easily provoked, and impossible to quash.

"Get back to the ship so I can kick six of the seven seas out of you, you mutinous bilge snipe!" Timbers hollered at the now openly weeping Oaf. Another plunging Lepre-fist grasped for the tussling pirates as Oaf hauled Whipstaff back up to share in the chastising tirade. The tiny first mate leapt onto the vast lapel, chuckling in spite of the imminent keelhauling he would likely receive, and hefting up a large sack behind him. "I took his wallet, let's be off." Fixing him with as much glaring anger as it was possible to muster with one good, button eye, Timbers motioned for his erstwhile comrades to follow as he skipped up onto the leprechaun's shoulder and made for the deck of the *Fathom*, still battling the current, and almost upon the recently pilfered pixie.

"Me gold!" The leprechaun cried, clutching for the escaping pirates as they darted across his ten yard long epaulette and sprang onto the waiting deck of the *Fathom*.

Marty had seen enough. His crew back on terra-*Fathom*, and with another giant probing hand angling towards them, he summoned up the best ship's captain order he could think of. "Up!"

With ample time and consideration, he could have possibly come up with something better, but it encapsulated everything he wanted to occur at that moment. Zephyr mercifully obliged, emitting a screech which seemed to tear the *Fathom* from its crashing technicolor wave. Angling upwards, everything turned vertical, as ship and giant robotic bird tore into the heavens, barely evading a final sweeping right hook from the still swearing giant leprechaun beneath them. As was usually the case with gravity, the overriding thought of human, pirate and koala became *hold on, and hope for the best.* In spite of the mast creaking, the shrieking of several random panickers, and the whooshing of the night passing around them, Marty almost smiled at the thought that this was what had been missing in his life, and that he really was becoming a grand master at completely and unashamedly winging it.

Above all the behemoth leprechaun protests, clown carnage and all-round mayhem that gripped the town below, the *Fathom* billowed out through the clouds into the starry black canvas of the night sky. Zephyr fluttered, steadied, and banked into a graceful glide as everyone on board the ship untangled themselves from everyone else.

Timbers, his mind clearly still set on punishment, was upon his mutinous crew in an instant. "Someone fetch my favorite plank, there's two deck scrubbing gold hoarders off for a short walk and a long drop, by my reckoning."

Whilst Oaf attempted to hide behind something ill-fitting for his bulky form, Whipstaff seemed oblivious to his captain's threats, shaking the sack he'd pinched from his mighty quarry moments earlier. A shining gold coin, the size of a sewer grate tumbled out, clanging heavily on the deck and came to rest, head side up. "Yeah, I know, bad form and all that, captain. But look at this. It's huge! Must be worth a fortune."

Timbers prodded the massive doubloon with his boot, unable to suppress his admiration of its undoubted shininess, before snapping back into the role of finger wagging captain. "Very nice. What good it is to us, I have no idea. Unless Paul Bunyan needs to make a phone call, it's about as much use as pigtails on Oaf."

Oaf cupped his hands to his ears. Already fearful of a plank walk, a trip to the hairdressers was just a step too far.

"It's gold," Whipstaff continued, unperturbed.

Timbers rubbed his face impatiently. "That's as maybe, but we have more pressing concerns at the moment, like why we're here. Why all that down there is here. What, basically, the hell is going on?"

"I know." The voice was small, apologetic, and almost indiscernible amid the frantic back and forth.

"We could melt it down," Whipstaff implored. "Bury it under one of those big X's."

"I know," came the whispered interjection again, and this time Marty heard it.

"Maybe you could hang it around your neck," Timbers barked, clearly still put out at his crew's disobedience. "It'd go down a treat at the next toy pirate swash-your-buckle convention."

Whipstaff lined up another imploring reply, but was cut off by Kate, who had clearly heard the whisper too. "Both of you, pipe down." She had turned towards Benji, who was peeping out of a barrel that he had apparently fallen into, mid-ascent. "Benji. What do you know?"

The little koala shone with a faint, white glow, and cleared his throat sheepishly. "I know what's happening here."

The eyes of everyone on board turned to the quivering marsupial, who cowered within his wooden hiding place. Even Timbers, who was still apparently not done with his admonishment, casting a *this isn't over* glare at his first mate, before turning his attention to the tree rat in the barrel.

Marty stepped to Kate's side. "And what is going on?" he asked, in a voice he hoped wouldn't drive the creature further into its hiding place.

Benji peered out at the crew, blinking uncomfortably at the sudden onrush of attention, and turning a bright shade of crimson. "The big shiny holes. The painted gentlemen. The wicked slinky things under the bed," he squeaked, seeming to grow smaller as the words flowed. It didn't help that Marty, Kate and the crew were advancing on him inquiringly, but he persevered.

"The biggest painted man with the…" Benji made large spherical motions around his already fairly bulging eyes. "He wanted to come through, and he found a way."

A tiny furry finger extended towards Marty. "You showed him how to do it."

Chapter Fifteen

Marty blinked, taking in the world which had suddenly ploughed to a silent crawl around him. Even the eyes upon him, some of which were attached to heads that shook in disbelief, registered only dimly as he took in what the little koala had just said.

Whilst a torrent of theories, questions, and mystifying recipes for cheesecake tumbled through Marty's brain, only one word managed to wrestle its way to his lips. "…What?"

Timbers was quick to flesh out the premise of the hastily uttered statement. "Are we talking about the same guy here? Scary guy, weird clothes, about the size of a smoking boot last time we saw him?" They all knew that Benji was talking about Mr. Peepers, but it had been much more manageable to deal with a horde of cavorting clowns without contemplating that the grand high juggler of all things unpleasant had somehow survived his cannonball close up.

Benji nodded solemnly, his body now emitting a deep blueish tint. "I saw him, outside the drinking place, right before I met Miss Kate. I was wandering for quite a while looking for something climb or eat worthy. We both saw him, didn't we?" He peered up at Kate, who removed her ward from his barrel, and cradled the little marsupial, as much for comfort now as for protection.

"I saw clowns," she imparted slowly. "One was bigger than the rest, sure, but they're clowns." She shook her head, as if trying to dislodge the supposition from her mind. "You've seen one, you've seen 'em all."

Timbers winced. "Ooh, that's a little clownist." He was no lover of red-nosed devils, but there are some lines one just didn't cross.

Marty had snapped out of his single syllable hypnosis, and

paced the deck. "I think we're getting a little off track here. Whether Peepers is here or not, the town has clearly gone turnip shaped, and we need to do something about it." He turned his attention to Benji, still glowing blue and clearly missing his barrel. "Do you know where they came from then, little koala fella?"

Benji flinched, flashing briefly crimson, before realizing that a reply was expected. "It's Benji, sir, and I couldn't say for sure. There seems to be quite a few of them everywhere. I thought perhaps they all lived here, at least until I saw the big tent."

Marty straightened, clues didn't often turn up with huge pointy arrows over them, but this one sounded very promising. "Big tent? Where is this big tent?"

"Just outside of town." Benji simpered, clearly not loving being the center of attention. "Looked like they were coming from there." The little koala nodded, as though confirming the story to himself as it was imparted. "Big tent, with a big swirly light in it. They came out of there by the bucket-load, and headed off towards town." Benji seemed to shrink within himself. "I followed them. I thought maybe one of them would know how I could get home, but when they started acting all murdery, I decided to stay put, munch on some leaves and see what happened." He motioned towards Kate. "That's when Miss Kate landed on...I mean found me."

Whipstaff grabbed Oaf by the arm and gave his crewmate an excited jostle. "They've got a shiny, too!" Oaf gaped down at his comrade in surprise. There were words happening, and he wanted to be involved, but he had been so beguiled by the brightly flashing teddy bear that he wasn't exactly sure what was being talked about. Absently, he threw out an arm which catapulted Whipstaff back across the deck. As Oaf replies went, this was practically a rousing speech.

"That's where they've come from." Marty snapped his fingers, glancing over at Timbers, who nodded silently in agreement. Benji nodded along with them, apparently trying his best not to be too scared by the sudden sound and movement all around him.

"Out of the swirly thing, yes. That's what I thought, since I saw something just as bright and swirly when I got here. It's probably where your little doll friends came from, too." He motioned towards the crew of the *Fathom*, who were in various states of revulsion at being labelled in such an unheroic and fully poseable way. "Look here, Ninny the Pooh," Timbers raged. "None of my crew has got *Made in China* stamped anywhere about our persons. You can check!"

Marty placed a steadying hand on the fuming captain's shoulder, fighting to suppress a chuckle. Benji once again flushed bright crimson, shining awkwardly and holding out his hands in a plea of frantic diplomacy.

Timbers waved a disgusted hand and strode back towards the quarterdeck, where Oaf furtively checked himself for a maker's tag. "And none of our accessories are sold separately," the little captain muttered angrily.

"Look, stow the bravado for a second." Kate was suddenly alive with intent, and Marty was given a glorious reminder of why he had so wanted to rescue this girl. Timbers halted mid-grumble, remembering just how hefty this wench's cannonballs were. "A couple of hundred feet below us, the town is receiving one hell of a custard pie to the face, and we're up here bickering like children." She huffed, squeezing her little koala ward reassuringly, and glanced at Marty for support.

"He started it," Whipstaff murmured, casting a half-hearted finger at Benji, before Marty stepped in to steady the ship. It was already steady, cradled in the crisp black embrace of the night sky, but steps needed to be taken, and Kate was right. They were going to get nowhere up here, and he had no wish to share his town with the cavorting denizens of his own nightmares.

"We need a plan," he declared, almost cringing as the words fell from his lips. Even in the heady throes of ill-conceived heroism, Marty's plans historically amounted to little more than half-baked logic, insanely good fortune, and basically charging face-first into mortal danger. He was not the millionaire vigilante with a basement full of impressive gadgets, or the ex-special ops mercenary with training in everything and a bullet proof ego. He was the other guy. He had always been the other guy, and nothing about this situation gave him anything more than a quivery bladder and a yearning to set sail for anywhere but here. Battling gibbering monsters from somewhere south of bed time was all well and good, but this was the real world, and here, he was just a guy who sometimes dressed as a dog from outer space and rode a bicycle to work. He stared blankly at the expectant eyes gazing back at him, and realized that finally something else was required of him. Wasn't this what he had been wishing for since he had arrived back in terra norma? Steely resolve arrived just in time to drive away the demons of his own uncertainty, or at least usher them into a holding pen to worry about later. Marty sighed. For now, that would have to do.

"We need to find Peepers, and get him back through this portal, or one like it. Then we need to figure out how this happened, and somehow sort out this mess." It seemed like a definitive statement, despite the fact that none of what he had said had resembled a plan in any way, shape or form.

Timbers grasped the railing of the quarterdeck, his one good eye gleaming intently. "Is that all?" he crowed. "Well let's get to it then? For a moment there, I was worried you might propose something ridiculously half-cocked and foolhardy."

Marty fought back the urge to point out that what he'd suggested was exactly that, and nodded cautiously at his captain.

"I mean, it's not like we've never gone up against the most horrifically evil clown ever to draw breath before. It's not like we've never swooped into a certain death situation with no apparent means of escape or victory."

Marty shifted uncomfortably. He wasn't even sure that he'd delivered anything resembling a plan, and having the possible drawbacks spelled out to him was not doing wonders for his resolve.

"It's not like we've got a history of failing in these situations. We've got out of almost everything we've recklessly thrown ourselves into in the past," Timbers added supportively. "I can't see any way in which we might find ourselves completely outmatched, and making up stuff as we go along in the desperate hope that blind luck will carry us to victory."

Marty cleared his throat, as the little captain prepared to continue with his magnificently doubt inducing speech. "Timbers, please stop talking."

The little captain blustered, carrying himself off to the quarterdeck in a huff. Pirates weren't particularly gifted in the supportive department, and he was already getting restless, since it had been a good four minutes since his last brush with mayhem.

Let him have his stamping fit, Marty thought. There'd be plenty of gold plated, banjo playing bedlam in the offing if they were to attempt any of what he had just proposed.

Much to his relief, Kate's hand found his, and squeezed reassuringly. "Marty's right. We could sit up here and watch the world go boom all night, but sooner or later, we'd have to go back down there and pay the fiddler. Let's get organized." Mixed metaphors aside, Marty felt energized by the like-minded ally at his side. It helped, of course, that this ally was all kinds of cute, and was giving him that unmistakable smile that spurred all foolishly heroic folk to embark upon something foolishly heroic. The sticking point, of course, was the latter part of her speech, which demanded further thought be put into his hastily cobbled together plan.

Getting organized was going to be problematic, especially when his crack team consisted of a crew of pint sized buccaneers, and a dayglo marsupial. The pirates had proven their worth countless times, albeit with an unpredictable dose of gunpowder and madness. Benji had proven no such worth, although he was quite soothing to look at.

"First order of business, as far as I see it, is to track down old balloon eyes." Timbers hopped down from his self-imposed solitude on the quarterdeck, having gauged that just under a minute was ample time in which to parade his displeasure. "The little red-nosed honkers seem to be fairly well distributed around town, so it shouldn't be too hard." He fell in beside Marty, delivering him a curt but amiable nod. Angry words could be spoken, and disagreements argued, but it was impossible to remain at odds with the little toy loon for long, especially when the weight of glorious shenanigans propelled him to fill in the gaps that had been left in a creaky and paper thin plan.

Kate interjected, using reality and good sense to swat at their lofty aspirations. "Great. Then what?"

Whipstaff scuttled up to where his captain had planted himself defiantly, motioning for Oaf to follow suit. The lumbering deck hand had been staring absently at clouds for the past few minutes, clapping his hands contentedly whenever anything shifted into a shape which was vaguely anything shaped. Realizing he was not destined to remain in his own little world of clouds and not much else, Oaf lined up alongside his crewmates.

"Then what?" Whipstaff echoed grandly. He paused, chewing at his sack cloth thumb, before turning to Marty. "Then what?" he asked, much more timidly than his initial assertion.

The familiar, half-baked lets-see-if-this-works coda crystalized in Marty's mind, and he threw caution and good sense to the wind, believing that justice invariably prevailed. And anyway, a man's time on this Earth was fleeting—why not garnish it with the sort of blaze of glory that a tepid, mainstream rock band might one day write a song about?

Marty wrestled with his thoughts, attempting to file them in some sort of order. Tricky at the best of times, without the prod of impending peril, and the fact that many of them were still about cheesecake. He cast his mind back to their previous run-ins with the psychotic travelling circus. How they had high-tailed it from the Hall of Mirrors, been chased through Stellar Island's inflatable funhouse, and scarpered from Downtown amidst much ice cream throwing and tactical confectionary wagon acceleration. Now that he came to think about it, much of his dealings with the clowns had involved either charging toward, or valiantly legging it from their nemeses, usually in short order after Plan A became Plan Oh No. Marty waved away the troublesome latter half of this train of thought, latching on to the intriguing, vaguely plan shaped idea which was forming in his mind.

"It's simple," Marty lied, although it was only a tiny lie. He hadn't really thought it out, and therefore it was very straightforward, and also ridiculous. He cleared his throat, hoping that a solid declaration would give his plan wings, and a decent smoke screen to hide behind.

"We go and find us some clowns. Then, we tactically retreat to the *Fathom*, and lead them back to the big tent, and this portal thingie. It's cat and mouse, bait and switch...taunt and, erm, run away." Marty was dimly aware of a history lesson about a battle in Olde England, ten-sixty-something or other. If memory served, this sort of sneaky play had worked out quite nicely for William the Wotsit, so it was going to work now. Probably.

"Let me get this straight." Timbers stroked his woolen beard thoughtfully. "You're proposing that we swoop into a nest of angry, clown sized hornets, drop our trousers and wave our backsides at them, then pull a one-eighty and head for the hills, like some kind of portal hopping pied piper?"

Marty squinted, his brow furrowing as the half-baked nonsense was spelled back to him. "Umm. Yes. Something like that," he mumbled, already hoping that someone had concocted a better idea.

"Isn't that a little half-cocked? Foolhardy? Not to mention ridiculously dangerous?" the little captain asked.

"Again...yes. Quite," Marty mustered.

Timbers grinned, clapping his hands together excitedly. "Fantastic, just making sure." He scuttled back up to the quarterdeck and turned sharply on his small cluster of crewmates, who were still clearly attempting to digest what had just been suggested. "Bobs, make ready to dive, we're going back in." His captainly orders returned to the deck. "Lads. And lass. And...rodent. Grab your best clown hunting gear, we're going fishing." Delivering a supportive wink to Marty, Timbers took up a position behind the wheel on the quarterdeck and set his feet firmly, in anticipation of the imminent descent. "Look lively!" he bellowed.

Amid the sudden flurry of activity on deck, Kate caught Marty's eye and arched an eyebrow uncertainly. "Marty, are you sure about this?"

"As sure as I have been about anything so far," Marty replied, in the closest thing he could find to confident assurance. Kate winced. "Ooh, that's what I was afraid of," she replied through a cheeky half-smile. "What the hell, we can't stay up here all night."

Benji had been quietly glowing a faint shade of yellow beside her, and sending out silent quivery objections to everything being proposed. "Excuse me, would it be all right if I stayed up here please?" he moaned feebly.

Whipstaff eyed the marsupial curiously. He was no expert in zoology, but he was sure that koalas weren't in possession of wings. He continued his scrutiny nonetheless, just to make sure. "I dunno, can you?" he asked, spying neither wing, parachute, or comedic cartoon umbrella.

Benji sighed, flashing blue before returning to his now apparently trademark chicken-liver yellow. "I suppose there'll be trees down there. I can hide with something to munch on while you folks go about your outrageously dangerous business." Whipstaff crowed at the mention of danger. Some laughed in the face of it, but being much more of an enthusiast of peril than a vanquisher of it, he preferred the way of the whoop, and delivered another excited punch to Oaf's shoulder to punctuate the sentiment.

Oaf absently tugged at a stray thread in his stitching, and turned to regard his crewmate with a mixture of surprise and more surprise. He didn't care either way about peril, so long as people spoke slowly and in words of one syllable or less.

Kate hoisted the tiny koala protectively in her arms. "You're staying close to us, Benji," she soothed. "Don't worry, you'll be safe with me." She smiled, that smile that Marty had seen a hundred times before, but only from Kate. Only she had that power to turn carnage into comfort, and clearly Benji noticed it too. He radiated a soft pink and immediately stopped quaking.

Timbers hopped from one foot to the other on the quarterdeck, clearly eager to get stuck into the aforementioned peril. "Are we off then?" he demanded. "Come on, I haven't shot at anything in at least ten minutes."

Marty hustled up to where his captain stood, and struck as heroic a pose as he could generate on such short notice. "Ready to get down there and goad some evil chucklers when you are, Timbers." He turned to the little corsair, awaiting the order to disembark. Timbers doffed his hat, a broad grin spreading beneath his wickedly gleaming good eye. "This is your town, squire. And your show. Give the order."

Marty returned the grin, bigger and backed by the gleeful prompting of the miniature madman at his side. "Bobs," he hollered up into the rigging. "Take us down!"

Chapter Sixteen

When your town is being overrun by all things giggly, bitey and explodey, quiet streets are at a premium. And yet as the *Fathom* drifted serenely back through the clouds and into the fray, it seemed worryingly fray-less, and bereft of anything that the crew had been gearing themselves up to face. Even old thirty story Seamus was nowhere to be seen, which was odd, since there weren't too many places a Cthulhu-sized leprechaun could effectively hide amongst the not too towering buildings of Main Street. The midnight sky had returned to its familiar twinkling serenity, and the rainbow which only moments ago had carried them on a torrent of technicolor had seemingly vanished along with its lumbering protector.

"This is no good. No good at all," Timbers muttered, pounding the ship's wheel with a tiny bunched fist. "I'd got my fighting trousers on and everything."

Zephyr fell into a glide, bringing the *Fathom* into a sweeping cruise, barely ten feet from the ground. Up ahead, a small municipal garden stretched out from the town hall, boasting a rather handy pond, with a path skirting around it.

"I must say, this town has gone out of its way to provide us with decent mooring facilities," Timbers observed, motioning for the Bobs to initiate a parking maneuver. "We'll have to send them a thank you card. Oaf, take a letter."

Oaf was readying the anchor for deployment, and stopped to give the order his full attention. "Which one?" he enquired. With twenty-six letters to choose from, it was important to get some clarity.

"Never mind all that, Oaf. There's an anchor that needs awaying,"

Timbers shouted, as Zephyr brought the mighty galleon to rest in the town's municipal pond. Those on deck swayed slightly as the boat connected with the still waters, and Marty immediately turned his attention to the slumbering town, which seemed remarkably untouched by the wrecking ball of clownish incursion. No booze fueled weekend warriors carried their impending hangovers homewards, no frantic taxi drivers ferried their rowdy passengers to their beds, and no hideous lunatics sprung jerkily out of the night towards them. The whole town appeared to be stuck in valium day at an old folks' home.

Timbers scampered down from the quarterdeck to join Marty in his muted surveillance. "Well, this is...dull," he ventured, cracking the silence which gripped the street. Marty could sense the disappointment in his pint-sized ally, and in spite of himself, felt a little of it too. He had been riding on the crest of a plan for the first time since rejoining his little gray life, and was now fighting to avoid the wipeout of impending safe tranquility. Had they all gone? Had the shadow of looming destruction and grease-painted Armageddon just simply left?

Whipstaff let out a cry of exasperation. "Is this it? Where are the clowns? The explosions? The heads to aim a flying boot at?" He huffed irritably and stomped across the deck to find something inanimate to kick.

Marty hoisted himself onto the gangplank which had been dutifully extended by Oaf. "They're out there somewhere. Things like this don't just pop out of existence."

Timbers tugged at Marty's leg. "Well, technically, they did just pop *into* existence, so..."

Benji, still cradled in Kate's arms, was quick to add weight to Timbers' point. "Yes, they've probably all just toddled off to where clowns go. Norway, or somewhere like that. Let's just call it a night."

Marty gripped the deck railing tighter. They couldn't just call it a night, because the morning wasn't far behind, and with it came the prospect of commuters and bystanders, and all manner of collateral damage for the erstwhile wrongdoers to bear down up. And worse still, he had to go back to work tomorrow. "This isn't over," he growled. "They're out there, somewhere, and we've got a job to do." How unfortunate that he should deliver such a line, with no camera and film crew to record it and craft some kind of movie trailer around it. Timbers, at least, was on hand to appreciate the sheer action-hero-ness of his words, and spoke up in support. "We've landed now. Least we can do is take a look see. Maybe there's some stragglers we can throw things at." He raised a half-hearted thumb in Marty's direction. Marty managed a strained smile in return. The flickering embers of his plan were still alive, and Timbers was doing his best to fan them.

Whipstaff ceased his quest for something on deck to smash, and returned to the gangplank. "Right you are captain," he chimed, apparently eager to find or start a fight. "Oaf, go fetch your mallet. There's got to be something out there we can whack."

Oaf trotted up behind his crewmate, hefting his mighty wooden hammer, and filed in behind the troupe of disembarkers as they made their way back onto dry land.

Marty continued to scan the street, expecting something to come slithering out of the darkness at any moment, but nothing moved, and it was beginning to bother him.

"How are we going to do this?" Timbers asked from beside him. "I can go fetch a megaphone to announce our presence if you like?" He scratched his head thoughtfully. "I don't know if I've got one, but it's the kind of thing I'd expect me to have lying around somewhere."

Marty shook his head faintly, his eyes still trained on the shadows. "No, I think we should keep the element of surprise for as long as possible," he whispered, taking a step closer to the road to get a better view along it. "We should find a bunch of these creeps first, then we can make all the noise we want."

"What do you propose?" Whipstaff chimed in. "If we're going up in the *Fathom* again, this town had better be known for its extensive collection of municipal ponds."

"We don't need to get airborne to reach higher ground." Kate was already moving at a cautious trot, still clutching her tree dwelling companion. She pointed across the street, to where an impressive looking building reached up out of the gloom and into the night sky, much taller than its neighbors. Standing some five stories high, the structure had once been Acey's department store, before it had gone bust a few years back. Now it stood, a flaking monument to consumerism, and was used for little more than storage of old stock. It was certainly a useful vantage point from which to recon the surrounding area, and more importantly, it sported what looked like an old, gothic clock tower on its roof. From there, they would be able to get a full three-sixty of the town. *If only I had a sniper rifle,* Marty thought. Such locations were tailor made for, and almost demanded the use of something stealthy and scoped, but alas, this was the real world after all. Marty wasn't even sure if he owned a set of working binoculars. Such are the drawbacks of not living in an action movie.

Leaving the Bobs to mind the ship, and without a sound (no mean feat when in the company of tiny, excited pirates), the crew ducked into an alley beside Acey's, and crept around to the rear of the building. It too lay in quiet stillness, empty save for a few old pallets and several overflowing bins.

"There has to be a fire escape or something back here," Marty whispered, scanning the wall which was predictably light one fire escape. "Health and safety would have a field day. No wonder this place closed down," he tutted. Stepping forward, Whipstaff made mock rolling up actions to sleeves he didn't have. "Right, looks like we're doing this the old-fashioned way then." He hopped up onto the nearest bin, which lay beneath a grubby window. "Oaf, pass me your thumper." His lumbering crewmate clutched the precious hammer to his chest momentarily, before giving it up to the grabbing hands of Whipstaff.

The list of things one can do with a hammer and a window is a very small one, and Marty put two and two together just as Whipstaff began his arcing swing. "Whoah! Easy on the breaking part of breaking and entering. We haven't even looked for a back door yet."

Whipstaff sighed. "Oh come on, Marty. I live for this stuff. If I'm not allowed to break a window, why did you even bother bringing me along?"

Kate nodded in agreement. "He's right. We do have sort of a higher purpose here."

This was all the incentive Whipstaff needed, and he launched the hammer once more towards its target. "The ayes have it. You can't make an entrance without breaking a few windows," he declared, and gleefully sent the pane shattering inwards.

Marty might have expected a few whoops of approval, given the company he was in, and was surprised as something inside him sent a small cheer up to join the chorus. Even Kate seemed to enjoy the forced creation of a new entrance to the building. Aside from the increasingly familiar sight of a cowering Benji wholly not getting involved, it was safe to assume that everyone was a fan of breaky noises.

Even before the dust had settled, the crew of the *Fathom* had vaulted up to the stricken window frame and peered inside, like excited children on Smashmas morning. Oaf turned back towards Marty, brushing dust from his face. "It's all dark," he moaned.

"'Course it is. It's night time, genius," Whipstaff chuckled over his shoulder as he hoisted his captain through the aperture. "Careful sir, Some pointy bits there. They could have a man's stuffing out." Marty wondered if Timbers still had his sewing kit handy, but decided not to pose the question as Timbers jostled through into the blackness beyond. A clatter, followed by gruff pirate swearing signaled the captain's arrival on the other side of the wall. "Who puts a tin of paint right under a window like that?" an angry voice squeaked from inside. "It's almost as if they didn't want visitors."

"Visitors probably use the door, Timbers," Marty replied, suppressing a grin, and moved to where Whipstaff and Oaf were now just two pairs of waggling feet in the window hole.

"Let me get through, then you come after."

"I can't, I'm in now."

"I wouldn't call this 'in'. Did you learn nothing from the cat flap incident?"

The bickering ceased as both pirates cork-popped through, and judging by the returning expletives, onto their captain.

By the time Marty, Kate, and Benji made it through into the store, the arguing seemed to have settled, however. Whipstaff was already snooping, as was clearly his preference these days, whilst Oaf peered nervously into the dingy gloom of what appeared to be a loading bay. Beside Marty, Timbers was busy shaking white paint from one leg of his trousers. The boot and once shiny buckle appeared to be beyond rescue, a trail of thick emulsion leading back from it to the offending overturned paint can. "If this doesn't wash off, I'm coming back later and broadsiding this place," he grumbled.

Aside from a few piles of carefully stacked junk, there didn't appear to be anything of interest in the bay. Small and grubby, its dimensions were only discernable due to the pale moonlight issuing through the broken window. Marty pointed over to the far wall, where a heavy hinged door stood next to a small box on the wall, helpfully marked 'Keys'. "I wonder if they label all their valuables too," Timbers huffed. "This is too easy."

"Never say it's too easy," Marty whispered, glancing furtively behind him. In his experience, fate had a nasty way of making you regret dancing around in front of it and sticking your tongue out. "We'd better get a move on, we've got a few stories to tackle before we reach the top."

A weathered steel table stood against one wall, laden with this and that, and Kate turned from it, brandishing a torch that she had found amongst the debris. "Check this out, lucky or what?" she beamed. Marty replied with a smile of his own, delivering a wink that he now kept on standby for whenever she did something awesome. He used it a lot. *Maybe this IS too easy*, he mused, before telling his mind to can it, or risk the wrath of fate.

Several keys later, Marty heaved the rusty door open, and peered tentatively into the gloom of Ground Floor: Menswear. A shaft of bright yellow light shot past his shoulder as Kate played the torch across the vacant rows of clothes rails and hangers. Aside from a swirling fog of dust, nothing peered back at them from the darkness. Fate, at least for now, seemed to be appeased.

"Over there. Stairs." She motioned, training the light on the far corner of the room, where a small flight of steps disappeared up towards Sporting Goods. They darted, and in some cases scampered, over to the stairwell, trying not to make a sound as they ran. As far as midnight pirate incursions into deserted department stores went, this was a particularly stealthy one, Marty thought, and once again allowed hope to wave a little flag inside of him. Nothing lay in wait for them on the stairs, and in moments they were making swift progress across the vacant Sporting Goods floor. Marty had memories of camping equipment, fishing supplies, and hunting paraphernalia that he had not been allowed to touch when he'd been here as a child. None of that remained, and only a few racks stood now, holding nothing but dust, and the ghosts of long extinguished camping stoves.

With the torch light dancing in front of them, the second stairwell sprang into dim view, the upward pointing sign above it declaring 'Second Floor: Bedroom Furniture.'

"Brilliant," Timbers chirped quietly. "Fancy a nap, Marty? Get us all back home?"

Marty turned to his pint sized compadre, a half-smile on his face. "What, click my heels? There's no place like Lucidity Junction?"

Timbers beamed back at him, scuttling towards the stairwell. "Just a thought. Come on, we've got clowns to find."

The little captain was already on the second floor when Marty and the rest of the crew arrived at his side. Whoever had cleared this place out when Acey's had gone under had apparently not been able to count to two, as cabinets, wardrobes, and beds stretched out and away into the dark corners of the store. Worryingly, those dark corners seemed to spread throughout most of the floor, so much so that even the beam of the torch seemed unable to throw its light more than a few feet. The thin celestial rays that threatened to pry through the grime smeared windows seemed to be choked by the all-consuming gloom that rolled in to spoil the party.

"Whoa!" Timbers rasped, squinting out into the blackness. "It's like the inside of my eyepatch in there. Good job, we've got the torch. Hey, wouldn't it be awful if the batteries died, y'know…?"

Marty sighed. Whatever stay of execution fate may have given them was surely about to imminently run its course. "Like you see in movies?" he ventured, wearily.

"Yeah, like you see in…"

Timbers' reply was cut short as Kate's torch flickered, and blinked ominously out.

Chapter Seventeen

The thing about total darkness, is that it is usually followed by complete silence. Nobody wants to wake the sleeping monster, or advertise their whereabouts. It was something of a mystery therefore, that Timbers, Whipstaff, and Oaf had taken this opportunity to embark upon an impromptu game of hide and seek.

Marty stood frozen to the spot the moment the torch light had gone out. It was an involuntary instinct, borne solely and unashamedly from nights of thunderstorms and x-rated movies he had been too young to see, and more recently, from a brush with the monster under the bed. Standing as they were in the bedroom furniture section of Acey's department store, Marty had made a judgement call to stand as quietly and motionlessly as possible, for the foreseeable future. It seemed that Kate had decided upon a similar course of action, and Marty flinched as a hand grasped his in the pitch blackness. Beside him, the faint yellow glow of a petrified Benji did nothing to allay the void, and the little koala's repeated mantra of, "Oh no. No, no, no," only served to fan the flames of panic inside him.

Somewhere out in the smothering nothing of the store, voices cropped up here and there, as the pirates taunted each other from their respective hiding places.

"You'll never find me," sang a voice that sounded liked Timbers.

"Oaf, where are you?" Whipstaff called from somewhere off to the right.

"I'm in the wardrobe," Oaf replied, provoking uproarious laughter. "No. I'm not. I'm definitely not in the wardrobe." He clearly had about as much grasp of the rules of hide and seek as he did on the rest of life.

Marty edged forward, feeling Kate moving just as tentatively alongside him, and hearing her muffled curses as she attempted to slap the torch back into life. His leg brushed against something wooden, and he staggered, flopping down onto what might once have been a finely sprung mattress, but was now little more than finely sprung garbage. Something below him gurgled expectantly, and bright plumes of bristling panic shot up Marty's spine. He managed a rasping *SHH!* which seemed to draw more movement from beneath the bed, before silence once again fell upon the department store.

"Who's shushing? That's not in the rules." The voice was off to Marty's left, and could have been Timbers. The thing under the bed seemed to like it, and a flurry of movement and shadow slid fluidly out into the store. Marty squinted, trying to see what had spilled forth from beneath him, but it was just shadow. Shadow that moved, significantly more than shadows had any right to move.

Marty's mind wrenched him back to the incident earlier that night, and how it had been so similar to the nights spent huddled under the covers as a child. *You never saw the monster, but you knew it was there*, his mind chided, and he fought against the 'keep quiet, keep still' reflex which was now putting his friends in danger. "Timbers, stay where you are and be quiet. Something's coming," he managed, as the dark shape he watched stopped and floated back towards him.

I hear youuuuu, the shadows chattered out of the darkness. Marty tightened his grip on Kate's hand. Mercifully, she had taken his advice, and aside from a trembling koala in her arms, stood statuesque beside the bed.

"I'm not going anywhere Marty. This is the daddy of all hiding places, there should be an 'X' over me, it's so good," Timbers crowed, somewhere amongst the rows of bedtime regalia.

Again, the shadow shifted, back towards Timbers' voice. *I like it when they hide*, something cooed malevolently.

A faint stirring jerked a nearby chest of drawers from its inanimate state, and the hidden thing paused, drifting over to the cabinet and reaching out with hazy, intangible limbs. It caressed each drawer, hissing malevolently as it probed for evidence of concealed prey. The top draw rattled and shifted again, and the hissing became more urgent, rising almost into terrible melody. *If you move, you're mine. Those are the rules,* seemed to be the crux of the dreadful chant, and Marty's eyes widened as the top drawer slid jerkily open, borne by some force that he could not make out.

"Oy! You're not a registered hide and seeker," A voice from within the cabinet growled. The barrel of Whipstaff's blunderbuss poked out of the open drawer, plunging into the ragged mist of the encroaching shadow. "Bugger off!" The roar of the shot sent the cabinet rocking backwards, and wrought the mystery shadow thing into a million fluttering scraps of swirling void. The noise shattered deafeningly through the department, sending instinctive fingers that were mercifully his own into Marty's ears. He removed them, scanning the floor for signs of their ethereal assailant, but only the sound of scuttling feet remained, as Whipstaff relocated to a better hiding place.

The swirling, shattered creature hung in the air momentarily, mingling with the dust and gunpowder, before closing in on itself, and settling in a rapidly expanding pool of unpleasant darkness on the floor beside the now vacated chest of drawers. *I bet I've got more lives than you've got bullets,* it cooed, laughing emptily, before oozing a path to where Timbers had last spoken.

Beside Marty, Kate had ceased her torch cajoling, and waited, quite literally it seemed, with baited breath. Evidently she too knew about the monster under the bed, and was reluctant to draw the gaze of the mysterious phantom. It headed back towards Timbers, though, and Marty summoned up what words he could to halt its pursuit. "Find a light. Get into the light." Again, the shadow changed course, moving back towards the wide-eyed Marty, whose hand now clasped firmly across his mouth in a feat of bodily self-preservation.

There you are, the shadow gurgled, fronds of darkness wrapping around the foot of the bed and inching towards Marty's feet. If he moved, that would be all she wrote, and yet tendrils of black nothingness inched closer to him along the mattress. Something snagged Marty's boot as the unseen terror probed ever closer, and he finally gave in to the scream pestering to be let out of his chest. "Light. Light. LIGHT!" he ranted, much to the apparent glee of his stealthy stalker.

"Oaf!" Timbers shouted up from somewhere beyond Marty's sight. "Light your lantern up, big lad. Marty's got a case of the heebies."

As the command cracked through the stagnant air, the shadow creature veered away, searching for the new voice, and a door swung open beside Marty's head. Oaf stepped out from the wardrobe, his trusty lantern held out in front of him, casting a brilliant glow, and sending the shadows sneaking back whence they came. Marty sprang up from the bed, distancing himself from the hiding place of the darkness dwelling nightmare, and wrenching Kate and Benji along with him. He stood, gasping for the breath that he had been holding, next to his light wielding savior.

"What the hell was that?" Marty managed, breathlessly surveying for any sign of returning nastiness.

"Looked like the thing we barged in on you scuffling with earlier," Timbers replied from his apparently unfindable hiding place. "Well, I say looked like, it didn't really look like anything, except maybe angry smoke."

"It lives under the bed." The voice was quivery, cautious and Australian. "It lives under all the beds. It comes out when you make a sound, make a move. It eats kids." Benji quaked in Kate's arms. "Now it's here, looks like its menu has expanded." The little koala shuddered, and Kate squeezed him tighter, perhaps to fend off the notion that he had just given voice to.

Not wishing to fan this new fear any further, Marty turned to Oaf, who still held his lantern aloft as though it were some kind of holy talisman against evil. Right now, that was probably exactly what it was. "Oaf, why didn't you light that thing earlier," Marty panted, resisting the urge to hug the tiny giant.

Oaf shrugged, hoisting his lantern and peering out into the blackness. "Miss Kate lady ma'am. She had the big light, and that glowing penguin. Didn't think we'd need it."

Kate knelt and squeezed Oaf warmly, whilst Benji tutted at yet another anthropological affront to his lineage.

Marty aimed a thankful nod at the blushing Oaf, before casting his gaze across the gloomy shop floor once again. "We should get out of here before that thing comes back."

"But you haven't found us yet," a pleading duet yelped from

somewhere in the bedding section of the second floor.

"We're out of here Timbers, you win, ok?" Marty called back, much to the dismay of Oaf, who hadn't even begun to look for his crew yet.

"Boom! I never lose at hide and seek." The voice was jarringly close, and Marty wheeled around to see Timbers at his side. "What? How the hell? Where were you?"

Timbers patted his nose smugly. "A pirate never reveals his hiding places." He winked cheekily, and made for the stairwell. "Plan B then, is it?" he called over his shoulder.

Kate glanced at Marty. "What's Plan B?"

Marty had no idea, having only half-concocted Plan A, but followed the little captain to the stairs. Coming up here to scope for clowns had been a great idea, but he wasn't about to wait around for whatever came out when the lights went off to make another appearance.

Several leaping steps later, they were back on the veritably well-lit first floor, with nothing but darkness and silence behind them.

Marty sighed. It had been Kate's idea to come up here to cast an eye over the town for clownish behavior, but he had really hoped that it would work. Now they would have to go street to street, and that was far more of an unpredictable course of action. Not that this had ever been any sort of deal breaker in the past.

Behind them on the stairs, something stirred. A rustling, scampering, galloping sound of something hastily following them. As one, the group adopted defensive positions, except Benji, who adopted a familiar cowering, trembly stance. The footfalls grew closer, and a shape clattered into the stairwell behind them, barreling into Oaf, who was still trying to figure out what floor he was on.

"You bilge rats never came to look for me," Whipstaff gasped, getting back to his feet amongst the pile of Oaf. "And you scarpered without telling me. I'm invoking Section Five, Subsection B of the Hide and Seek code, therefore I win."

Timbers grimaced, plodding back towards the ground floor stairwell. "Damn. He always wins on the technicalities."

Chapter Eighteen

The crew were part way through the tricky and wholly grace-less maneuver of returning to the alleyway through the broken loading bay window when Marty spotted something.

Across the square, past the tranquilly bobbing *Fathom*, a blinking blue light flitted through the sparse trees flanking the town hall. As he watched, it was joined by another, and another, until a cluster of the strange beacons were faintly visible in the darkness, like regimented fireflies. Marty wasn't aware of such behavior in clowns, but then, up until tonight, he'd had no clue that they were also walking confetti bombs either, and this was certainly an odd enough site to warrant investigation.

Timbers appeared at Marty's side, peering first at his transfixed companion, and then off into the distance at whatever had caught his attention. "What is it, Marty?"

Marty shrugged. "No idea, but it's weird and shiny, so that ticks at least two of the boxes that normally has you guys chasing after stuff."

"I want to chase after it," Timbers confirmed, his one good eye as wide as a dinner plate. He snapped out of it long enough to shoot an approving grin up at Marty. "You're learning, lad. We'll make a pirate out of you yet." With that, the little captain set out across the still deserted street towards the mysterious lights.

"Hang on, Timbers. We can't just go galloping into something we know nothing about," Marty hissed, calling a halt to Timbers' charge. The pint-sized plunderer tutted loudly. "But that's my favorite part. I'm a pirate, not a Sunday school teacher. Caution is for people who don't want to get shot at, chased, and return home with scars and awesome stories." It was hard to argue with that.

"Well you're going to have to wait." Kate arrived beside Marty, a look of concern on her face, and a rapidly strobing koala in her arms. "We've got to do something about Benji, he's freaking out."

"I don't want to get shot at, or chased," the meek marsupial stammered, flashing brilliant yellow, before imparting another seizure inducing technicolor volley. "I want to go home. I don't like clowns, I don't like shadow monsters, and I *don't* like adventure. Small furry animals are not cut out for such things." Marty raised a hand to comfort the trembling, fluffy disco ball, causing Benji to flinch and recoil, hiding his face against Kate's shoulder.

"We're going to have to make a stop at the *Fathom*, guys." Marty sighed. "We can't take this little fella off into the dark again, look at him." He turned his attention back to Benji, taking care not to make any sudden movements. "Would you prefer that, Benji? If we drop you off at the ship? You can stay with the Bobs, they'll look after you, and you won't have to sneak around in the dark, how's that?"

Benji's frantic flashing slowed, then drifted into a steady pink haze, and he withdrew his face from its hiding spot. "Yes. Thank you. I'm sorry, I'm just no good in these situations." The tiny ball of fur looked past Marty, a look of faraway melancholy etched on his face. "I normally just meet up with my dream person, and we run in the grass, gaze up at clouds, munch on eucalyptus. Well, that's just me usually, but there's certainly no shooting or chasing or mortal peril of any description." Benji lowered his head sorrowfully. "I'm not really of any help here. I'm sorry."

"He got that bit right," Whipstaff muttered. "Not unless Oaf runs out of lantern oil." He chuckled, stopping short as Oaf shook his head disapprovingly. Kate, too was not amused. "It's not his fault, leave the little guy alone," she chastised. Whipstaff hunched his shoulders and kicked at the pavement grumpily.

Timbers clapped his hands together, attempting to bring the focus back to the matter in hand. "Come on then. We'll swing by the *Fathom*, drop Kate's gerbil off with the Bobs, and get after those fantastically shiny things." He made a trotting start towards the ship, turning mid-canter. "Come on!"

A brief sneak across the deserted road brought them back to the *Fathom*, where the Bobs were busily involved in some sort of stock take. Bob scampered across the broad planks which made up the deck, numbering each one with a stick of chalk. As he did so, Also Bob scribbled in a tatty note book. Marty wondered just how important it was to ensure all the planks of the deck were still there, and filing them all in number order, but decided not to make the enquiry. Clearly, it was a pirate thing.

"Do they ever leave the ship?" he whispered to Timbers, who was ushering Benji up the gang plank.

Timbers turned, glancing up at the plank labelers as he did. "The Bobs? No, not really. They're as much a part of this ship as old Zephyr. They're happiest here, making sure everything works, and is where it should be." He lowered his voice further, ushering Marty down to his level. "Probably for the best to be honest. Bob's stitching is coming undone, and Also Bob has asthma. Still, I recruited them on a two-for-one deal, and they keep the place tidy, so I can't really complain."

Marty found himself struggling for a reply, as if one was needed. Why wouldn't this make perfect sense tonight of all nights? And anyway, Benji was now emitting a contented white glow on the deck of the *Fathom*, and off in the night behind them, something else, probably less fluffy, and certainly more bizarre was waiting for them.

"Are we off then?" Timbers chimed, mirroring Marty's sentiments, as a toy who had been with him since childhood rightly should. Light one koala, the remaining crew hunkered down against the walls of the nearest building, and skirted across to where they last saw the blinking blue lights. Although they weren't there anymore, sounds of muted mayhem snaked out from the nearest side street. Sounds that drew simultaneous dread and hand rubbing, depending on whether you were a gung-ho toy pirate, or nervous human, intent on surviving the night.

Forming a cautious line, the crew crept along the walls of what appeared to be a slumbering office block, to an intersection of alleyways. Somewhere off to their left, something that had previously been intact, boomed explosively and, in all probability, lost its intactness. "Over there," Timbers barked, clambering over a clump of shrubs and into an adjourning alleyway. There was no time to raise the calming hand of reason, and the group followed into the darkness, which gave way into a street that appeared to have been touched by the dainty hand of utter carnage.

Kate had vacated The Pickled Judge less than two hours ago, and yet the crumbling booze fortress which stood before them as they sneaked out of the alley bore no resemblance to the shabby local she and Marty knew only too well.

Huge holes in the main facade dripped masonry and plaster, and flames still murmured amidst the rubble that had once been the main entrance of the stricken pub.

"Wow, the clowns really did a number on the Judge." Marty sighed, wondering if there was any chance the pumps remained undamaged.

"Did? Looks like the siege is still in progress," Timbers warned, pointing at the sea of bobbing shapes which closed on the blasted doors. Marty squinted into the darkness, which was being punctuated by the flickering blue and white lights they had been following. They darted in and out of focus as dozens of silhouettes crept towards The Pickled Judge. Scampering into one of the few remaining intact streetlights, a smartly dressed monkey paused, turning to urge his comrades onwards, and pressed on to where figures still hunched in the depths of the Judge.

"Bar's still open!" Whipstaff crowed excitedly, and a little too loudly for comfort, sending several shushes rasping in his direction. It appeared, however, that the first mate was correct, the bar was indeed open, and although the doors hung on their shattered hinges, Old Mad Bill seemed to be in the mood for a lock in. The disheveled publican stood atop the sign of his beloved watering hole, bracing himself on the roof with a delicious array of flammable liquor lined up at his feet. He grimaced as the first line of monkeys presented themselves on the other side of the street and let out a roar which stopped them in their scampering tracks.

"Keep your hands off my patrons, you damned, dirty beer monkeys!" he bellowed, launching a flaming bottle of Hawkins Mind Scrambler Rum into the mass of strobing beacon-headed simians.

Whipstaff lurched forward, barely restrained by his captain as the forty percent proof bomb exploded impressively, sending whooping apes leaping for cover. "That's quality grog, the fella's a madman!" he shrieked, clearly upset at the spillage of perfectly good happy juice.

As rattled as the first mate was, it paled in comparison to the encroaching monkey horde, which parted to avoid the boozy napalm's blast radius, hopping across car bonnets and street signs, and screeching with manic, but clearly well-organized intent. "Want some more, do you?" Bill hollered from his perch atop the Judge. He scanned the bottles at his disposal, evidently looking for something befitting of the occasion, although Marty couldn't see what difference a really good year would make.

Another, much less intelligible battle cry rang out, as two equally fiery bottles of Crimson Death Chihuahua Tequila sailed end over end towards the pub's assailants. One plumed in pools of Mexican immolation only a few feet from where Marty hid, whilst the other dropped over the fence at the opposite side of the street. Someone screamed, glass shattered, and the unexpected sound of an alarmed sheep rang out from behind the fence, and still the monkeys advanced.

"Perhaps we should help him," Kate offered, her willingness to jump into a fight impressing both Marty and Timbers, albeit for markedly different reasons. Marty glanced from the attacking throng to the stricken building, it was a big ask, and although the beer monkeys had obviously come through the portal, their presence and agenda wasn't high on their list of priorities right now.

The squealing sobriety patrol had reached the pub when he looked up again, and were scaling the walls, darting in through caved in windows, and generally pouring across the road like an endless tidal wave of uniformed, shrieking nuisances. As they flashed through the glow of the streetlights, Marty could see in each of their hands, the same miniature polo mallets that he had received a first-hand introduction to upon waking up dreamside. They meant business, they had their quota, and they weren't going to stop until every dribbling alky in The Pickled Judge was suitably hangover laden.

"This isn't going to be pretty," Marty muttered. "We should go."

"Hold on," Timbers interjected, clearly reveling in the carnage. "The nutter on the roof's not finished yet."

Old Mad Bill was indeed far from beaten. He had taken over stewardship of The Pickled Judge untold years ago, and had been its proprietor through rough times and smooth. Mainly rough.

Even from across the street, Marty could see a fire in his eyes, and a solidity in his stance, but more specifically, he saw the giant wooden gavel which usually hung over the bar, resting in Bill's mighty paws. The sturdy barman lofted the makeshift bat over his head in a show of aggression, and barked at the apes which were scurrying up the walls of his beloved pub.

"Let's be havin' ya then. Old Justice is waiting!" he cried, bringing the gavel down hard on the first head that appeared at the edge of the roof. More appeared, and Marty thought he could almost hear Bill laughing as he brought down the hammer again and again, engaging in a demented game of Whack-A-Monkey.

"This is brilliant." Timbers chuckled, peering at the bedlam and hopping up and down on the spot. "Has anyone got any popcorn?"

Kate edged towards the door, the intent to rush in and assist still being held at bay by good sense. "No, it isn't, Timbers. This is serious."

Timbers, turned and held out a calming hand. "Stay your blade, lass. They're just hangover technicians. There'll be no plank walking tonight. They just want to get in there and tap some drunken heads. It's all very official." He smiled reassuringly. "They've dropped in on all of us before. No harm, no foul." He stopped, considering his words. "Well, actually, it isn't that harmless, and it is pretty foul, but the swillers will live to buy another round, mark my words."

The little captain seemed to be right, as the hangover technicians swarmed through the smashed entrance of The Pickled Judge, brandishing their mini mallets high and strobing their little blue lights.

Above them, his rooftop perch now bereft of monkey targets, Old Mad Bill craned to view the interior of his decimated establishment, and the wholesale head knocking that was occurring within. He dropped the giant gavel and fell to his knees, aiming a rebuke up into the sky.

"You maniacs! You're sobering them up! Damn you...damn you all to hell!"

On the other side of the street, Timbers jumped down from his vantage point at the window, straightening his coat and regarding his companions.

"Well, that was all very theatrical. Shall we go?"

Chapter Nineteen

Somewhere amongst the rubble left by giant leprechaun footfalls, in and about the clownish forays through dark alleyways, and what can only be described as a unicorn stampede through the center of town, officer Michael O'Riley made the decision that police work was not for him.

He had seen many things in his day. Admittedly, most of them were about as close to his beloved TV cop shows as the ad breaks which punctuated them, but such was the noble legacy of protecting and serving the trouser end of nowhere.

There were no heists, or high speed pursuits in shiny and totally impractical sporty numbers. No drug deals going down at the docks. There weren't even any docks, if you didn't count the sleepy harbor over by Stellar Island. The only drugs you were likely to find over there came in little child proof bottles and gave the blessed high of mild headache relief. It was hum drum, it was boring, but dammit, you could at least walk your beat without worrying about mythical uni-horned steeds, or the grim prospect of being juggled to death.

This was the problem with fantasy, O'Riley mused from beneath his squad car hiding place. It presented a world which seemed fanciful and exciting, but gave you no tools to deal with its resplendent horrors once they came tumbling in a magical tidal wave into your back yard.

Daydreams were a nice place to visit, but you stood no chance of living more than twenty-four hours there.

O'Riley watched from his vantage point, for who knows how long, as a procession of innocent bystanders illustrated his point. A group of wayward partygoers found themselves the unwitting cattle in a clown rodeo which had ended in a way that he had not been willing to witness. Something malevolent and unseen had gathered up into the shadows a young couple, who had perhaps started the evening with romantic intent, but had ended up wishing they had stayed home with a bottle of wine and a machine gun. Worst of all had been the troupe of cub scouts who had barreled down the road beside him, pursued by a gang of heavily armed, and murderously driven cartoon woodland creatures. That sure as hell hadn't ended with a sing-a-long around a camp fire. At least one pixelated deer, minus its mother appeared to have gotten some form of revenge, though.

Something way off in the land of wonder and joy had apparently broken, come loose of its moorings and spilled forth its unfettered mayhem into the world. O'Riley didn't hope to understand it, and why would he? The best he could hope for would be to survive the night without being amazed into tiny pieces.

Somewhere off to his right, something plumed with Molotov splendor. "At least the locals are fighting back," he muttered, immediately regretting the words that might give away his position. A voice behind him confirmed once again the age-old discretion and valor argument. "Look who it is," it purred horridly. "Officer Hide and Seek here to read us more rights." The face craning under the car behind him was ghostly white and grinning, and precisely not what a person would prefer to see tugging at their feet whilst hiding beneath a police car.

"Come and play with us, officer." The clown shrieked, a gloved hand already invading some serious personal space. "Hiding is boring, and so much fun at the same time."

Hiding was fun. He had been very good at it as a child, not that there had been any awards for it in the mercifully clown free days of his youth. Right now, he had been rumbled, and the thought that he who fights and runs away doesn't get something unspeakable done to him with a balloon animal flew into O'Riley's mind.

In an instant, he was up and away from the probing jester. He had faced down his fantasies back in the horror show at the police department, and aside from a few mystifying eruptions of confetti, being the tough guy hadn't gotten him very far. Maybe this wasn't the time for glib one-liners and unlimited ammo. The fantasy world had arrived in town tonight, and it was not the penny in the well, or the wish upon a star kind. It was the clown in your closet, and the reason you kept the light on at night variety.

"If it's all the same to you guys, I think I'll let you be 'it' this time," O'Riley gibbered, the last remnants of his wish to deliver clever comebacks still throwing possibilities.

The clown under the car righted itself, and loped towards O'Riley playfully. "How delightful. Shall I count to ten?" it leered. "One. Two. Three." Like moths to a countdown, three of its cohorts appeared from somewhere within the night, joining in the gleeful head start declaration. "Four. Five," they chanted, as more devilish harlequins appeared.

Tonight, the stuff that dreams were made of appeared to want to know what O'Riley's insides were made of.

With that in mind, he boldly turned tail and sprinted off down the street, the sight of an impressively moored pirate ship looming large in his frantically darting line of vision.

Chapter Twenty

"**D**ammit, I wish there were some clowns here."

It was a statement that felt unusual and redundant as Marty gave voice to it, and with good reason. It was probably the first time in the history of the spoken word that such a sentence had been uttered. Nobody wanted more clowns, or in all honesty any clowns at all. On the face of it, it was a shame, since the merry jesters seemed singularly happy and carefree, with laughter and mirth their only mission in life, who could begrudge them that? There were probably genuine examples out there, happy to amuse and entertain, and turn up jarringly at children's parties. All completely harmless and fun, until the lights went out. Once they got into your dreams, these benevolent circus fools became unstoppable, giggling psychopaths, and inherent self-preservation took over. For this reason, unless you were a hand wringing child who would one day turn into a serial killer, nobody wished for the presence of more clowns, until now.

In Marty's albeit brief experience of encountering, escaping from, and now hunting clowns, he had never openly welcomed their presence. And yet here, walking through decimated streets, he felt like he was out on safari with an invitingly bloody slab of steak tied around his neck.

"Is it always like this, Marty?" Timbers muttered, prodding with his boot at a section of curb that had recently lost a fight with carnage. "I can see why you come over onto our side every night." The little pirate continued with ill regard on his face.

Marty was busy scanning for areas of his town that hadn't been touched by the ka-boom fairy, and quickly decided to end that particular train of thought. If you could think it, you could dream it, and he really didn't want a run in with a tutu wearing, bazooka wielding soldier sprite. "It's usually less horrifically mangled than this," he absently replied, picking through a pile of what he dearly hoped were skittled mannequins at the side of the road. "You've kind of caught us at a bad time. Usually when the circus comes to town, they don't try to set fire to the patrons." He kicked what was mercifully a very plastic shop dummy head and turned back to regard the empty street. The plan was not going, well, to plan.

"This isn't really going to plan, is it?" Timbers echoed. Pirates could be so damned intuitive sometimes. "Don't worry about it." The little buccaneer delivered a supportive pat to Marty's kneecap, and smiled up at his friend. "The night is young, and the unfathomable possibilities are multiplying by the hour." Timbers' good eye shone in the flickering glow of a burning chunk of Marty's town, he may have been on the real side of the fence tonight, but that glint had faced off against rampant despair before, and no amount of moping would dampen it. Marty had seen it before, and although a fair degree of running, shrieking, and hiding had followed it, the day had ultimately been won, and that was no small comfort.

"I'm glad you're here, Timbers." Marty smiled down at his unswervable comrade. "Over here, I'm just a guy in a space dog suit, and that's on a good day."

Timbers' face caught a frown for the briefest of moments. "Have you gone soft, matey? Look around you." The little pirate waved a pointing cloth hand towards Whipstaff. The cackling first mate chased Oaf across the street, holding out a wooden pole with a disembodied mannequin head upon it, much to the hand flapping disapproval of his lumbering companion. Marty eyed Timbers quizzically, as the captain closed his fist, and plunged a thumb back over his shoulder. The hazy shape of Zephyr sat amongst galleon rigging in the haphazard light of the randomly toppled streetlights. The mighty bird stood motionless, a faint whistling melody dancing out of the night as the *Fathom*'s metallic courier sang itself a steam-driven lullaby. "All this came from inside your head, lad." Timbers' pointing finger was now trained firmly on Marty. "You're the maker of worlds, the thinker of long thoughts, and the leader of tiny cloth men." The little squeak gravel voice grew quieter, but seemed to boom through Marty's head like an angelic fanfare. "Over here, over there, doesn't seem to matter too much tonight, does it? I don't care what suit you wear when the sun's up. The moon's hanging high tonight, and there's a bucket load of trouble to be gotten into. If memory serves, you're not too shabby at getting into, and out of that. What say you?" A gold flecked toothy grin punctuated the speech, and Marty realized that there was only one answer he could give, and that answer could neither be spoken, nor needed to be. A broad smile delivered a wordless high five to the nodding Timbers, and Marty turned again to view the beleaguered street, the flickering glow beginning to shine in his eyes.

Timbers arrived back at his side, a tiny sentinel, a beacon of barefaced, reckless lunacy in a world full of what ifs and yes buts. "Think big, do bigger" the little maniac chuckled. He leapt up to slap Marty's back, managing only an awkwardly impromptu low five. It was more than good enough.

"Anyway, what else are we gonna do tonight?"

Marty knew exactly what else they were going to do tonight. Fueled by pirate gusto, and no small percentage of captainly goading, the plan had roused from its listless meandering and was dancing around in front of him like an excited child. "Follow me," he sang, almost vaulting into the street before them. Timbers was at his heels in an instant, beckoning for Kate and the crew to follow. "The plan. THE PLAN," he crowed, as though he had seen Marty's intent, and sought to give it wings.

Whipstaff cornered Oaf, and advanced with his mannequin headed poking stick, whilst Kate looked on with the look of a jaded, but amused babysitter. All eyes (even those belonging to a sadly decapitated and be-poled shop dummy) shot to where Marty and Timbers were galloping off into the distance, and they gave chase, unaware of where they were going, but happy enough to follow in the knowledge that the caper was back in full, glaringly dashing and possibly perilous effect.

A few dozen hurried paces ahead of them, Timbers struggled to keep up with the newly invigorated Marty, but managed a panting query nonetheless. "So, what's this way?"

Marty had his eyes fixed on a group of buildings which huddled in a miraculously unannihilated group across the street. "You'll see," he breathed, new purpose blooming in his voice. "There's no clowns here, so how about we make some?" He glanced down at the puzzled expression which had sprung up on Timbers' face.

"Make some? You can't grow clowns, they come creeping out from Satan's backside or something," Timbers chuckled.

Marty grinned, maybe to dream it and to do it weren't such bad things after all. If you have the keys to Pandora's box, why not get a keg and invite the neighbors over? If the mountain wouldn't come to Mohammed, then perhaps he could paint a big smiley face on the mountain and see what else came along to play.

"How's your juggling?" Marty asked as Timbers arrived beside him in a tatty old shop doorway. Timbers looked up, reading the sign which hung limply, advertising Fancy Schmancy Dress. His gaze trailed back to Marty, who was gasping for breath through an ominously mischievous smile.

"This can't be the plan," Timbers groaned. "I *liked* the plan."

Behind them, Kate and the rest of the crew came to an untidy halt at the steps of Fancy Schmancy Dress. In its windows, all manner of party finery hung on display. Roman centurions stood, much more impressively than their headless mannequin in the street behind. Vampires, cowboys, even pirates lined up in a row which ended with the sobering figure of their nemesis. Shop window clown stared back at them blankly, no less terrifying than the biting, clawing psychopaths that had arrived that night to tear the town a new one. Marty pointed up at the window, towards the macabre, hanging jester costume, and fixed Timbers with a knowing gaze. "We're going undercover. Grab a fluffy wig and a balloon."

The little captain sighed, shaking his head doubtfully. Beside him, Whipstaff crossed himself and uttered a barely audible sea faring prayer. Oaf, already beguiled by the bright colors and sparkly outfits in the shop window let his jaw fall open. "Balloons?" he chimed, clapping his hands together.

The large glass door of the shop stood closed, a helpful sign hanging behind the glass to emphasize the point, and Marty cupped a hand up against it to peer inside. It was oppressively dark, and several figures lurked within the gloom, although they seemed only there to model the many resplendent and garish outfits that the place had to offer.

"Are we knocking, or what?" Kate ventured, peering past Marty cautiously. Whipstaff was at her side in an instant, having again swiped Oaf's mighty hammer. "Too right we are, missy." He hefted the club and swung it through the delightfully yielding glass of the shop front, sending splinters of glass flying inward, and a surprised Marty stumbling outward. He turned to rebuke the first mate, but Whipstaff had already hopped up and through the shattered doorway, no doubt eager to resume an already busy evening's exploring and wholesale looting. He turned to meet Marty's look of bewilderment. "What? I thought we were doing this now." He dropped the hammer, and Oaf scuttled forward to collect it, holding it against his barrel chest protectively. "You let me do that last one." During the last few hours, nothing that even approached logic had reared its methodical head, yet this statement was making a solid case, and he grudgingly nodded, following Whipstaff inside the store.

Only a few feet inside, it became apparent that this was something of a gold mine for those willing to put reality on hold in favor of far more important things, such as messing about and generally treating life like a playground. Marty smiled as the others filed past him. This was exactly why he had always loved Fancy Schmancy Dress. On more than a few days off, he had frequented this glorious establishment, if only to while away the hours donning amusing masks, or pushing buttons which would faithfully deliver comedy sound effects. Outside these doors, the world plodded on, getting on with its day to day trudge through tedium, whilst in here, he could be the hooded vigilante, off to rescue the local orphanage from an unfortunate penguin related catastrophe. He could be the hero who saved the day, armed only with a piñata and a trash can lid. He could be the other guy, and he frequently was.

Costumes, props, and other paraphernalia lined either side of the dimly lit central corridor of the shop, and the crew wasted no time in rushing to check out the various weird and wonderful wares on display.

Marty picked his way through pieces of recently hammered doorway, scanning the shelves for plan-worthy items, as Timbers gingerly offered an opinion from behind him. "This isn't going to be as much fun as it looks, is it?"

Marty waved a scolding finger at the captain. "Fun's where you find it." He was remembering more than a little reckless abandon from his time aboard the *Fathom* in his own dreamspace, and his soul embraced it like the return of a prodigal, if somewhat problem child. Timbers' nervousness was starting to galvanize him. In these last few minutes, roles had apparently been reversed, and Marty reveled at the helm of this speeding train of mayhem that he was in no way attempting to steer.

Amazingly, the train seemed to pull in at Timbers' stop, and he brightened, offering a hearty thumbs up. "Right you are then," he chirped, and scampered over to where Whipstaff and Oaf were trying on zombie masks. Beside them, Kate twirled amidst the clinging grasp of a feather boa, and caught Marty's eye with the first genuine 'Kate smile' he'd seen that night. She fluttered briefly, seeming to almost levitate in a shaft of light that obviously wasn't there, and Marty replied with a smile borne from the belief that everything was going to be okay. He had no idea of any such thing, but a smile like that could not be answered in any other way.

"This place is great," Whipstaff piped up from a corner of the shop. He had donned a pair of jamjar spectacles which made his eyes look like hubcaps, and he staggered forward, knocking over a display of amusing hats that Timbers had been eyeing gleefully. "But what exactly are we doing here?"

Still grinning, Marty smacked a palm to his forehead. Given a plethora of playthings, and a clown free setting, it seemed that your average pirate would forget almost anything, even a freshly rekindled plan. "Like I said, we're going to bring the noise by being the noise." Marty stepped forward, holding out a brightly colored wig, and a cherry red plastic nose that he had liberated from shop window clown. The headwear stopped the cavorting pirates in their tracks. Oaf dropped the face paint he had been using to draw a crude picture of himself next to a giant treasure chest on the wall.

"Street performers drop a little cash into their hat to get the money flowing," Marty continued, as Timbers wrestled with Whipstaff for control of a rather fetching sombrero. "We've got no clowns, so we're going to make some." The sombrero toppled to the floor, and several button eyes darted in Marty's direction at the utterance of the 'C' word. "If we make them, they will come." It seemed a disservice to one of Marty's favorite movies, but the point was valid, and he intended to run with it.

"So what did you have in mind?" Whipstaff asked, the look on his face making it clear he really didn't want to know the answer.

Marty moved quickly across the store, planting a fluffy, brightly colored wig on the first mate's head. "Well. This." Chuckles rang out across the gloomy shop floor, and Whipstaff sunk into himself, like a child who had been told to eat his greens.

"Maybe we can just spray paint the massive afro under your bandana," Kate offered quietly, provoking a hasty *shush!* from Whipstaff. He patted disapprovingly at the mass of cotton candy hair that had invaded his head and shot a glance over to his captain.

"I'd have gone with red, personally," Timbers giggled. "Matches your temperament."

Despite the obvious clown connotations, Whipstaff failed to suppress a smile, and launched into a high kicking jig, which threatened to bring shelves, displays, and Oaf crashing to the floor.

All right, Marty thought. This was the time to do it: when the pirates were distracted by amusement, brightly colored things, and a frankly death defying dance. Quickly, he gathered up a handful of fancy dress gear, and darted through the store, fitting a red nose here, and hoisting a hideously oversized pair of pantaloons there. Within minutes, he was finished, just as Whipstaff completed his dervish of a performance and looked down at himself.

"What the...?" the first mate yelped, pulling halfheartedly at the bright checked waistcoat that had arrived about his person. "You've clowned me!"

Moans and cries of objection rang out from his shipmates, who had found themselves similarly be-jestered, but Marty stood defiant, a small pot of greasepaint and a brush in his hands.

"This isn't my hat."

"What am I wearing? Is this even a real color?"

"These shoes are actually quite nice."

The last statement, uttered by Oaf, drew stares from every corner of the room, which instantly erupted into laughter. The freshly harlequin-ed giant looked up in surprise, before nervously giggling along with the group, because something amusing had obviously just happened, and he never really got stuff anyway.

Timbers composed himself, stepping up to where Marty

brandished his brush. "Come on now, Marty. What's this all about?" He moved a hand up to his head, in an attempt to silence a cluster of tiny bells that jingled with every movement. "It's not wise to mess with a pirate's ensemble." The bells jingled again, and the little captain grimaced. "It's like putting a floral bonnet on a werewolf, or giving a supermodel a cheeseburger. You're upsetting the balance of the universe."

Marty paused, checking the words queueing up on his tongue for rationality and sense. None of them seemed to make the grade, but then this was an evening not fully acquainted with the sane protocols of normality. He chose a few of the easiest sentences and pressed on. "Look, Timbers. We're fishing for clowns without any bait."

Timbers huffed, finally losing patience with the chiming around his head, and throwing the bells to the ground. "I'm not a worm on a hook, me hearty." He stomped over to Marty, his hackles on fire at the very notion. "My lads'll take on an army of those red-nosed monsters, and come out of it with tales to tell and songs to sing, but they sure as shingle ain't wriggling maggots in a bucket."

Marty's eyes widened. He was staring down at his friend, who had raced into, and spectacularly out of battle alongside him on more than one occasion. Now the little pirate stood before him, with no clowns in sight, with his hand resting on the hilt of his cutlass. Clearly he had messed with the pirate code, something that should not be taken with a pinch of salt, let alone a glob of greasepaint, and he lowered his brush.

"Okay, I get it. I'm sorry." He raised a hand to stay any potential swordplay that was in the offing, in no small part due to the fact that he was not packing a blade himself. Marty sighed, raising a hand to cover his eyes. Another volley of random insanity lined up in his mouth to spill forth and no doubt complicate matters further, when another voice spoke up.

"Timbers, you're not bait."

Marty withdrew his hand as Kate appeared by his side. "You guys are pirates, right?"

Whipstaff had fallen in beside his captain, who was still bristling, and both nodded guardedly. "What gave it away?"

Not much, you look like a miniature circus parade, right now, something inside Marty tried to say. Good sense beat the thought to death before it could make it out of his mouth.

"I bet you've been on all kinds of adventures. Missions. Super secret, behind enemy lines stuff, am I right?" Kate continued, smuggling a barely visible wink towards Marty. Some part of him could see where she was going with this, and he smiled back, hoping that she had this covered. The smile took root and spread. Maybe he didn't have to be the man with the plan all the time. At no point since he had known her had Kate been anything less than on the ball, and she was sprinting towards the end zone right now.

"Adventures?" Whipstaff stepped forward, his little chest puffed out, and only slightly less impressive due to the sequined waistcoat upon it. "We've done this, we've done that. You tell me who's done this and that." The chest inflating increased. "We've been here and we've been there. I only know a few folk who have been here, and those who did would soil their britches at the thought of going there." The little first mate's eyes darted about him. Clearly he was running out of places to wax lyrical about. "We've done...well, we've done a lot of stuff. You wanna go here and there, you talk to a pirate."

Timbers glanced over at his crewmate, who breathed heavily, apparently exhausted by his rant. "Good show, Whipstaff. I remember going there, it was brutal."

Whipstaff turned to his captain and smirked. "Boatload of fun though."

Kate rolled her eyes and cleared her throat. Nostalgia was going to get them nowhere, although Marty was rather curious to hear more of this 'there' place. "What I'm saying is, are there any more qualified fellows to go on a covert mission than this fine crew?"

The bluster fell from the pirates' sails like a fleeting squall, and they looked to each other uncertainly.

Kate mocked surprise, holding her hands theatrically to her face. "You mean to tell me that you guys have never been on a covert mission? Sneaked into a stronghold and plundered some booty, and then soared off into the night like a bunch of stealthy nin...er... pirates?"

Timbers raised an eyebrow. The rift between ninjas and pirates was well documented, and yet a challenge had been given. "What

Whipstaff said is true," the little captain declared finally. "There's not a this or that, a here or there that we haven't braved." He patted Oaf on the shoulder, and the little giant turned to join the conversation, wearing a pair of oversized googly eyes that he had been busy trying on.

Kate clapped her hands, fixing the pirates with a sugar-coated look of awe. "Then you're the very ones to undertake this daring, clandestine mission!" She pointed out beyond the broken doors of the shop, into the empty street. "You can go out, infiltrate the clownish hordes, and bring them back to the *Fathom*, get them right where we want them."

Whipstaff slapped his thigh enthusiastically, turning to deliver a similarly purposeful smack to Oaf's shoulder. "Yeah. We can do that. We're pirates, there's nothing we can't do."

Oaf nodded happily, seemingly at least partially aware of what was going on. His googly eyes lolled and swung from his face, and he raised his hands to signify his agreement.

"It's settled then," Timbers crowed. "We go in all sneaky and stealthy like, and we drum up some evil juggly action."

Cheers rose from the ranks, and Timbers rode the crest of his crewmates new found purpose. "We're gonna beat these freaks at their own game, and then...just beat them. With sticks. What say you fine fellows?"

Tiny cloth hands grabbed the greasepaint from Marty's hands, and in moments, three tiny, grinning clown-pirates stood in a row, eager and willing to get on with a night's subterfuge.

Marty stood, taking in what had just transpired, and turned to Kate. There were several more words jostling for position in his head, but none were needed, as Kate cupped a hand to his ear, and whispered a smile back onto his face.

"I knew what you had in mind. The plan is solid. I just Kated it a bit."

As the pirates hurtled back out into the quiet night which lay beyond the doorway, Timbers turned to Marty, flashing him a knowing smile. "Ohh, she's good."

With that, they cavorted out into the street, Oaf clattering into a rail of clothes as they went. Googly eyes were fun, but you really couldn't see a damn thing out of them.

Chapter Twenty-One

The street was exactly as they had left it. Decimated, ruined, and clownless. Except, that wasn't strictly true. Three miniature, pirate-shaped clowns trotted out into the middle of the road, and stood in a frustrated and slightly embarrassed line, as if waiting for ridicule.

"Well, no clowns. Can I take this ridiculous get up off now?" Whipstaff flapped, pawing at his technicolor wig.

"Hang on." Marty stared out into the darkness as a shambling figure made its way towards them. As it drew closer, Marty flinched at the downright clownishness of its appearance, making ready to dash back towards the *Fathom,* but something about the new vagrant on the block made him pause.

The stranger was old, that much was clear. A thick, gray beard hung over tattered garments which may have been brightly colored and merry several hundred millennia ago. It sported a jaunty, bell laden cap, and a faded red nose rested haphazardly upon its face. If this was a clown, it was about as daunting as a kiddie ride at Disneyland, and had probably been around longer.

"Hey, old timer!" Timbers was quick on the offensive. "Seen any clowns around here?"

The ancient jester flinched, as though he hadn't expected to be addressed, and craned a wrinkled white neck to regard his addresser.

"Oh! I've found you," he croaked. "You young whipper snappers scamper off so quickly, you never give us veterans a chance to keep up." He creaked towards the cluster of pirate-clowns, arms opening in greeting.

"What have you young scamps been up to? Breaking things I'll wager. In my day, we wouldn't set upon the scenery until every last soul had been scared witless." He sighed, wistfully. "Simpler times."

Timbers nudged Whipstaff, motioning towards the elderly harlequin and winking, as if to convey an elaborate scheme in one wordless gesture. "Yep, that's nice and all, but we seem to have gotten lost. This street hadn't been clowned yet, and...well, you know how it is."

The wrinkly circus freak gave out a huff, and shambled still closer. "Ah, where are my manners. the name's Wrinkles, and I can set you on your way. Why, there was a time when I would have joined you, but these old hands can scarcely rustle up a balloon anything these days."

Clearly the old duffer was in the mood for nostalgia, and the crew of the *Fathom* had neither the time, nor the patience for such clownish reminiscence.

"I came through with the others, but I'm afraid they were all too eager to spread chaos and merriment, and they went on ahead."

Whipstaff rubbed a hand across his face, "That's very sad, sir, but we'd like to get back to our fellow clowns. They're having all the fun, setting fire to things and chasing innocents and so forth." He turned to Timbers. "That actually doesn't sound half bad. Maybe we had these clown guys all wrong."

Timbers shot his first mate a withering glance, before chipping in with a further enquiry. "So if you could see us on our way, we'd be most grateful."

Wrinkles slinked up alongside Oaf, staring down at the tiny giant with eyes that seemed to telescope out on their stalks. Oaf shifted uncomfortably, wanting to say something, but all too aware that something important was happening, and still trying to maintain control of his own googly eyes.

"You don't look like the chaps I used to raise hell with," Wrinkles croaked, peering at the costumed pirates curiously. "Where'd you get those outfits?"

Timbers jostled his way between Wrinkles and the clearly panicking Oaf. "Lost and found. You take what you can get, there's a war on, don't you know?" He shrugged, blankly at his companions. This doddering clown was older than the Bible's publisher, there was sure to have been a war on when he had still had some of his marbles.

Wrinkles clapped his hands approvingly. "Good for you, pitching in and helping the war effort." He beamed, a smile that would have given any dentist within a ten mile radius nightmares for weeks. "I'll show you where the troops are converging, but you'll have to leave your...friends here." He eyed Kate and Marty cautiously, apparently offended by their lack of outlandish colors and greasepaint.

"We can't. They're our prisoners," Oaf piped up from behind Timbers.

Perhaps once in a lifetime, when the planets are in alignment, and the words in his head formed a magically relevant sentence, did Oaf pull a blinder, and this was that moment. he basked in the glow of this crystalizing miracle, as several eyes turned to add to the glow with a mixture of surprise and awe.

"Oh splendid! Well follow me then," Wrinkles replied curtly, clearly unaware of the gravity of the moment, before shambling off back the way he had come.

The crew stared after the departing clown blankly. "Should we...should we go after him?" Whipstaff ventured.

Timbers was already trotting away in pursuit. "What else are we going to do? Stand around looking like the lost and found box at Chuck-E-Cheese?"

Whipstaff glanced down at himself. He had forgotten for a moment that they were decked out in clothes that would make a seventies glam rock star embarrassed. He motioned to Oaf to follow, and scampered off after his captain.

Kate shot a cautious look at Marty. "This has all the hallmarks of an impending and comprehensive disaster." What should have worried Marty was that she was right. They were being led into the lion's den, with the ultimate aim of towel flicking a bunch of clowns' backsides, before legging it back the way they had come. Even backup plans held more water than that.

Marty felt a grin creep across his lips. "That's exactly why it's going to work. Because it shouldn't."

Kate shook her head, raising an eyebrow. "That makes precisely no sense at all."

Already a few paces up the street, in the direction of his departing shipmates, Marty hesitated, fixing Kate with what he hoped was a look of reassurance. "I know, but look around. Does any of this make any sense at all?"

Fighting reason with bare-faced anti-logic had been a skill Marty excelled at, even before the world had gone big topped shaped, and he knew Kate had no answer. She smiled back, throwing her hands in the air. "Dammit, Marty, why'd you have to be so damned right all the time?"

Marty grasped her hand, and took a wild stab at milking the moment. "I'm not, except when it comes to having no business being right in the first place. I've got that down to a fine art."

She giggled approvingly, pushing Marty towards the almost totally foolhardy plan as they ran. "That's what I like most about you. You're a complete idiot," she whispered, squeezing his hand. There was no way to take this as anything other than a compliment in their current predicament, and Marty would've smiled even wider, had they not caught up with Wrinkles and the crew of the *Fathom* at that moment.

The doddering jester had come to rest beside a lamp post, which he clung to as he fought for breath. Timbers and Whipstaff stood beside him, eyes wide and taking in the sight before them, as Oaf lumbered up to join his crew.

"That's your standard base of operations," Wrinkles wheezed, casting a tattered glove towards what seemed to be all the clowns in the known universe. They spread out like a wriggling patch of weeds in the shopping mall car park which sprawled out along the underpass beneath. "I sure wish I could be with them, preparing for the festivities, but like I said, I got a bit lost, and these old bones won't get me down there." The old clown sagged against his lamp lit crutch, letting out a sigh that seemed to deflate his entire body as he surveyed his unreachable kin.

"Wow," Kate murmured, tightening her grip on Marty's hand. "That is a hell of a lot of red noses."

"More on the way too," Wrinkles chipped in, having apparently found emergency reserves of breath. "There's still more of us coming through that big portaly thing at the edge of town."

Timbers and Whipstaff exchanged excited whispers, letting

words like *shiny* and *sparkly* escape into the air above them. The two quickly became aware that eyes were upon them, and straightened sharply, Whipstaff's eagerness to chime in with a final "Shiny!" cut off by a rasping, "Shh!" from his captain.

"Oh, we know about all that, of course," Timbers stammered. "We've just come from there." He glanced around for support from his costumed crew. "Haven't we?"

Whipstaff nodded way too emphatically, almost losing his wig. "Oh yes, and did all sorts of incredibly naughty things on the way over here. Why, just before we bumped into you, we smashed up a...we set fire to some..."

Oaf stepped up, his face set and determined, as though he was trying to maintain the roll he was clearly on. "We played some mini golf." Whipstaff peered at his comrade. "As devilish escapades go, that ranks up there with breaking wind at a Sunday school picnic, or mooning a busload of passing nuns." The little first rasped, grinning despite himself, and possibly making a mental note to do the latter at some point that evening.

Wrinkles rubbed his leathery chin dubiously. "Golf, you say. Well, times have changed since my day. I suppose if you laid mines at each hole as you went, that would count." He paused, his gaze drifting, before he returned to the point he had started to make. "In which case, bravo!" He exposed more orthodontic terror in their direction, much to the relief of the would-be clowns, and their pretend captives.

Timbers rubbed his forehead nervously, as if to coax more words with which to dupe the old geezer into getting them down to his cronies somehow. As he withdrew his little cloth hand, the ancient harlequin gasped in surprise and revulsion. Timbers glanced down at his paw, which was now dripping with freshly removed greasepaint, and hastily attempted to reapply it to his face.

"Mother juggler!" Wrinkles cried. "You're not clowns at all." He turned on creaky ankles and crowed an alarm to the assembled fiends below. "Interlopers! Tiny spies in our midst! Get up here, and bring sharp things!"

Wrinkles' pleas for assistance were cut short as he fell beneath a pirate pile-on, but seemed to have reached their target, as dozens of glinting, wicked eyes turned to view the frantic scuffle above them.

Marty took a step towards his scrapping shipmates, as shrieks of realization came swirling up from the car park. Kate's hand pulled him back, and her eyes stopped him from wading further forward. "We have to get out of here. All of us." She was right. At any moment, those gleaming eyes would start to get bigger as their owners made for the overpass. Even as she spoke, clusters of balloons were bobbling out of countless clownish waistcoats, and carrying their wearers skyward, a floating squadron of murderous airborne freaks.

Marty turned to where his pirate allies were enthusiastically putting the boot in on old Wrinkles. Oaf stared back from where he sat, pinning the old pie chucker to the ground, and waved happily.

"Timbers, stop abusing the elderly and get out of there." Marty cried. "We've got incoming."

The sound of several battered nose honks drew triumphant battle cries from the scrapping brigands, and Timbers' head rose from the chaos to reply. "You go ahead, Marty. We've got this crusty old balloon-atic." He chuckled to himself, although it was unclear whether it was due to the fighting, or the zinging one liner that he'd just delivered. "Once his mates land, we'll be right behind you. Get back to the Fathom and get ready for a quick exit." There was no arguing with the captain, mostly because he had underlined his point with a hefty elbow slam and returned to the melee.

"Come on. They can handle this." Kate repeated, tugging at Marty's arm. "If we don't get the Fathom ready, we'll be sitting ducks when the charge of the fright brigade gets here."

Marty cursed under his breath. He was not a fighter, but wasn't one to leave his friends in a fight, no matter how much they appeared to be enjoying it. Grimacing, he turned back the way they had come, and high tailed it towards the Fathom, with Kate sprinting alongside him, and the fire of several dozen ghoulish, clown eyes burning into their backs as they ran.

Chapter Twenty-Two

There is a deep, dark place that your mind goes to when faced with the absurd, impossible, and downright terrifying. In Officer O'Riley's case, that place was a small, groundskeeper shed just outside the town hall. He had stumbled into it, frantically casting glances over his shoulder, convinced that a white gloved hand would be resting upon it at his every step.

The tiny wooden hut offered little in terms of protection, but it had a door, and a lock, which was enough for now. O'Riley sank back into the sparse shelter, listening for signs of red nosed intrusion. Whether the abject silence which greeted him was reassuring or worrying—he could not decide—but it at least gave him the chance to catch his breath.

There wasn't much by way of furnishings within O'Riley's hiding new place. Several tools hung from hooks on the wall, and bags of something funky smelling were heaped up against the far wall. Beside him sat a sorry looking camp bed, no doubt a place to rest the weary head of someone down on his luck, or an employee lacking in horticultural motivation.

O'Riley's eyes shifted back towards the rough hewn doorway of the shed. No glaring eyes peeked their way into the gloom, and no darting hands sought access. He plonked himself down onto the camp bed and placed a quivering hand to his face. When would this nightmare end? *Probably when the sun came up*, he thought. That's when nightmares usually ended, wasn't it? When the break of dawn shot forth radiant beams of reality which put paid to the night terrors, and signaled another dreary but thankfully murderless day. The darkness closed around him, pushing the panic inwards, condensing it like a tightly packed lump of coal that would inevitably give way to a needle sharp, gleaming diamond of fear. O'Riley couldn't see anything now. Maybe the moon had passed behind a cloud, or maybe he had shut his eyes, he had neither the will nor the curiosity to decide which.

Slumped down again the bags of fertilizer, he barely heard the wispy voice drift down from the tiny window above him. "Hey. You in there. I know you can hear me."

It was an ambitious claim, as O'Riley craned up to the little aperture from which he thought he'd heard something. He had no wish to advertise his presence, but gave in to the last embers of regimented procedure that still flickered within him. "Who... who's there? Identify yourself." It came out as more of a plea than a command, but was markedly better than the stifled whimper that his mind had offered up as an alternative response.

"I know why you're here as well," the voice continued, ignoring the weak question. "And you should know that you picked the wrong evening to walk your beat, Mr. Policeman."

There was a diminutive quality to the voice, like a puppet who had somehow learned to speak, and possibly wield a knife. O'Riley had been uneasy when it had first issued into the shed, and what sounded like a thinly veiled threat did little to allay his rapidly blooming fears.

"Listen, I don't know who you are, but I'm not walking anything," O'Riley gibbered. "I'd place tonight's moonlight stroll in the 'running away' category, if anything."

The voice sniggered. "Indeed. You *don't* know who I am."

O'Riley winced. For all the terror, uncertainty and downright confusion that tonight had bestowed upon him, a sliver of annoyance had crept in as the mysterious whisperer continued to completely ignore him.

"Look. What's all this about?" O'Riley flared, gusto momentarily wrestling control of his senses away from self-preservation. "I don't care who you are, I'm just trying to get home, preferably with at least all of my limbs still attached."

The voice suddenly exploded into fits of shrill laughter. Whether O'Riley had discovered the secret of comedy, or this hidden menace had several hundred screws loose, he couldn't be sure. He was willing to hazard a guess, though. His question hadn't been that funny.

"Oh, my speeding ticket dispensing friend, you will find out soon enough what all this is about," the voice rasped excitedly. "As for your limbs. Well, that all depends on how adept you are at dodging nightmares."

O'Riley hadn't considered nightmare dodging to be an inherent skill. He'd survived this far through a merciful concoction of luck, abject cowardice, and the desire to wake up tomorrow, limbless or otherwise. He steeled his whirling mind against the barrage of thoughts, questions and prayers to deities, and pressed on. "What do you want?" That was the real kicker, the golden egg, the sixty-four thousand dollar question in the game of extreme hide and seek he'd been playing this evening.

More sniggering greeted his question. This willful outpouring of disregard would surely have awoken the action hero in him, had said hero not turned tail the moment the last of his bullets had been spent. Not having infinite ammo was another bugbear that he would be adding to his list of Hollywood gripes, providing he lasted the night. The giggling snapped off sharply, as the voice pitched forward with a ragged venom which caught O'Riley by surprise. "I told you, you will find out," the voice eased, as though its owner was struggling to maintain some kind of calm sanity atop what was almost certainly bubbling depravity.

"I just wanted to give you the option to scurry back whence you came before the fireworks really get going tonight. You've seen my servants at work. You really don't want to be around when the world stops taking its meds, do you?"

O'Riley was a good enough cop, albeit several vertebrae short of a full spine, to realize that this was not an empty threat. He was also good enough at being alive and staying that way, to recognize a 'get out while the getting is good' suggestion when he heard one.

Rounding up all of his analytical skills, O'Riley channeled his contemporaries: Holmes, Marple, Poirot, Crockett, Tubbs, Columbo, even the Greek, lollipop sucking bald one. "Mr. Peepers?" he ventured into the darkness.

Again, the hoarse whisperer chuckled. This was becoming an annoying trait, and his crime fighting peers collectively shook their heads in his mind. "Mr. Peepers? Close, but no cigar I'm afraid."

O'Riley cursed under his breath. This was starting to feel like a game of Cluedo, only he felt like he was staring down at his own body, in the shed, with the juggling balls.

"Peepers does my bidding, and tonight, over here, I'm running the show," the voice cooed. "I find it amusing that you think me a foot soldier in tonight's festivities. No matter, I just wanted to be nice, and give you a chance to head for the hills." There was a pause, as though the evil mastermind behind whatever plot was unfolding expected a response. "What? I can be nice if I want to be," came the almost offended afterthought. "It won't matter anyway, because after tonight, heading for the hills will be pointless…because we'll be there. In the hills. In the streets. Everywhere in fact." There was a faint huffing sound, as though the harbinger of all things apocalyptic had run into a dead end of sinister foreshadowing, and was somewhat stumped by the degeneration into small talk.

"If it doesn't matter, I think I'll just stay here a while," O'Riley mumbled sheepishly. "At least until you've gone anyway. No offence."

The voice continued, not a hint of affront in its tones. "That's up to you. I came over to warn you off, thinking that you might be a hardened cop on a one-man crusade to vanquish evil, like in that movie."

"What, you mean *'The Hardened Cop on A One-man Crusade To Vanquish Evil'*?"

"No, the sequel."

O'Riley simultaneously wished he was, and was relieved that he wasn't.

"Anyway, now I see that you're only here to give my clowns something to chase after, so I will leave you to cower in your bolt hole."

"Good," O'Riley ventured, unsure of how to end a conversation with a criminal mastermind. "Umm, bye then."

The unseen doomsayer appeared similarly stumped, as several thrashing noises outside signaled its semi-successful attempt to vacate. Amidst various sounds of wrenching foliage and muffled curses, O'Riley spoke up, since he had no wish to peek nervously out of the slatted window for clarification. "I thought you were going?"

"I am! There's just a lot of shrubs and junk back here. It's quite difficult to...ow! Nettles!" More puppet-shrill protesting rang out, but further away, as the outsider found what O'Riley guessed was a way back to the town hall gardens.

Now was the time for action. Something inside him demanded steely resolve. It cried out for him to throw open the rickety shed door and chase down the departing evildoer. It screamed inwardly for justice.

It groaned as O'Riley shuffled uncomfortably into a kneeling position, and cautiously peered out of the little window.

Outside, nothing stirred. There was no evidence of the scornful being which had been there moments earlier, and O'Riley almost hated the fact that a sigh of relief escaped his lips at the sight. Beyond the creeping thickets and leftover gardening tools, the gardens stood motionless, bereft of anything that could leap in terrifyingly at him, and almost normal in what had been an evening of anything but. Aside of course, from the enormous pirate ship in the town pond.

With everything that had happened so far that night, he didn't even question what it was doing there.

Chapter Twenty-Three

Marty had never been a big fan of surprises. Even on Christmas morning as a child, he would sneak downstairs when all but the most diligent of partygoers had collapsed into their beds, or a close approximation to it. He would shake, poke, and pry at the myriad of wrapped goodies beneath the tree mere moments after his paren…ahem…Santa had placed them in the moonlit living room. Even then, the not knowing would drive him crazy. All the guessing that the tiny, box-shaped gift in the corner was in fact a bike wouldn't change that. It was, after all, the mission of every child to ponder endlessly about what goes on out of their sight. Curiosity might kill the cat, but such portents held no fear for a youngster, especially when the prospect of shiny new free stuff bestowed upon them by a mysterious, fat bearded stranger hung like pixie dust in the air.

This child-like hunger for answers had followed Marty into pseudo-adulthood, and it jabbed him impatiently in the ribs as all manner of unseen shenanigans exploded violently in the shrouded street behind them.

Kate squeezed his hand, as though she sensed his pensive curiosity, and stared out into the chaotic void as something exploded, maddeningly just out of sight. They stopped to wait for their pirate allies, with the *Fathom* in sight, and the imminently arriving clown reinforcements now shrouded in the darkness.

"I've got this one in a headlock, that means he's mine," a voice cried out from somewhere in the gloom. "There's a bunch more over there, go play with them."

A red nose clattered down the street and came to rest at Marty's feet.

"Oaf, get off! I'm on your side. Aim for the taller ones."

More whup ass escaped its constrictive cans behind them, and still Marty could make out nothing of the melee which was so obviously going down.

"I'm sorry, was that your face?" Came a much deeper, Oaf sounding apology.

Marty bunched his fists, much to the displeasure of Kate, who was still holding one. This was like playing a video game with your eyes shut. "This isn't right," he muttered. "We should be in there, helping them."

Kate shook her head slightly. "It sounds like they're doing okay on their own."

An order rang out from Timbers, as if to emphasize Kate's point. "Whipstaff, go easy on them. We're supposed to be getting them to follow us, not making them explode."

"I can't help it," another voice chimed in, with enough enthusiasm to sink a battleship. "They just go off like paper fireworks. I'm only hitting them a bit. Okay, I'm hitting them a lot, but hey, fireworks!"

Much giggling, followed by what sounded like an explosion in a piñata factory ensued, and Marty darted a nervous glance up the street, then back towards the *Fathom*, silhouetted against the night ahead of them. This was not shaping up to be a textbook execution of the plan, unless that textbook had been written by an Austrian cyborg on a sugar high.

Three pint-sized shapes galloped out of the cloaked chaos behind them, carrying various trophies of the fight which had disappointingly unraveled without Marty, and darted past, back the way they had come. Timbers was, of course, leading the charge. He was holding what appeared to be a freshly scalped clown wig, which was unravelling back to whatever rapidly balding horror he had accosted in the battle just moments earlier.

Whipstaff followed close behind, clutching a pair of freshly liberated pantaloons. Marty had no idea how that little skirmish had panned out, and had no wish to delve further into that line of enquiry.

Bringing up the rear, Oaf appeared, holding proudly aloft a potted plant. Whether this item had been in any way connected with the epic coming together of clown and pirate in mortal combat was unclear, but the lumbering buccaneer cradled it like a new born puppy, and Marty thought it best not to probe too much into the whys and wherefores of its origin or purpose. In any case, the guttural shrieks of protest, and juddering shapes which appeared in pursuit were sufficient incentive to send both him and Kate sprinting after the departing pirates. It appeared that they had snagged the attention of the marauding circus hellion, and although that had been the plan all along, Marty grasped at the logic behind it, which had seemed such a good idea only moments ago.

A few fleeing strides brought him level with Timbers, who was already on the home straight back to home base, and Marty aimed a frantic glance down at his still chuckling comrade. "I think we've got their attention, Timbers. Maybe drop the hair?"

Timbers was in full flow, caught in mid-adventure, and shooed his friend's suggestion with a flapping, wig filled hand. "No chance, Marty. I got me a scalp, like one of them Cherokee fellows. This'll go great with the red nose and Peepers' boot in my trophy cabinet."

They were running parallel to Main Street now, and turned collectively on a heel for the final stretch to home straight, with the *Fathom* looming silently before them. There was a simplicity to this that made Marty almost break stride as it sunk into his brain. There were no meetings, no traffic jams, no minimum wage to this life. Throw a rock, watch it hit and run. It was as close to his childhood as he had come in twenty or so years, and the sheer carefree abandon of it forced a smile onto his face. He turned to Kate, wondering if some semblance of reality remained with her, waiting to drag him back into the nine to five and remind him of his inherent realness, but she grinned back. Clearly responsibility had taken just as much of a hit as the town, and it was time to embrace what had rudely arrived in its place. Wholeheartedly in the 'run' portion of this scenario, Marty's only wish was that he had been present at the 'throw the rock' part.

Ever the sage, albeit blithering lunatic, Timbers seemed to catch a whiff of Marty's epiphany. "Look lively, lad. There'll still be plenty of clowns when we get back to the *Fathom*. Man a cannon and you can pop as many of them as you like." He winked, and streaked off ahead, a pirate on a mission to get back to his ship, and make ready with the plan. Marty's plan. The grin was spreading, and setting up a decent argument for permanent residence. This wasn't reality, or at least the reality that had imposed itself on Marty's life. This was his road, and he was currently hurtling down it with a bunch of toy pirates and the girl of his dreams. Aside from the clowns pursuing them, it didn't get much better than that.

Life, of course, has an evil way of demonstrating just how much worse it can get. As the group reached the *Fathom*, Marty gazed up at its deck, and almost stopped dead in his tracks. There had been who knows how many clowns at their backs, braying and cackling in a demented pursuit of their prey, but none of the crew had given any thought to the hordes which might be lying in wait for them. Clowns are a wily bunch, and when not falling foul of wonderfully half-cocked, and amazingly working plans, can be found concocting strategies of their own.

Upon the deck of the *Fathom*, a dozen or so of the scheming harlequins ran hither and thither, hooting, creeping, and making a general nuisance of themselves. High up in their crows' nests, the Bobs cowered, clearly outnumbered and with no backup, whilst Zephyr sat motionless, apparently in some sort of recharge mode.

Marty called out to Timbers, hoping it wasn't nearly as desperate and panic stricken as it sounded in his head. "They're on the ship, Timbers. They've boarded the *Fathom*!"

The little captain shot a barely discernable glance upwards as he hit the gangplank. Territorial indignance had taken hold, as quickly as a tiny clothed hand met the hilt of the blade at his side. "You are in direct violation of the plan, and you're on my boat. Prepare to meet your fluffy maker, you gibbering bilge rats!"

Even as Timbers sprang onto the deck of the *Fathom*, his loyal crew adopting similar modes of attack behind him, the clownish interlopers were in motion.

As Marty and Kate finally reached the jetty, the clowns slithered back to form a tight circle in the center of the deck. They bared countless yellow teeth, and hooted frantically at the advancing crew. From somewhere in the middle of the hideous huddle, a new voice sprang forth, high pitched and pleading, as Benji was hoisted above dozens of brightly wigged heads like some kind of squirming trophy.

"Miss Kate!" Benji struggled against the grasp of his leering captor, as the crew of the *Fathom* stopped dead in their tracks. "Don't let them take me. I don't want to be a koala bear picnic."

Kate turned, wild eyed, towards the whimpering marsupial. Benji shot from yellow, to green, to radiant white as the monster holding him turned its face upwards. Like a painted anaconda, the clown's jaw dropped, unhinging, and Kate's mind dragged her unwillingly to thoughts of Sir Reginald in the alley behind The Pickled Judge.

"Benji! No!" Marty grabbed Kate as she flung herself helplessly across the deck. The ghoulish face loomed further towards its prey, and the tiny koala dropped, strobing, out of sight into the slavering clown's now impossibly gaping mouth.

For a searingly long moment, everything seemed to come to a standstill. Marty turned to the crew of the *Fathom*, his mouth hanging open, although not quite to small furry creature swallowing capacity. Timbers' blade dropped, and a blinking, quizzical look flitted across his face. Even the clowns, still panting and full of murderous mirth stood rooted to the spot, as if waiting for something to happen.

"That's not supposed to happen," Timbers ventured, shaking his head vaguely. "We win. We always win." He turned his attention to the waiting jesters. "You can't do that. Undo that right now, bad show!"

Appearing to enjoy this little outburst, the clowns erupted into fits of shrieking laughter, snapping the shell-shocked Kate from her stupor. Marty let go of her, stunned at what had happened, and only realized that his hand was Kate-less when she shot past him, Oaf's mallet already sweeping in a lethal arc over her head.

The nearest clown was still giggling manically when the force of a woman wronged dropped wooden retribution onto its head. Hell predictably followed, reducing the unsuspecting creature to a pair of oversized shoes, jutting out from a pummeled flat wig on the deck.

Clearly this was the cue the other clowns were waiting for. As one, their waistcoats parted, and a flurry of balloons cascaded forth, peppering the air with brightly colored plastic. As they drifted into the sky, Timbers flailed at swiftly departing devils, throwing hastily crafted insults at the ascending jesters.

Kate crashed back onto the deck, her sobs rattling through Marty in heart wrenching tremors. It was safe to say that the plan had flown out the window, and was currently being trodden under the flappy size twenties of the angry clowns still chasing them in the street below.

Up on the quarterdeck, Timbers was at the helm. "Bobs. Wake up Zephyr. We need to get airborne, sharpish." A look arrived on the little pirate's face, filled with more determination and purpose than Marty had ever seen in his admittedly limited interaction with living toys.

His sword was still drawn, and his intention was clear. With enemies above them, and more incoming, the order came swift and direct.

"Nobody eats a koala on my ship. Follow those balloons."

Chapter Twenty-Four

Marty sank back against the railing of the *Fathom's* deck, as a million thoughts, emotions, and questions wrestled for priority in his head.

Yesterday, his most pressing concern had centered around whether his socks had one more day's wear in them, and whether to have ham or cheese on his sandwiches.

As the *Flying Fathom* soared silently back into the heavens, his mind was beset by thoughts possibly more befitting of a madman. What were they going to do when they reached the big top full of psychotic clowns at the edge of town? How would they deal with dozens of similarly demented jesters currently at their backs? How exactly does one console a significant other who has recently lost their talking koala?

The latter thought pushed all others aside as Kate's sobs played wrenching power chords on Marty's heart strings.

"He didn't want to hurt anyone," Kate wailed, clutching her knees and rocking to and fro on the deck. "He didn't even want to be here." She paused, collecting herself, before following up with the sort of unintelligible mass of syllables any mortally upset person imparts in an attempt to sum up their feelings. "Ebeeweefoteeweemeeeee!" Kate sniffed, blinking up at Marty through teary eyes. "You know?"

Even though Marty hadn't caught the words, he had understood the sentiment, just as he knew that a hug would not help, but delivered one anyway. Words came next, although he acknowledged that they would be equally redundant. "I know you don't want to hear this, but right now we have to concentrate on the job in hand." Marty winced at his words. Never mind redundant, those had been downright unhelpful. He pressed on, hoping that his follow-up would be more comforting. "And anyway, what better way to get back at these red-nosed gits than by booting them, arse first back through their portal?" Although better, they still weren't the verbal medicine that he'd intended them to be.

Nevertheless, Kate straightened, sniffing back tears and nodding deliberately. "You're right," she croaked, rubbing her eyes and springing to her feet. "They've crossed a line, and now they'll have to pay." Marty decided to forgo any further words in favor of another hug. Kate was stronger than he could have ever imagined, and right now he was looking at a girl with one thing on her mind. Revenge. Knowing what he already did about Kate, Marty decided he'd take that over a tactical missile strike of the big top any day of the week.

Turning to glance over the side, he surveyed the night sky around them. The gang of koala munching clowns had disappeared in the distance up ahead, but there were still plenty more on their backs, no doubt hot on their sails. He tried not to think about the hovering shapes, borne beneath countless billowing balloons, behind them. "We'll figure all of this out. We always do." He summoned up the best smile he could muster, and was simultaneously surprised and relieved as Kate managed a defiant one in return. "Even with clowns to the left of us, and..." The remainder of the question was lost as they both succumbed to nervous, uncomfortable laughter.

"These creeps are cannon fodder," he declared, gaining strength from her smile. "We beat these guys before armed only with ice cream, remember?"

"And pirate ass-whuppery," a voice from the quarterdeck interjected. Marty looked up to see Timbers hanging over the rail and delivering a cheerfully supportive wave. "Don't you worry, Katie lass, we'll be over the big top and raining down the good stuff on 'em before you know it." Marty suppressed a fist pump. There was a time and a place for such gestures, and he wasn't done consoling his lady.

"But what about the ones behind us?" Kate asked, a hint of uncertainty creeping back into her voice.

The *Fathom* descended soundlessly down towards the gray slumber of the town beneath, as exactly far too many floating clowns bobbed and snaked out of the night in pursuit. They sure as hell weren't going to outrun these balloon-borne monsters, Marty thought, and it seemed Timbers concurred as he issued the order to dive.

They were approaching the outskirts of town as they dropped adjacent to the various shops and office blocks skirting the street, but there was still enough urban maze to exact some devilishly brave and foolhardy evasive maneuvers amidst.

A tall, steely building which looked boringly clerical cast a reflection back at the crew of the *Fathom*, and Marty took a moment to remember just how awesome a flying pirate galleon looked, mid-swoop. The *Fathom's* sails billowed in the night air, and the slow arc in which Zephyr was carrying them drew a mirror image of the ship's mighty deck from the tower's shining facade. "Damn, we're pretty," Timbers crowed, adjusting his hat, and twirling his flintlock in a dashing pose which would surely have made it onto the cover of *Toy Pirate Weekly*.

"No time for looking awesome, Timbers," Kate pointed back the way they'd come as several dozen flying lunatics drifted into a V formation behind the *Fathom*. Timbers stamped a disapproving foot, and leapt from the quarterdeck. There was always time to look awesome.

The little corsair hit the deck at speed, nodding at Whipstaff as he took up a position at the railing. His first mate was already hurrying to the aft of the *Fathom*. "Don't you worry about them. We dream pirates have ways of dealing with noisy neighbors." Timbers winked at Kate.

As one, Kate and Marty stared over at where Whipstaff had taken a seat upon a large, cast iron apparatus, moored to the rear of the ship. It stretched out behind the *Fathom* like an oversized artillery cannon, which sat upon a metal cage that Marty felt sure he should have noticed at some point before. "It comes up out of the deck, specifically for situations like this," Timbers explained, as he rested on a lever which presumably had brought forth this impressive tailgun. "We don't venture onto another plane of existence with only our wits and finely stitched good looks to fall back on you know." He beamed.

Whipstaff leapt into the operator's seat, and used a complex array of gears and winding things to pivot the big gun. Beneath him, Oaf took up position beside the cage, and looked back at his captain, awaiting the order to fire. Above him, Whipstaff jiggled and bounced in his seat. "I've been waiting to use this bad boy for ages!" he squealed.

Marty got to his feet, taking a few steps towards the mighty cannon. Behind them, the clowns veered ever closer, and Whipstaff wheeled the gun to bear upon them, an oversized gunsight framing the lead group of hellspawn harlequins. "This is just like that movie," Marty called out.

"What? *Gone with The Wind?*" Whipstaff replied, still playing with his many levers.

"Yeah, that's the one," Timbers chimed in. "Whipstaff. When you're ready, lad. Give 'em a dose of mutton mayhem."

With the order given, Oaf ushered a weakly bleating sheep into the back of the cannon, which closed behind it.

"Wait, no!" Kate cried, jumping up from where she sat. "That poor sheep!"

"Fear not, m'lady. We keep a paddock of completely mechanical livestock on this boat. No animals are harmed in the use of the Mutton Musket. A whole bunch of clowns are about to get mullered, though." Chuckling, Timbers levelled his sword at the advancing jesters and issued a bellowing command. "FIRE!"

A cackling Whipstaff trained the gun on the nearest cluster of floating harlequins, and pulled the trigger.

A booming retort sent the robo-sheep hurtling from the barrel of the cannon, and pitched the *Fathom* forward. Whipstaff craned from his seat, watching as the sheep whistled through the night air, bleating mechanically as it flew towards its target.

From the ground, this whole spectacle might have looked like a page from the *Big Book of Unhinged Bedtime Stories*, which was exactly what it did look like to a cluster of passing students, heavy laden with stomachs full of cheap alcohol, and heads full of beer tornados. Somehow, they had managed to stumble through the calamity that the evening's nightmares had wrought, and giggled with inebriated wonder as the floating pirate ship berthed a mildly complaining sheep into the sky above them.

It reached the first row of floating clowns in seconds, and exploded in a plume of wool, cogs and brightly colored, paper clown guts, drawing raucous applause from the massed ranks for drunken academics in the street below.

"Home run!" Timbers cried, punching the air. "How'd you like them sheep-shaped apples, you swarthy balloon blowers?" He pitched a thumbs up at his first mate, who gleefully repositioned the gun at the second phalanx of advancing jesters.

The street ended abruptly up ahead, and Zephyr pitched the *Fathom* hard to port, bringing the ship around into a sweeping fly-by of the local drive-in theatre. Marty clutched the rail as they coasted sideways across the massive screen, which danced merrily to the tune of a fifties, sci-fi B movie. The *Fathom* lurched creakily level, guaranteeing that any passenger not in full possession of their air legs would most likely be enjoying a close reunion with their lunch.

Still the clowns pursued, although a number of them were now being pelted with popcorn and plastic cups. The discerning patrons of the drive-in had clearly decided that the addition of an all too realistic 3D element to their evening's entertainment was unacceptable. A few of the clowns broke rank and dove at their concession wielding attackers, although not enough for Marty's liking, as his eyes returned to the pressing flanks of circus freaks, now gaining on them.

He had seen a hell of a lot following his re-acquaintance with the plush pirate brigade, but this seemed absurd, even by their standards. His mind quickly rewound to the impressive explosion they'd caused moments earlier, and he wheeled on Timbers. "Wait. Sheep now? We're firing sheep at clowns?" A frantic giggle sneaked out of his mouth. "That makes absolutely no sense."

Timbers paused, mid-command, and rolled his good eye. "Which part of this whole thing does make sense, matey?"

He had a point, and Marty wasn't sure what his follow up question was going to be, but he readied it anyway. "Yeah, but why sheep?"

"What better way to send your enemies back to the land of nod, in this case in several pieces?" Timbers beamed. "Plus, the added bonus with these critters is you don't have to count them. You get to one, and you're pretty much done." As always, the little captain's logic was tenuous, completely insane, and bang on the money. Satisfied that he'd explained himself adequately, Timbers returned to the matter in hand. "Bring out number two, Bessie," he ordered, prompting Oaf to fish around in the cage and pluck out another mechanical bleater. Bessie sported a red number two on her flank, and duly shuffled into the loading bay of the Mutton Musket.

"Ready to fire, captain," Whipstaff screamed, clearly loving the opportunity to shoot something big and explodey. "Lamb in the hole!" Another apocalyptic boom rang out, as Bessie sailed from the musket's muzzle, fixing the oncoming clowns with a determined, robotic gaze. She ploughed through their ranks, sending balloons and oversized shoes streaking from their owners in a shower of sheepy fire. The impact also served to pepper the screen of the drive in with what was once clowns, but was now nothing more than pluming showers of glittering debris. The moviegoers groaned and threw more light refreshments, although in truth, this intrusion had probably been more entertaining than the movie.

Timbers leapt into the air, fueled by the effectiveness of his farmyard ammunition. "Sleep tight!" he shouted, before issuing another command. "All right Oaf, time for number six, Mittens." As requested, Mittens the sheep, a big red six emblazoned on her side, was readied for deployment. "Aim for that big bunch of red nosed gits off to starboard, Whipstaff."

Buffeted by a sudden descent as Zephyr plunged further floorward, the eagle eyed first mate twirled the gun effortlessly to bear on the flanking sortie of clowns and fired. Again, the woolen harbinger of doom blasted forth and detonated, sending her clownish targets to their presumably chuckling maker, and bringing forth more whoops of triumph from the deck of the *Fathom*.

Marty glanced over the side, gripping the rail worriedly as he realized they were mere feet from the floor. Trees, cars and bemused onlookers whipped past as the *Fathom* gunned towards the wafting flags and inviting lights of the MacWenCastle diner. "Cheeseburgers!" Whipstaff cheered from his perch in the command chair of bleating destruction. "Who's got change?"

Timbers scampered across to the gangplank, apparently gauging their speed to drive thru window ratio. "You're buying, Whipstaff," he called back to his first mate. "That is, if they take giant, lepre-coins." Whipstaff had no time to object, as the *Fathom* screamed through the drive thru, faster than the beleaguered clerk could take in what he was witnessing, let alone their order. Barely edible, cow based treats would have to wait for another day, it would seem, as Zephyr flung the *Fathom* out through MacWenCastle's exit, and back up into the heavens with all the grace and poise of a blind shot putter throwing sloppy joes through a wind tunnel.

Amidst the various laments about unrequited junk food, Marty glanced over to port, just as a group of twenty or more clowns dropped out of a cloud and drifted up alongside the *Fathom*, close enough to see their bared teeth and frantically grasping claws. "Timbers, port side!" he shrieked, pulling Kate back towards the quarterdeck as their pursuing assailants swooped in for a surprise attack.

Timbers' odes to rapidly departing sandwiches ceased, taking with it his gleeful smile, as the new danger filtered into his field of vision. Marty knew that the smile would return—it always did. Timbers had unfathomable sleeves upon which to draw an ace, and Marty was not about to doubt his pint-sized ally, when he had seen that grin re-emerge countless times before.

Almost on cue, Timbers gave voice to a near impossible, teeth baring beamer. "Whipstaff. Turn the musket to port. Oaf, bring out number nine, Mrs Cottonbomb.

The name alone demanded some kind of fanfare, and possibly a deep voiced introduction. Marty felt as though he should brace himself as Oaf hauled out a wholly terrifying looking sheep with the number nine etched upon her side. Mrs Cottonbomb was the A-Bomb of farmyard animals. She strutted up to the loading bay with a determined look in her eyes, and flicked her robotic tail defiantly. As Mrs Cottonbomb disappeared into the Mutton Musket, she bellowed out a battle cry that sounded like the hounds of hell playing fetch with a nuke. The following explosion was no less cataclysmic, as the most violently terrifying sheep in existence plummeted headlong into the thick of the clown offensive.

Marty just had time to hear Timbers yell, "Hit the deck!" as the world's biggest firecracker erupted beside them. He threw himself to cover Kate as the midnight sky turned a bright shade of daylight, and everything decided to collide with everything else.

In his peripheral vision, a tiny point of light became a ball, and then a horizon, before filling the night sky with brilliant, sheep borne fire.

Several whirling, wind whipped moments passed, during which Marty was sure he felt his eyebrows singeing, before the buffeting ceased, and the *Fathom* came to a drifting rest. Like passing thunder, the noise drifted back into silence, and Marty opened his eyes, checking to see if he still had the normal amount of limbs. The rest of the crew were in various stages of recovering from the atomic blast around him, and Kate stared out into the inky blackness which had returned to the night around them.

Off the *Fathom's* port side, no clowns threatened to board them. Behind, upon the rapidly diminishing canvas of the town, nothing threatened to pursue. Beside Marty on the quarterdeck, Timbers picked himself up and surveyed his ship. Oaf stood next to the musket cage, looking bewildered. Since this was pretty standard for Oaf, nobody really paid any attention. Above him, Whipstaff sat in his gun seat, blackened, and blasted. Singed hair stuck out from beneath his bandana, and random articles of his clothing still smoldered. "Wow," he muttered, staggering down from his perch. "Mrs Cottonbomb. What a sheep."

Timbers sheathed his sword, nodding in reverent acknowledgement of the shearly departed. "What a sheep, indeed. I would say we packed her with too much dynamite, but come on." His trademark grin reappeared. "That's just crazy talk. There's no such thing as too much dynamite."

Marty chipped in worriedly, "Hang on, Timbers. Weren't we supposed to be leading those guys to the big top?" He leaned over the side of the *Fathom*, regarding the clown-less sky behind them. "Essentially, all we're doing now is dropping in on the incoming pie chuckers."

Timbers hitched his thumbs into his belt, fixing Marty with his one good eye. "We've just dropped a sheep nuke on Peepers' army. He'll have seen that, and he'll come running. All we've got to do now is take the big top, and wait for the head harlequin to come home."

Marty raised a hand to his mouth, in a vain attempt to suppress the smile beneath. "Is that all?"

Timbers winked, apparently seeing through Marty's disguised attempt at incredulity. "Yeah, that's all. Come on lad, you've flown with me before. Haven't you learned by now that this is how we do things?"

Marty removed the hand, but not the smile. He was in, and they both knew it. Kate stepped up alongside Marty. She was not smiling, but the intent in her eyes conveyed that she too was in.

"Okay," Marty conceded. "So how exactly do we do that?"

Timbers scampered up to the bow of the *Fathom*, turning back to deliver a jovial shrug. "I have absolutely no idea."

Chapter Twenty-Five

All things considered, and given the flavor of the evening thus far, the flight had taken a serene, almost normal turn. Mechanical whirring from Zephyr's huge metal wings rang out like a pulse through the night air, and only the sound of gently creaking rigging accompanied it. That, and the soft clunking and gentle swearing which signaled the crew's stowing of the Mutton Musket back below decks.

Marty hadn't strayed far from Kate since they had dispatched the clowns, and although she put a brave face on, he could tell that her mind was fixed on her little koala casualty. Marty took a seat on the steps to the quarterdeck, where Kate had stationed herself against the forward mast. She absently scored lines into the wood, and staring emptily into the night ahead of them. Marty took her hands and gave them a gentle squeeze. "Better not let Timbers see you doing that, or he'll throw a fit." He smiled, as supportively as he knew how, and tried to illicit a similar one from Kate. "We don't want to walk the plank right now, that first step's a nightmare. Literally."

Kate shifted her hypnotic gaze and blinked weary eyes. "There's going to be a hell of a lot of giggling bodies in that tent when we get there. How are we going to pull this off? We're not cut out for this sort of thing. Hell, I only stopped off for a drink on the way home from work tonight, and now I'm mourning a talking koala."

Marty nodded, immediately aware of how that felt. When he'd woken up dreamside, the conversations with his own mirror self and the smart mouthed cuddly toy from his childhood had left him feeling like a passenger on a driverless train for a time, and he knew full well how disconcerting it was.

"Hey. Remember when Timbers got toy-napped, and we barged recklessly into the heart of enemy territory, just a paper-thin plan, a wing and a prayer away from being juggler bait? I seem to recall you were just as dubious about the ins and outs of the process then, too." He smiled, as though recalling a treasured memory, which for all the running and screaming, it was.

"The point is, we got in, and we got out. We didn't need a finely crafted strategy, concocted by some master tactician. We did it on the back of bare-faced foolhardiness and a bit of luck. Okay, a lot of luck. And an ice cream truck." Marty reigned in his thoughts, which threatened to derail his speech. "What I mean is, we have the tools and the guile to get us through this. Every obstacle we've faced, we've dealt with, because we're frankly awesome at this."

Kate looked up into his eyes, as though she heard what he was saying, at last.

"I get through the days because I have to. In the real world, you get by because the bills need to be paid, and the food needs to somehow find its way onto your table. You get by, and you make it work as best you can, because there's nothing really at stake, and at worst, you have to hand in your Space Beagle costume."

Marty pressed on, now as sure that he didn't belong in reality as he had been when he woke up to the assaulting beer monkeys in his own subconscious, even if he hadn't fully realized it at the time. "But here, here we get through the days because we *can*. I'm sure I wasn't put here to wander around dressed as a cosmic hound and entertain bored kids. Were you put here to push tickets through a slot?"

She knew the answer, and he knew that she did.

"We'll get to the Big Top, and we'll do what has to be done, because we can. Because it's not something we can just shrug off as a bad day and forget about when we punch our clocks at the end of our shift." Marty cleared his throat. He was saying this as much to himself as he was to Kate, and it scared part of him. That piece of him lived in the before, though, and the part that mattered cheered him on, throwing more words into his head. "This, right here, right now. This is real. This is what matters, no matter how crazy it seems. It's important to us, and so it gets done, by any means necessary."

Marty breathed out a sigh, along with the remaining ties he had with the real world, and Kate joined him in the exodus.

"That was some speech," she replied, after a moment's consideration. "If I didn't know what was going on, I'd probably have you committed." She held a serious look long enough to get Marty a little worried, before cracking a smile. "Fortunately, I know of your escapades in the land of the surreal, sir. If you say we'll get it done, I believe you."

Marty squeezed the hands in his grasp again, and urged their owners to their feet. They must surely be approaching the edge of town by now, and action needed to be taken. Kate pulled Marty back as he made for the pirates. "Just so you know, after all this is over, I might still have you committed."

Marty grinned. "You'd be doing me a favor. There's a staff meeting Monday morning, and I'd take rubber walls over that any day."

"Who's having a rubber meeting? Also, what's a rubber meeting?" Timbers had finished his duties, and strode across the deck beside them.

"Nothing, Timbers," Marty replied. "We were just questioning our existence, and our place in this wholly make believe world." He turned towards the captain, positioning himself so that Timbers couldn't see the vandalized mast. "That was some pretty hefty sheep deployment back there, are you sure it'll be enough to get Peepers' attention?"

Timbers cocked his head and made a pondering face. "Marty, we're in the business of clown removal. Land, sea, and air. I'm chalking this one up as a victory. Peepers? He'll take it personal, trust me."

Marty half-smiled. Although his compadre had a point, they had been on a mission to lead the clown ranks back to the big top at the edge of town. Now, all the circus freaks followed various tufts of smoldering wool that drifted back down to earth behind them. "We were supposed to be doing the whole Pied Piper bit, and taking the chucklers back to where they came though, remember?"

Timbers stroked his beard thoughtfully, not that there was any other way that one could stroke one's beard. "This is true," he mused. "And therein lies my point. We lit up the sky with enough exploding jugglers to make even the devil sit up and take notice."

He snapped off brisk nod, "Oh yes, that guy's a clown, make no mistake." Marty was in no mood to argue. Beelzebub could be a roller skating walrus singing show tunes, and he wouldn't bat an eyelid tonight. "You can bet your bottom doubloon that Peepers saw, or at least got word of his army getting the old lamb treatment, and you'd better believe he'll come running." Again, the logic, which hung in ragged strands amid the canopy of the night's activities, was irrefutable. "All's we've got to do now is get to this big top, lay low till he shows his crimson honker, and then chuck him through the shiny portal." By now, his bluster was unstoppable. "We've landed a fair few weighty boots in his checkered britches before, this should be like taking candy from a baby, giving it to a monster, and then running away."

Marty felt almost apologetic in the face of such intent, determination, and twenty-four carat recklessness. "Yeah, that actually sounds like it might work."

Timbers tipped his hat. "See? Always thinking. Even when I'm not thinking." He prodded his temple with a cloth finger and leaned back on the grandeur that he had amassed with his speech.

"Sometimes I forget that we're somewhere south of normal right now," Marty conceded. "Me and Kate were clocking in to work and thinking about how to avoid rush hour only a few hours ago, don't forget."

Timbers huffed. He had spotted the scratched mast, and his eyes narrowed disapprovingly, before the beaming warmth returned in abundance. "Well, you're a part of the crew, aren't you?" He shifted uncomfortably, eyeing Kate with his good eye. "Listen Kate, lass. I didn't really have any love for your little tree midget, but it's not right, what happened." Timbers lowered his gaze, kicking at the floor, and shook his head slightly, as though attempting to wrestle awkward thoughts out of his brain. "I want you to know that we're fighting for your cause now, too. We'll stuff Peepers and his cronies through that portal, but we'll do it for Barney."

"Benji," Marty interjected, prodding the little captain with a not so subtle whispering prompt.

"Huh? Oh yeah, him too," Timbers stammered, mustering a sheepish shrug. Kate couldn't miss the intent behind his words, it seemed, as big, blinky tears welled up in her eyes. "You're one of the good ones, Timbers," she managed, wiping the tears from her face and replacing them with a smile. "I think Benji would have appreciated the sentiment."

Timbers waved a dismissing hand, seemingly embarrassed by the notion of sentiment having any place in the life of a buccaneering daredevil. "Yes, well, that's all splendid then, isn't it?" he blustered, looking for a reason to get back on course. "Well, look lively you two. There's trouble afoot, and work to be done."

Kate leapt to her feet, also moving to stand between Timbers and the etchings she'd carved on the wood. "You're the boss, captain. So long as you don't have us scrubbing decks."

"Ah, you're all right there, lass." Timbers smirked, motioning back towards his crew. "That's Oaf's job, especially after he lost at poker the other night."

Oaf trotted up to join his companions, as though summoned by the mention of his name. "They only give me three cards. It doesn't seem fair," he muttered, grabbing a mop and getting to work anyway.

High up in the rigging, one of the Bobs piped out a shrill whistle, and gestured towards the horizon. "Looks like we're coming up on our target," Timbers sang out cheerfully. "How about we take a look-see?" He hopped up the steps to the quarterdeck, motioning for Kate and Marty to follow, and taking up a position at the very front of the *Fathom*.

As they arrived at his side, Timbers stared purposefully through a brass telescope at the shadowy, rolling hills that stretched out ahead. He sighed, dropping the device to his side, and pitching a thumb in the direction he'd been peeking. "Looks like I won't be needing this. We're here, folks."

Marty grabbed the railing, and peered over the side. They'd travelled quite a ways out of town, and currently glided over Harper's Meadow, its tree lined expanse stretching out silently beneath them. There was nothing beyond it, except miles of sprawling fields and farmland. Just grass, more grass, and an imposingly huge canvas tent which seemed to reach up to the heights at which the *Fathom* currently cruised.

"Looks like the circus has come to town," Whipstaff growled. He had joined the others on the quarterdeck, and leaned over the side to view the spectacle.

"Umm, yeah. I think that's kind of a given, seeing as how we've encountered more clowns than you can shake a balloon at tonight," Marty interjected.

Whipstaff deflated slightly, moving away from the edge of the ship. "Yeah, I suppose. Sorry, I was just trying to be all dramatic and such." He blushed, in as much as a toy pirate can turn an embarrassed shade of red, and went back about his duties. Beside Marty, Timbers chuckled. "He's not wrong, mind you. Looks like this is where your town's little infestation is coming from."

Below the *Fathom*, a steady line of clowns trooped out from the entrance to the Big Top, like grease-painted, demonic ants, heading back the way they had flown, towards town.

"There's so many of them," Kate murmured, taking a few steps back, and clutching the ship's ornamental steering wheel. There was, and Marty felt himself moving backwards as well. "What do we do?" he asked, aiming his enquiry towards Timbers.

"I thought you had a plan?" the little pirate replied, his one good eye raising a quizzical eyebrow, which demanded a response.

Marty's head went into another spin cycle. He did have a plan, but would it work? What was the best way to get to the end of this journey without being horribly killed in some way? There were way too many caveats to this undertaking, and he was still only half sure that the first part might, possibly work.

As with all half-baked ideas, however, the proof of the pudding lies in plunging your finger into the mix, and hoping that it isn't bitten off by one of the awful, devilish ingredients that you tipped in there.

Marty turned on his heels, and caught up with the departing first mate of the *Fathom*.

"Whipstaff. I need a word." Marty turned to address Timbers as he left. "Get the lifeboat ready."

Chapter Twenty-Six

The woods past Harper's Meadow were, as the saying goes, dark and deep, and Marty had never explored them in their entirety as a child. As they drifted down from the heavens, he was relieved that the thick fronded foliage was sufficiently dense to hide a decent sized pirate galleon.

They were scarcely a hundred feet from the silently billowing big top, which spat forth a torrent of clowns like some unholy circus artery, but the night and the trees hid their stealthy landing. Oaf leaned over the deck rail as the *Fathom* came to rest, mumbling complaints about how there was no water here, and that it he would probably be on hull repairing duty in the not too distant future. Timbers continued with his intent scanning of the scene through his telescope, while Marty whispered super top secret orders into Whipstaff's ear.

The little first mate flapped and groaned as he received them, as though he were being asked to take latrine cleaning duties for the rest of the millennium. "This doesn't sound like fun at all," he moaned, "Can't you get Oaf to do it?"

Marty straightened slightly, glancing over at the tiny giant across the deck. "Sure, he'll have to go with you, to steer." He fixed Whipstaff with a glinty eyed look. "Look at it this way, you get to…" the ear whispering continued, and Kate craned towards the conspiratorial duo in a vain attempt to catch the rest of the gambit. Whatever it was, it seemed to lift Whipstaff's spirits, and he tried in vain to suppress a giggle. "Yeah, that does sound like fun. Okay, I'm in." He scuttled over to where Oaf was still complaining to nobody in particular and tugged at his shipmate's waistcoat. "C'mon, big lad, we're on secret mission duty. I hope you've got your ninja pants on."

Oaf ceased his grumbling and held out his hands, displaying his tattered moleskin trousers. "These are my only pair. Will they do?"

Whipstaff chuckled, patting Oaf's shoulder. "Most ninjary pantaloons I've ever seen, my friend."

Seemingly pleased by this observation, Oaf fell in behind his comrade, and made ready the lifeboat.

Up on the quarterdeck, Timbers had given up trying to see anything through his telescope. It was dark, and there were dozens of trees, and besides, he seemed to be holding it up to his patched eye. "I hope we know what we're doing, Marty." he mumbled, watching his crew prepare to set sail, before adding, "What *are* we doing, Marty?"

Marty was only half listening. He hadn't been on a roll this impressive since managing two whole songs at the Pickled Judge karaoke night without having something pint shaped thrown at him. The curious captain needed answers, however, and whilst Marty realized all this tiny pirate army had done for him, he was reluctant to give voice to the burgeoning brainwave which still lurked somewhere in the realms of actually working. "Trust me. I know what I'm doing," he lied, before heading across the deck to keep an eye on clownish proceedings beyond the tree line.

Timbers threw his hands up in frustration. "Do you know what he's up to?" he asked a silently watching Kate.

She looked past him, a hint of thinly disguised confusion on her face. "I can't possibly imagine."

"I can," Timbers muttered. "That's what's got me worried."

Marty was beyond all thoughts and musings of what may or may not be going on in his head. What had started as a mere plot, made up of hopes and possibilities, had somehow mutated into some kind of many faceted bucket o' subterfuge. Marty was further down the rabbit hole than he had ever been, and more certain than ever that this deep-fried lunacy might actually work. Behind him, the *Fathom's* lifeboat gusted into the air, with Oaf at the bellows, and Whipstaff staring excitedly out into the night.

"When you get back, give us a signal. We'll be ready," Marty called at the departing pirates as quietly as he could manage.

Whipstaff smirked and nodded in the affirmative. "Don't you worry, lad. When we get back, you'll know about it." He turned to

Oaf, who piped another bellow blast into the lifeboat's sails. "Look lively, big lad. we've got important, secret stuff to be doing."

With another gushing whoosh, the lifeboat arced up into the heavens, and angled out of sight beyond the thin light that the moon was casting.

Back on deck, Kate resumed her pacing, and Marty joined her. "We should be getting in there." She motioned towards the imposing tent before them. "Oaf lent me his mallet, and I think it's time I got to using it." She was already moving towards the gangplank as she outlined her vengeful intentions. "Let's get moving."

This was as simple as it got, Marty thought. Infiltrate demonic clown tent, find the big, shiny portal, then unleash untold shenanigans and wait for the cavalry to arrive—textbook. Of course, that was all reliant upon said cavalry charging the line before a certain eight foot tall, gibbering grandaddy of all hellish clowns arrived on the scene. Marty's brow furrowed as he realized that this was, also, exactly what they wanted. It made no sense, in as much as it made perfect sense. Had he not recently spent a day in the company of his own dream manifestations, such a quandary might have driven him to insanity, but right now, who was to say what was sane anymore? It was almost empowering.

The epiphany was short lived, as Kate hopped over the side of the *Fathom*, landing in a clutch of shrubbery, and creeping over to a line of trees that ran parallel to the big top. Oaf's mallet swung with grim intent by her side, and it was clear she meant business. Marty snapped to his senses, this was not the time for getting all misty eyed at the prospect of going deliciously insane. Kate was once again proving to be the impetus to his musings, and he wasn't about to sit idly by, when wheels had already been set in motion.

It was only a short scamper to the edge of the tree line, and beyond that, the vast canopy of the big top plumed up into the air, blocking out most of the thin moonlight that peeped through the clouds.

"This is all a bit spooky isn't it?" Timbers peered around a bunch of saplings, surveying the scene. "Shame we don't have an ice cream truck."

Marty squinted out into the gloom, scanning for any sign of snapping teeth or errant juggling balls. "I don't think that'd help us very much, Timbers," he whispered. "We're not trying to get away from them this time, remember?"

"Who's talking about getting away? I just really fancy an ice cream." Marty had become accustomed to Timbers' penchant for lightening the mood in certain death situations, but as he turned his gaze towards the little pirate, no cheeky grin shot back in reply. "Hey, the stomach wants what the stomach wants," Timbers moaned, patting his complaining belly.

Kate was growing noticeably restless beside them. "Come on, you two. There's no time for munchies." Timbers raised a cloth hand to his mouth, shock pouring from his face.

"I know, I know," Marty assured. "There will be time for munchies. Don't worry, Timbers, I bet there's all sorts of candy coated junk in there." He motioned towards a small, untethered flap at the rear of the tent. "Damn thing's probably made of cotton candy."

Timbers grinned happily. "You're lucky Oaf isn't here to hear you say that. We'd have to pry him off that thing with a crowbar." He took a few steps towards the big top, turning cautiously. "It isn't though, is it? Made of cotton candy, I mean. Because if it is, problem solved." He rubbed his hands together, deflating slightly as Marty shook his head.

"Sorry, Timbers. Looks like we're going to have to do this the old-fashioned way. Besides, looks like Kate's in the mood to redecorate."

Kate heaved the hammer up onto her shoulder, and strode past the pair, towards the back entrance of the big top. "Hell yeah," she growled.

Marty paused for a second, a smile of admiration taking hold. As much as this reinforced his belief that Kate was, in fact, a badass, and as much as he loved her for her passion, determination and inner strength, it also made one thing perfectly clear.

Never tangle with a woman whose pet koala has just been eaten by clowns.

Chapter Twenty-Seven

The interior of the big top looked very much how one might expect a giant circus tent to look. If that tent happened to be run by goth demons with a fetish for decorating their home with the souls of their victims.

Everything was black. Thick drapes hung from the ludicrously high rafters. Balloons the color of midnight bobbed and weaved across the canopy, perhaps searching for a way back into the night sky. Here and there, boxes, tables, chairs and other random furnishings littered the large room into which Marty, Kate and Timbers crept. All of them as colorless as a void, and equally as inviting.

As they tiptoed into what looked like a manic depressive's summer home, Marty clattered into a sign which stood inconspicuously atop a shining obsidian pedestal. Not surprising really, since it sported black letters against a black background.

'Big Top Tradesman's Entrance - Trespassers Will Wish They Hadn't'

"Not exactly rolling out the red carpet, are they?" Timbers huffed.

Kate gestured towards the floor. "Well they did, sort of." Beneath them, a long, lavish carpet swept from the back entrance, and snaked off into the darkness ahead of them. It was black.

"This is horrendous," Marty rasped, peering after the dread carpet. "It's like the inside of my head on a Monday morning in here."

"Just don't touch the walls." The voice was Kate's, her face a mask of disgust as she shuffled back to join Timbers and Marty. Just like a *Wet Paint* sign, though, the suggestion was like an invitation to do exactly that. Stretching out his hand, Marty immediately wished he hadn't, as it touched what felt like wet leather, which had been soaked for several days in pure evil.

"Ugh! Get a maid or something." Timbers appeared, shaking ick from his paw. This was clearly not a circus to bring your kids to.

Ahead of them, the tent opened out, and was intersected by a corridor running parallel to it. Although for all they knew, it could just be another wall. Everything had a way of looking like everything else in here, and none of it was good. "Let's keep moving," Marty whispered. "My mind is running out of ways to process all this non-color."

Somewhere in the darkness, a light blossomed, turning the gloom only slightly less horrendous.

Marty turned to where Timbers stood, holding aloft a lantern. "Is that Oaf's lantern?"

"Yep."

"Did we just nick all of Oaf's stuff, then?"

"Pretty much."

Timbers waggled the glimmering lamp enthusiastically. "I figured we might need it in case that shadow beastie showed up again."

Kate patted the little captain on the shoulder. "That's boss thinking, Timbers. Way to use the old gray matter."

Timbers cocked is head, tapping it with a cloth paw. "Oh, I don't know about that. For all I know, it's all stuffing up there." He grinned, nonetheless, and scuttled over to where the corridor began. Marty's mood brightened. This was going to be a good deal easier with at least one of them thinking a few steps ahead.

A few steps ahead, Timbers crashed into something unseen and swear inducing. Clearly he hadn't thought *that* far ahead.

As they edged forward, the dim glow from the lantern afforded a little more of a clue as to where they were headed. The passageway before them sloped upwards, an unlikely direction to be taking in a circus tent erected on a flat, featureless field, but then these were unlikely times. And anyway, what was essentially the back porch was about as inviting as an open day at a sewage plant, so they pressed on.

Halfway up the magically elevating corridor, Marty caught up with his pirate friend. "Timbers, once all this is over, how are you guys going to get back? You know, providing we don't all end up horribly destroyed in some way."

The pint-sized captain strode on, not taking his eyes from the dimly lit path before them. "I don't know, Marty. Maybe we make a dash for the shiny portal. Maybe we stay and get jobs at your theme park. We can be spacey, I have a sparkly outfit. How does that sound?"

Marty chuckled quietly. "You'd be bored before lunchtime. Imagine all the chaos, lunacy and adventure we've had tonight, then take away all the chaos, lunacy and adventure."

Timbers shuddered. "Avast, what sort of life is that? And you live here?"

Marty almost dropped a stride. What sort of life *was* that? His mind flung him back to the conversation with Cabbie, in which he had been a catatonic participant earlier that evening. Twenty years down the line, he could be that empty, babbling soul, filled with regret and tall stories. Providing of course, as was pointed out just now, they weren't all clownhandled by the minions of chaos tonight. That was some choice. Death, or vacant routine. It wasn't really what he had planned for his life, and he felt sure that Kate wouldn't be opting for doors number one or two either.

"Maybe we'll come with you," he ventured, after a moment's silence.

Timbers whistled, taking a leap into the air, mid-scuttle. "That's absolutely crazy talk, Marty. Absolute grade A, twenty-four carat, crayon chewing bonkers." He tilted his head up towards Marty and delivered a wink. "Fortunately, I am fluent in such talk, and we'd be happy to have you."

There was no time for sentimentality, or plans to settle down somewhere white picket fence-y inside his own dreamspace, as the trio crept out of the corridor into what appeared to be the main chamber of the big top.

Although still murky, and not entirely the sort of place one would choose to spend a vacation, the central room of the big top sprawled out before them in multi-colored, awful splendor.

It was not unlike the sideshow carnivals that Marty had been dragged along to as a child. A large, sawdust filled center circle covered much of the ground, and from it, hulking posts sprang up from the ground like massive candy canes, reaching up into the lofty canvas, far enough to be intangible in the darkness. Marty thought that he could even spy a trapeze wire amidst the ridiculously tall rigging, although the roof of the tent was so high, it was hard to make out what was actually hanging up there. It was probably best not to ponder too much about that.

Much more discernable on the ground, however, were the clowns. Marty had expected them, Timbers had expected them, and judging by her demeanor, Kate had hoped for them, and here they were. The sawdust circle crawled with them. A broiling, swirling, unholy juggling mass of them.

"I've said it before, and I'll say it again," Marty whispered. "That's a lot of clowns." He ducked back into the darkness of the passageway. "What do we do?"

Timbers drew his sword. He'd expected long odds in this caper, and from the look on his face, was already calculating his blaze of glory through the manically juddering sprawl of brightly colored bodies.

"There's an old pirate saying," he began, fixing Marty with a defiant look. "Maybe I'll tell it to you, after we've dropped a Yo-Ho-Ho-Bomb on these balloon chuffing cartwheel chuckers!"

The grinning corsair dashed into the vast chamber as the words reached Marty's ears, and he flinched as Kate bolted past in pursuit, Oaf's hammer raised and ready to greet unholy harlequin.

Marty sighed. As with all best laid plans, whether concocted by mice or men, they invariably broke down and fizzled out when the prospect of a good rumble was in the offing. Choosing the nearest group of cavorting jesters, he let out what he hoped was his best battle cry, and followed his charging allies into battle.

Depending on how you wanted to look at it, fortune, or ill fortune brought Marty into the melee faster than he had expected. A group of unicycling clowns turned to face him as he galloped forward. Their faces lit up in a hideous array of wild eyes and gnashing teeth, their hands moving almost automatically to beckon the onrushing Marty.

There were two ways to tackle these monsters. Either gauge their weak spots, and attempt to pick them off one by one, or barrel into them with limbs flailing. Marty silently cursed his lack of ninja training as he opted for the latter, hitting the clown gang at full speed, and sending them skittling in all directions. Luck was on Marty's side, since it is hard to recover from a body tackle, even when you're not perched precariously atop a single wheeled bicycle. Shaking his head at the impact, Marty watched as several wheeled freaks clattered, slewed and tumbled in every direction except the way he had come. He punched the air, inadvertently connecting with a passing jester, and momentarily wondered if spectacularly winging it might actually pay off, before remembering that it had on countless occasions before. Adrenaline paid a visit to brain, and left a calling card which simply said, 'This is going to work!' It was all Marty needed, and he set off in search of more prey to run blindly into.

Off to his right, he was dimly aware of several heavy *whumping* noises. They thumped into sharp focus as Kate cannoned past, sweeping Oaf's mallet like a vengeful wooden reaper. He slowed to watch as she sent six, seven, and eight looming harlequins pluming into showers of freshly whupped confetti. Still picking up speed, she charged at a close grouped bunch who seemed to be practicing lethal juggling techniques. Several dozen balls fell to the floor as their owners met the business end of the wildly flailing hammer.

Marty made a mental note never to leave the toilet seat up.

On the far side of the sawdust circle, Timbers had somehow made his way to a cluster of gibbering circus hellion, who had caught wind of what was happening, and glared at the advancing pirate, shrieking and drooling like gaudily painted harpies. Timbers seemed to be laughing as he reached them, and twirled in a tiny buccan-ado which relieved the ranting monsters of their bottom halves.

"Damn," Marty muttered, a hint of awe in his tone. "Why didn't I think to bring a weapon?"

The thought was punctuated, as Timbers somersaulted to a screeching halt before the only survivor of his chosen quarry. It sneered hideously, and licked its blood red lips, before charging with a whooping cry. "C'mere, little toy."

Timbers planted his feet, and held his blade out behind him. If this were an action movie, Marty felt sure that some kind of slow motion effect might be called into action at this very moment.

In the here and now, the flurry of movement and flashing steel registered as little more than a blur, as several clown parts skidded past the twirling pirate, who landed gracefully enough to impart a trademark one liner.

"I am not a toy."

Marty steeled himself, galvanized by the wholesale ass-whuppery that his friends were delivering, and shot out a blind fist which connected heavily with a clown bearing down behind him. All they needed to do was keep this up until Whipstaff and Oaf arrived with the cavalry, and they were home free.

Marty gagged on the thought as it sneaked into his mind. *'Come on, Fate. I didn't mean it. Let us have this one. Go on, please'.*

Fate, it seemed, was bored of Marty's constant dallyings with optimism, and a line of clowns formed ranks up ahead, covering the whole of the far side of the circle. Kate lowered the mallet, with nothing more to drop it upon, and Timbers ceased his cajoling at a random clown head that he'd found in the dust amongst the confetti.

Ahead of them, the clowns advanced, slowly, unstoppably, and gleefully. They didn't charge, or speak, or even grin. This was a phalanx of circus spawn intent on one thing, or more specifically three things, and those three things suddenly realized that they were hopelessly outnumbered.

Marty glanced back at the corridor from which they had arrived, but the encroaching clowns had circled them, and still they approached.

"Well, at least we gave it a shot," Timbers growled as he fell in alongside Marty and Kate. They were rapidly running out of room, and for all their bluster and intent, they would need an army to carve their way through this line of foul harlequins. As they backed up to form a tight circle, the clowns pressed still further inward, jerkily closing in with smothering, dread intent.

"STOP."

The voice came from behind the clowns, somewhere high up, maybe in the stalls which surrounded the center circle.

The carnival horrors halted, as though frozen to the spot, every beady eye still trained on Marty, Kate and Timbers.

"It looks like you fools can be counted on to fall into a carefully woven trap after all." The voice was steady, deliberate, and familiar.

"I'll take it from here, minions."

As commanded, the clowns fell back, forming a path to where the stalls sat in anonymous darkness. From within the shadows, something dropped to the ground, and sauntered slowly into the light.

Marty gaped at Kate, who replied with an equally open mouthed look of sheer disbelief.

"Well, I'll be a squid sandwich," Timbers spat. "It's you."

Chapter Twenty-Eight

"Well, I suppose I have some explaining to do," said Benji, the mood koala, as he strolled between the massed ranks of clowns, rubbing his glowing hands. "Isn't that the remit of the criminal mastermind? Divulge my fiendish plot in ridiculous detail, before leaving you to escape in a heroic and completely unlikely way?" He chewed his furry lip thoughtfully, before shaking his head. "No, not doing that. I've seen too many movies." He gestured to the row of ghouls to his right. "Take these two away. Peepers wants them. Do whatever you want with the doll."

"Doll!? Why you flea bitten…" Timbers was rolling up his sleeves when Marty stepped between him and the advancing jesters. "Wait! You got eaten. We all saw you die." Whilst not being a particularly complex or compelling reply, it seemed to snag the little koala's attention.

Benji turned back to his captives "No, no you didn't." He sighed, little paws flapping outwards irritably. "True genius is never fully appreciated. I don't know why I bother to concoct such devilry, when folk can't even grasp the basics." He blazed a fiery red, before trotting back towards Marty. "I had to hitch a ride in the mouth of one of these drooling psychopaths, or your little plan might well have succeeded." Benji tutted as blank looks flew up in greeting of his great epiphany. "All right, let's take this down a notch or two, for the people at the back. Why am I here, do you think?"

"Probably to take over the world," Timbers muttered sarcastically.

"Yes, exactly!" Benji seemed pleased that someone had picked up his thread, and completely missed the sardonic tone. "I made a bargain with Peepers; I'd get him over here, get him his prize," he pointed at Marty, winking sickeningly. "And in return, I'd get to hitch a ride with him and his chaotic cohorts, so that I could rejoin my brethren, and rule over this realm." Benji beamed smugly, adopting a defiant stance within which to take in the awe and horror that his wicked master scheme would no doubt reap from his prisoners.

Marty blinked at Timbers. Timbers blinked at Marty (or more specifically winked with his one good eye). Kate gaped at both of them, still processing what was happening.

"Erm, your brethren?" Marty offered at last.

"Yes! My armies of koala kin. I hear that they have set up a base of operations in one of this plane's larger islands. From what I can gather, it's somewhere down under, but that makes no sense, since my kind are not subterranean."

Timbers stifled a chuckle. Marty shooed him with a flapping arm, himself fighting back a giggle which was charging up from his lungs. "An army? Of koalas?"

"Yes? What of it?" Benji was growing impatient, and his aura pulsed rapidly brilliant white and void black.

"You haven't really done your homework, have you me hearty?" Timbers cackled. "I've been over on Real Side less than a day, and even I know that there isn't a koala from here to there that would pat its own backside if it was on fire."

Benji's strobing fell into thick blackness, and the air seemed to deaden around him. "Nonsense! Impertinence!" he cried. "We koalas are Alpha Predators. We sense the emotions of others, we are master tacticians, and are not to be trifled with."

Marty gained control of the burgeoning laughter rattling around his ribcage. "You're really not. As far as I know, you're the only one who even does any glowing. Your army are basically stoners. You sit around in trees all day, eating eucalyptus, and looking cute. That's about it, at least on Real Side."

Benji shrank visibly, which is dangerous for an already pretty small mammal. "No, you're lying. I am born of the tree, and I crafted this master plan, and I am running the show here. So, what you are saying makes no sense at all." He stomped angrily between the row of clowns and his captive audience, plumes of thick vermillion throbbing outward from his tiny body.

"How else could I have gotten you here, and gotten here before you?" The blood red light Benji emitted was dazzling. "I was all set to realize my dreadful scheme, when your girlfriend gatecrashed my base of operations." The diminutive critter glowered at Kate, who was clearly still struggling to come to terms with what was transpiring. "I couldn't just go on my way, how could I, when I had been compromised? And anyway, the blasted woman wouldn't let me, damn near abducted me. " Benji shuddered, brushing irritably at his shoulders, as though attempting to shake humanity from his fur. "I *hate* being picked up!"

Timbers ceased his chuckling, and prodded Marty's shin worriedly. This was quickly turning into the rant of a madman, or mad beast. Either way, it didn't bode well.

"What was I to do?" Benji continued, unabated. "If I was to slip away, you bald monkeys would just come looking for me. And then it hit me." Benji flared momentarily in a flashgun of brilliant white light, a look of assuredness melting across his angry features. "Any koala worth his twigs has a backup plan. Like any good general, I used my foes weakness against them."

Marty noticed the trappings of a blithering lunatic in the little koala's tirade, but wasn't about to interrupt. Every moment that Benji strutted his furry ass in mocking swathes of monologue brought his own plan closer to fruition.

Obligingly, the certainly evil, apparently genius continued. "I had to think on my feet, warn the troops. So, I gathered my intel, and faked my own demise, hot-footing it back to home base to arrange this welcome for you fools." Rage red now cascaded from Benji, adorning the canvas walls of the big top, and turning everyone in it a frantic shade of angry.

"I'm sorry, it's true," Marty chipped in, playing for time. "Head over to the local zoo if you don't believe me. See if any of the koala inmates share your obsession for world domination, or would actually rather just scratch itchy parts, and chew whatever happens to be in their hands."

"Or take a trip to Australia," Timbers interjected, cheerfully. "You look like you could use a vacation. We'll sit here and wait for you…honest." He raised his cloth paw in a scout salute.

Benji's seizure inducing light show halted abruptly. He turned slowly from his fervent stomping, a wry smile now set upon his face. "I see what you're doing. You've spent an evening in my presence, and you think you can adopt the ways of the koala." He grinned, a glinting smile that any of his waiting lackeys would have been proud of. "You're lying to buy yourselves some time. Well it won't work! My koala army will sweep across the land, with only a short interlude to hang out in a tree and munch some leaves, maybe." Benji shifted uncertainly, eyeing Marty and Timbers, who tried their best to maintain a straight face.

"Your words are lies, lies I tell you!" The little koala finally snapped, sending a wave of yellow light cascading through the tent.

"You're scared," Timbers crowed. "It's no use trying to hide it. You can't. Everything you feel is a fireworks display, and a fairly dull one at that. Ever thought of going all sparkly? That would be much more impressive." The captain's giggles sparked off another furious gust of crimson.

"Enough! Let's take this outside. Peepers will be along imminently, and he can deal with you how he sees fit. Then I can get to work with my koala battle horde, who are *very real*, and *utterly terrifying*, thank you very much!" With that, he snapped his fingers, and the line of clowns fell in dutifully behind Benji's prisoners.

Marty glanced over at Kate, who was still catatonic at the sight of the creature she had come to avenge. The very beast that had been plotting their grisly end all along. Marty grabbed her hand and headed towards the entrance to the big top. Its heavy flapped canvas drapes yawned out into the waiting stillness of Harper's Meadow, and past them, the gibbering cheers of countless grease-painted monsters drifted through to coax them out into the night.

Timbers scampered up alongside Marty as they marched out into the throng of circus wrongness. The field seemed to be floodlit, and as they emerged from the big top, several sentry towers trained unfathomably large guns in their direction. The procession halted before a crowd of whooping, slavering clowns, and at their cusp, the biggest, most grotesque circus maniac of them all stood waiting.

Mr. Peepers leered down at the small line which Marty, Kate and Timbers had formed in front of him, and let out a shriek made of one hundred percent distilled nightmares.

"There, you see?" Benji smirked, falling in beside his horrendous ally. "Here they all are, as I promised. All for you, except the toy of course."

Peepers scowled at Timbers, who puffed out his chest, and did his best to fix a pair of eyes that would turn most men to stone.

"Ah yes, the toy," Peepers slithered. "I have no need of the toy. I have what I came for right here." He swept an impossibly long arm out towards Marty and Kate, who stood rooted to the spot. "We'll be off now, back to the land of carnival delights for these two young morsels." He gestured towards the far end of the clearing, where something brilliant, bright and portally undulated in a way that nothing had ever undulated in Harper's Meadow before.

"Take the good captain away, and make me a hat out of him, or something."

Marty gulped down the urged to vomit, or bolt, or both.

"This doesn't look good for you, me hearty," Timbers whispered.

"Doesn't look like a pleasure cruise for you either, matey," Marty replied.

"There's always Whipstaff and Oaf, right?" Timbers seemed to be smaller than Marty remembered, with a hint of sheepish uncertainty in his eye that had never been there before. "They'll get us out of this. They'll stick to the plan...whatever it is."

Marty breathed deeply, the realization hitting him now more than ever that this was reality, and winging it rarely paid off on his side of the dream.

"They'd better." Marty glanced up into the heavens, hoping that salvation might be somewhere up there in the ether, and that Whipstaff had listened to at least some of his instructions.

He turned his attention back to the field, backing up as a legion of grasping hands and wicked grins advanced. There was nowhere to run, they were stuck, somewhat implausibly between a clown and a shiny place. Timbers raised his sword, scanning the approaching phalanx intently.

"It's no good, there's too many of them to take on," Marty said.

The little pirate sighed heavily, appearing to be trying his best to squeeze the last vestige of pirate gusto from within his tiny frame. "I know, I'm just picking the ones I'm going to take with me." The smile arrived, but Marty could tell that resignation lurked behind it, and for the first time since his reunion with his childhood partner in crime, reality tapped him on the shoulder, pointing to its watch impatiently.

This was it, then. Marty reached for Kate's hand and tried to find a way to look brave without coming across as constipated. Whatever combination of features settled upon his face, it seemed to work, and she half smiled back at him, hefting Oaf's hammer onto her shoulder. "I'm with Timbers. Let's go down swinging."

Marty cursed under his breath. He had been so sure that this would work.

Abruptly, somewhere behind the marching lines of impending doom, and out of the tomb quiet stillness of Harper's Meadow, all holy Hades was let loose.

Chapter Twenty-Nine

Constable O'Riley had come to the horrible conclusion that he was not cut out for the life of the gritty cop, or the one-man army.

As he had wholeheartedly legged it from the gardener's shed beside the town hall, he had harbored only one thought: Self-preservation.

The clowns that had jerkily charged in from all corners of the night had strengthened his desire to not grab a gun and take them on single handedly, and he had retreated to the closest and safest looking place he could find.

He hunkered down, in the bowels of the *Flying Fathom*, having stowed away below decks before all the shouting and ruckus had started. He had clung to something heavy and wooden in the ship's hold as the rollercoaster ride of his life unfolded around him.

He may, or may not have parted company with his breakfast, lunch, and dinner as the vessel pitched and rolled around him, and only he knew if he had quietly wet himself as the solid crash of ground meeting hull signaled his arrival back on sweet *terra firma*.

Somewhere, in the dark, quiet and possibly now damp confines of the *Fathom*, Police Officer Michael O'Riley had a good talk with himself, as who knows what went on outside. There had been a good deal of commotion somewhere beyond the wooden hull, also in his trembling gut, as he cautiously poked his head out of the deck hatch. But something else, deep down within O'Riley had also piped up, having been held down for too long beneath the endless layers of cowardice and desire to stay in one, unmolested piece.

It was oppressively dark outside, and the voice within O'Riley had sparked up with some half-remembered speech from a movie, which he was only partly paying attention to. As he crept through the bushes towards the massive tent which had somehow arrived in Harper's Meadow, something else seemed to be spurring him on. Maybe it was curiosity, or perhaps adrenaline. It could of course be the need to locate a dry pair of trousers. He didn't know, or care, as something feral and instinctive drove him towards the source of the light, noise and no doubt danger up ahead.

O'Riley's head swam with all manner of synaptic conflict. What had descended upon his town tonight? Why was he the only cop on the beat? Should a martini be shaken or stirred?

None of it seemed to matter as he approached the front of the tent. From his slightly elevated position on a convenient grassy knoll, O'Riley took in the spectacle before him. Clowns, lots of them. The mystifying presence of a koala, and a couple of kids with what seemed to be their pet dog in a pirate costume.

Not far from where he hid, a tower rose from the ground, and atop it, another of the painted maniacs, not unlike those that he had taken in and singularly failed to keep in custody. It stood, leaning on a wicked looking sentry gun, apparently intent on proceedings down in the clearing.

This was it.

If O'Riley was ever going to seize his destiny, and impart to the world the action hero one liner of a lifetime, it was now. A stealthy dart over to the ladder of the tower caught him almost completely by surprise, and he was at its top before anything inside him could point out how incredibly reckless he was being.

The clown manning the gun was too focused on the apparent main event outside the entrance of the big top to notice the interloper in his nest, and O'Riley hesitated, wondering how best to realize his newfound bravado. A list of quips filed into his head, begging to be used.

"Nice night for a swan dive."

"About time you flew the nest."

"Excuse me, would you mind awfully if I pushed you to your death?"

Just as O'Riley discounted the last one for being way too British, the clown turned to face him, baring its teeth and advancing with grasping arms out stretched. Why were clowns always so grabby?

Did the hunger for human suffering call out to them in the night, or were they just desperate for a hug?

The constable dropped his head and launched towards the approaching ghoul, sending it tumbling over the side of the tower, to its vibrantly confetti colored end on the ground below.

"Okay, so not particularly cool, but effective," O'Riley muttered to himself, turning his attention to the gleaming cannon which took prominence at the center of the nest. It sat impressively, with a long barrel, and a sturdy metal box beside it, presumably containing the teeth of this mighty beast. The controls appeared to be mercifully simple, much like your standard point and shoot arcade game. There was a joystick, a satisfyingly red fire button, and a huge metal crosshair, which O'Riley hauled over to train upon the throng of clowns beneath him.

This was too perfect. Not only had O'Riley been visited by the cojone fairy, but he was now in the position to visit paramount justice upon his town's assailants, from the safety of his own sniper's nest. He took a deep breath, summoning all the newfound gusto that fate had suddenly chosen to bestow upon him.

It was time for a weapons check. The cannon was undoubtedly awe inspiring, but O'Riley didn't want to be running out of ammo halfway through his initial volley of incredibly witty taunts. He hauled the lid off the box, which fed the mighty gun, and peered in at its contents.

The smell hit him first. Blueberry, gooseberry, apple, rhubarb. It was the most deliciously scented box of death he'd ever encountered. Within the box's metal casing sat rows of freshly made pies, all sitting in line, waiting to be delivered into the faces of the unrighteous. O'Riley paused to take in the sight before him, simultaneously fending off the desire to take a bite out of one of these fruity bombs. Why the hell not? Clowns were invading the world, the monster under the bed had come for its quota. It seemed only fitting to send them back whence they came with a volley or two of pie shaped doom.

The constable hopped into the gunnery seat, pivoting it to face the field up ahead.

A giant, hideous jester, much bigger than its cronies fell into his crosshairs, and all at once the life of a gritty vigilante, bestowing rough vengeance on the silver screen seemed to fit O'Riley like a newly purchased suit. A suit made of bullets, fire and piping hot baked goods, apparently.

This was his moment, and he wasn't about to let a pair of damp trousers, or the rapidly diminishing voice of reason spoil it.

With a bellow, O'Riley announced his presence to those who were about to rock, and pulled the trigger.

"Dinner is canceled, who's up for dessert?"

Chapter Thirty

The sky surrounding Marty, Kate and Timbers exploded in a torrent of fruity death, and the closest dozen clowns squealed as a pastry apocalypse introduced them to their makers.

In an instant, Harper's Meadow was a flurry of frantic activity. Ahead of them, rows of jesters scattered amidst a torrent of cream and jam. Behind them, Peepers sought cover, hissing out orders to his fleeing horde, as Benji tried his best to curl up into the tightest ball possible.

Marty poked his head out from beneath a berry peppered podium that he had hastily dove behind. Somewhere in the tree line, a lone figure launched delicious mortar fire into the field, cackling and spraying out equal amounts of questionable zingers.

"I used to protect, but now I'm serving!"

Timbers tugged at Marty's shirt as a volley of raspberry tartes darted overhead. "It's time we were elsewhere, me hearty, before the fat lady stops singing and comes looking for dessert."

It was hard to pose a counter argument, as more booming reports sounded from the edge of the clearing, fetching down another clutch of shrieking clowns in the process. Marty decided to agree wholeheartedly with Timbers proposal, and ducked back down behind the podium.

"I agree wholeheartedly," he cried, as if to emphasize his own decision. "But where? There's nothing but clowns, crust and confetti out there."

Timbers tapped a cloth finger to his nose. "Trust me, this is all going according to my plan."

"Your plan?" Marty bellowed, almost inaudible over another volley of bakery blitzing. "You had nothing to do with this! It's that maniac up on the hill. You were a clown hat two minutes ago."

"Don't bother me with details," Timbers barked over his shoulder as he crawled to the edge of the podium. "Just follow me."

Various pantalooned legs scurried hither and thither beside their hiding place as Timbers held out a halting hand. Some of the clowns still laughed as they dashed. Perhaps that was all they could do, or maybe they were gleeful in anticipation that the manner of their demise would deliver them to the circus equivalent of Valhalla. Die with a pie in your face, and take a seat beside your balloon huffing ancestors in the clown afterlife. It wasn't something Marty wanted to think about in any detail, mostly because a giggling clown in its death throes was still terrifying. He was almost relieved when Timbers gave the gesture to move, and the trio made a frantic sprint for the nearest tent pole, still standing wide and fruit spattered in the fray.

"Okay, where now?" Marty panted as a harlequin juddered past them, unsuccessfully dodging a barrage of vanilla trifle.

"I love the smell of strawberry flavored napalm in the morning!" The unknown sniper roared from the tree line.

"This is getting ridiculous." Marty muttered. "Where the hell is Whipstaff?" He ducked instinctively, as a clown ceased its retreat beside their hiding place. It leered hideously at Marty, grabbing his arm with taloned claws, just as half a dozen shells that smelled distinctly of banana shattered the circus brute into its component streamers. Marty shook the remaining, disembodied hand from his arm, and scanned up ahead for means of getting the hell out of here.

"Over there," he shouted, pointing over at a large tree which had somehow managed to remain free of confectionary decoration.

"Are you insane?" Kate snapped out of her daze, and pointed to the very swirly, and distinctly shiny portal which hung like a rip in reality beside their would-be hiding place.

Marty pointed at the mad gunman atop his tower. "We're almost out of his range here. We can make it."

"Capital idea." The voice behind them was low, guttural, and bone jarringly familiar. Mr. Peepers loped across to where they were standing, pies skittering and sluicing across his path as he approached. "We were going that way anyway." He levelled an impossibly long finger at the portal, his grin snaking from ear to

ear. "Let's not dawdle, it seems we've outstayed our welcome here."
More thumping cannon fire interjected, the man on the trigger was
clearly having fun up there on the hill.

"Delivery for Simple Simon!" Came the cry from above.

Timbers shook his head. "This guy is an amateur. I'd have gone
with *Stop, Jammer Time.*" Pie tins and their innards clattered past
as Peepers bore down on the trio. Benji cautiously crept out from
behind the towering hellion, glancing warily at the source of the
tasty barrage, and fell in alongside his despicable ally. "It comes to
this," he spat theatrically, as both sides formed ranks, facing each
other.

Timbers swatted his blade through the night air, as Kate heaved
Oaf's hammer to bear. Marty felt almost naked, with no impressive
tool of mayhem to wield, but mustered the best standoff stare he
could. Twenty feet lay between them and the daddy of all clowns,
his evil mastermind marsupial ally crouching beside him.

All in all, today had been a bit of a headscratcher, Marty thought.
Culminating in a face-off with Satan's jester and his evil koala,
amidst a barrage of exploding cake, and equally incendiary circus
folk. In hindsight, he wished he'd thought to bring a machine gun.

All thoughts, sane or otherwise, flew chaotically out of the
proverbial window, as Peepers launched forward. Benji, being
apparently the sort of koala who would prefer to observe battle
from a distance was less proactive, but fell in on the shirt tails of
attack nonetheless.

Marty darted a glance at his allies, who were already hurtling
towards their foes. Timbers arced through the air, his sword raised
to meet his clown nemesis, and Kate brought her hammer to bear
at the onrushing koala that she'd protected for the best part of
the night. Marty momentarily wished he had someone to charge
daringly at, if only for the sake of symmetry, before all thoughts of
the job, and screaming maniacs at hand dissolved in a whirlwind of
noise and movement.

High above them, something plummeted from the heavens.
A small, boat shaped something, carrying two pirates who were
currently engaged in an ear splitting battle cry. The *Fathom*'s lifeboat
pitched out of its dive, and shot past, a length of rope trailing behind
it. Marty forgot what was before him, and threw a fist into the sky

as the vessel passed them, the rope jolting and twisting against the giant gold coin that it was carrying. The same oversized nugget that had been purloined from a certain magical, and decidedly cranky leviathan that very evening.

""Whipstaff!" Marty shouted after the lifeboat, as another, much deeper voice bellowed through the trees of Harper's Meadow. Huge, thumping footfalls followed it, as a thirty story leprechaun galloped across the field, grabbing at the coin at the end of the rope. "That booty's mine! Give it here, you thieving pirate fleas!"

A gigantic, shiny buckled boot fell into the thick of the circus horde, sending dozens of them to Clown-halla, and Marty just had time to hear the chuckles of the lifeboat crew, as Kate flung herself into him, sending them both out of the imminent footprint which the boot now made in Harper's Meadow.

Everything stopped. Clownish antics, epic battles, even the gunfire from the hill, as the giant leprechaun landed on the big top, squashing it like a brightly colored paper cup. The colossal sprite surveyed its surroundings, spying the lifeboat which carried its precious cargo, and took off again. "I want me gold back!" It stomped angrily towards the swooping lifeboat, which was now openly fishing for giant fairy folk above the gaping portal. The boat steadied, before gunning towards the advancing mega pixie.

Marty glanced over to where death had been coming for them moments earlier. Peepers and Benji stood, transfixed by the absurd airshow, as Oaf piped more air into the lifeboat's sails, and threw it plunging upward into the night sky.

It seemed that every set of eyes in the meadow was now trained on this gigantic party crashed, and several of the clowns' searchlights swept over to converge on the new arrival. The mighty sprite threw an arm up to shield its eyes, and stumbled backwards, trampling a row of bleachers, and a few lines of grinning fiends that had taken up positions along them. The searchlight clowns in their machine gun nests wasted no time, and emptied torrents of sickly sweet vengeance at the towering green blimp, turning its smart waistcoat an alarming shade of everything.

The lifeboat made another pass as two of the clown turrets were dispatched by angry leprechaun fists the size of pickup trucks. It seemed that Irish eyes were not smiling tonight. Whipstaff leaned over the side as the tiny boat dove in a spiraling arc around its quarry. "Avast, you dung-faced hobgoblin. Come and get your gold before I melt it down and spend it on booze."

The leprechaun squealed in a manner completely ill-fitting of its enormous stature, and made another swat for its errant treasure. It trailed along behind the lifeboat as Oaf sent them swooping through the giant's legs, and soaring from its clawing grasp. "Haha, you're about as graceful as blind humpback in a washing machine," Whipstaff taunted, clearly having spent most of his journey thinking up ways to enrage the humungous imp. "Not even close, you massive bearded fairy."

The lifeboat pitched in a tight circuit of the meadow, sailing fast and low to bear on their furious target. It wasted no time in barreling towards them once more, kicking up dirt, clowns and circus paraphernalia as it charged. Whipstaff roared another exultant battle cry, and the boat slewed forward once more, heading straight for the onrushing behemoth.

As an enthralled observer of this unbelievable joust, Marty couldn't help but recall the story of David and Goliath, although had this been an accurate representation of the biblical fable, he felt sure that he would have paid a lot more attention in Sunday school.

Mere moments before tiny wooden hull, and enormous Gaelic hulk collided, Oaf blasted everything the bellows could offer into the sails, and the lifeboat heaved into a sharp climb, dodging the giant's jaunty green hat by inches.

The leprechaun screamed, clutching at the dancing coin as it flew into the heavens, and stamped a solid leather boot down firmly on the portal.

Marty hadn't been certain what would happen, in the unlikely event that everything he had planned had come to pass, but flung a protective arm over Kate and Timbers anyway, as a precaution against something world splitting happening.

In hindsight, the prospect of a skyscraper sized leprechaun careening into a rip in the fabric of reality was always going to result in something cataclysmic, so his fears were well founded as the world and its entire contents turned inward.

Almost instinctively Marty grabbed the tent pole, flailing with his free hand to find Kate as the portal burst outwards and instantly engulfed a group of clowns in its wake.

Marty had often wondered what it would feel like to have his life flash before his eyes as he died, and this was as close as he had ever come to it, as the world seemed to hurtled past him into the shining maelstrom at his back.

Mercifully, Kate's hand found his. Peepers skittled past, grabbing a tree limb to steady himself against the whirling vortex which was now forming where the portal once stood. "Looks like you're coming with me either way, Marty. See you on the other side." He giggled and let go of his mooring, cascading towards the portal, end over horrendous end. The giggles stopped abruptly, as a mighty leprechaun foot planted itself into the ground, and pancaking the wretched clown flat.

Marty smirked, forcing himself not to impart a one liner of his own. This was not the time.

Around him, the contents of Harper's Meadow were swirling, whirling, blurring into the shiny abyss. One of the big top's masts tore free of its mooring and threw its canvas coat into the eye of the storm. The clowns which once stood as an army, now charged helter skelter in a myriad of horrible shapes behind it, and Marty fought to hang on to Kate, and also to reality.

Somewhere over behind the tree line, something groaned and creaked into motion, and as more debris sailed past, the vast, dark shape of the *Flying Fathom* drifted up into the sky. Timbers was at Marty's side, clutching a row of seats as the mighty vessel pitched sharply sideways. "Zephyr! Migration Maneuver. Fly south, big lad!" he barked, his words falling inward with the rest of the big top towards the screeching portal.

Whatever command may have been uttered fell short, as the Fathom veered into a sheet of canvas tent rigging and raked the ground, throwing up a torrent of grass and dirt as it turned against Zephyr's toiling wings and dragged up a cluster of clowns in its crashing wake. Wood splintered as the squawking bird fought to maintain control, but the force pulling them back to dreamside gripped the world with inexorable fury.

Timbers dropped his cutlass as the *Flying Fathom*, *his Flying Fathom* blazed past in a whirling mass of wood, metal and Bobs, sucked finally through the portal and out of sight.

Marty felt his grip relax as the shock hit him, before realizing that one of his hands held Kate. She flapped and flailed in the wind, her feet mere meters from the shrieking vortex. He shot a look back into her eyes, and remembered their first date, when his awkwardness had gotten the better of both of them. Her hand was slipping, as Benji tumbled past, issuing redundant cries of protest, and equally empty flashes of light as he disappeared into the light.

Marty recalled her walking in on his dream, making him wake up, in more ways than one. Their hands were only fingertips touching now. his mind showed him their first, post dream date, and the kiss that had followed, screaming at him that he had to save her.

Their fingers drifted from each other, and Kate dropped silently into the portal, following the sprawling wreck of the *Fathom*. Something boomed loud enough to shake the heavens, before darkness finally settled on Harper's Meadow.

Chapter Thirty-One

There wasn't a lot left of Harper's Meadow, when police constable O'Riley poked his head out from the debris that was once his sniper's nest.

Whatever giant, pixie presence had taken hold of the field was now gone, and the silence felt almost painful in comparison. O'Riley was full of beans. He had been filled to bursting with righteous, trigger pulling, murderous beans, and now there was nothing more to shoot at. Rather fortunate really, since his weapon of circus destruction was now nothing more than kindling, a bed of mulch that he was now scrambling from.

He took a moment to survey the site of his great triumph. Confetti littered the scene, smoking and flitting through the air, with no evidence that it had once been a gang of marauding demons.

Something at O'Riley's feet clanked as he moved, and he smiled as he looked down, to find that his mighty pie cannon had survived, He checked the clip; a half dozen Lemon Fancies and a couple of armor piercing Cranberry Tartes would be sufficient to continue his quest.

Heaving the cannon onto his shoulder, O'Riley wandered away from the chaotic scene he had wrought. This was exactly how he had pictured it in his dreams, minus the whipped cream of course. There was even a sunrise into which he could wander. There would certainly be straggling do-badders from this procession of insanity, somewhere back townwards, and the job that he had pretended to do his whole adult life, suddenly became the job he was born to do.

He hoisted his trusty pie chucker onto his shoulder, searching for a clever quip to bookend the moment. Fate had given him his moment. It had bestowed upon him a lease upon life that blazed like freshly stirred embers in his soul. It sadly fell wanting in the sunglass donning zinger department, however.

Within moments, constable Michael O'Riley was back on the road towards town, and woe betide anything, clown or otherwise, that got in his way.

Marty brushed several layers of ex-clown from his face, and turned to Timbers, who stared at where the portal once stood.

The lifeboat came to a gliding rest beside them. Altitude, it seemed, had saved the tiny vessel and its occupants from the world warping events that had occurred below. Now it stood, the only remaining vestige of the *Flying Fathom*, in a blasted field littered with pieces of broken everything.

"Good thing that guy's into sunrises and guns," Whipstaff muttered, dropping to the ground, and picking his way to where Timbers and Marty stood. "Seemed like the sort of no nonsense vigilante cop type we wouldn't want to mess with." Oaf poked his head out behind the first mate. "What guy?"

Timbers remained silent, staring out at where his ship had vanished. Marty stood beside him, having also lost something dear.

"So. What now?" The request was almost apologetic, as Whipstaff sensed the tone of the moment.

Timbers lowered his head, staring at his feet. Momentarily, he wandered over to a patch of ground not festooned with the remains of the clownish invasion, and picked up his sword. He turned to Whipstaff, a surprising glint in his eye. Marty had seen the look before, but never with such serious intent. Timbers clearly had a plan, but there was no cheeky aside or clever retort to accompany it. This time, the stakes were higher than they'd ever been. This time, the little captain meant business.

"Whipstaff. Oaf, see if you can find any of the spotlights those juggling scumbags left behind. Marty, come with me."

There was something unsettling in that command, as though they had been playing war, and the big kids had suddenly arrived. All at once, the clarity of the situation fell upon Marty. Maybe he had been in shock at losing Kate, but reality was now banging on the door, and it wanted his lunch money.

Following Timbers' lead, Marty began sifting through the debris of the big top, not altogether sure of what he was doing. "What are we looking for?" he eventually asked, having turned up little more than a few red noses and handfuls of colored paper.

"This," Timbers declared, pulling a small, wooden cot from the wreckage. "Whipstaff, angle one of those spots over here." The first mate duly obliged, training a light that he had plundered from the other side of the clearing at where Timbers and Marty stood.

"Jump on," Timbers commanded flatly, motioning towards the bunk. "We may have lost the battle, but by Blackbeard's britches, we're not going to lose the war. Whipstaff, kill the light."

Marty was slightly disconcerted by the monotone emptiness of Timbers' words, but jumped aboard the creaky bed nonetheless. Clown beds seemed to be no more than a plank of wood with a sheet over them, but they served a purpose, and that purpose soon arrived under cloak of night.

Someone's stirring, I can here you. A voice issued from beneath the bed. It sounded horribly familiar, as Marty turned to press an ear to the wooden mattress. *You're up there somewhere, aren't you? Give me a sign.*

In the darkness, Timbers nodded solemnly to Marty, who duly stuck a leg out and rested it on the floor. *That's it, time to go.* The voice issued out again from under the bed, and this time, something grabbed at Marty's ankle.

"Oaf! Now!" Timbers shouted, prompting Oaf to leap from his hiding place beside the bed. He grabbed at the dark tendril circling Marty's leg, and hoisted whatever was beneath out into the open. Timbers was quick on his heels, launching at the blackness with flailing limbs. It was all the prompting Marty needed, and he flipped over onto his front, dropping onto whatever Oaf had got twisting in his grasp.

"Gotcha, you sneaky bilge rat!" Timbers shouted. "Whipstaff, lights!"

The spotlight streaked a beam of searing light onto the bed, and whatever lay beneath the dogpile of Marty, Timbers and Oaf shrieked. *Let me go. I don't do well in the light, and I only take people one at a time.* The voice pinched into a mewl. *Dammit, this is why I don't do sleepovers.*

"Quiet, you." Timbers held something, although none of them

could see what. "I'll cut your gizzard if you don't help us out, or whatever it is I've got hold of here."

Please, don't hurt me. The unseen creature simpered. *This is just my day job, everyone has to make ends meet, you know. What is it you want?*

Timbers looked up at Marty, who was also jostling with an unseen limb. He winked, and familiar pirate mojo sprang forth from his tiny face. Timbers had a plan, and an even bigger purpose. "What is it we want?" he echoed to Marty, already knowing the answer.

"We want you to take us Dream Side," Marty commanded, Timbers' motive suddenly flaring brightly in his mind. "You're going back under the bed, and you're taking us with you."

The shadow creature emitted a bowel loosening groan, thrashing against its captors and rocking the bed on which Marty still sat. A few moments later, the commotion ceased, and the voice spoke again, *oh, is that it? Fine, sure. Follow me.*

Marty released his grip on whatever the hell he was holding, and it slithered under the bed. He fixed Timbers with a look, which told the little pirate everything he needed to know.

They were going to find the *Fathom*, and they were going to find Kate, one way or another.

The crew dove beneath the frame of the makeshift bed, and vanished from sight. Marty took one last look at reality, and scrambled after his crewmates. He wasn't sure if Timbers had realized the other intention which flashed out from him, brighter than any evil koala could have mustered.

He was going home.

About the Author

Arriving in the rainy isle of Great Britain in the late '70s, James quickly became an enthusiast of all things askew. Whilst growing up in a quaint little one horse town that was one horse short, a steady diet of movies, '50s sci-fi and fantasy fiction finally convinced him to up sticks and move to Narnia--also known to the layman as Wales. Since there was no available qualification in talking lion taming or ice sculpture, he settled for a much more humdrum degree in something vague but practical, and set out to find a talking lion to make an ice sculpture of.

Mystifyingly finding himself behind the desk of a nine-to-five job, he kept himself sane by singing in a rock band, memorizing every John Carpenter movie ever made, and learning the ancient art of voodoo. Finally deciding to put his hyperactive imagination to good use, he ditched the voodoo and picked up a pen. A few months later, his debut novel, *The Forty First Wink*, was born. With a clutch of short stories in the offing, James is now loving his new life as an author, and still sings when plied with alcohol or compliments.

He also recently developed a penchant for fiercely embellishing his past. He really was a singer, although *The Forty First Wink* may not have brought about world peace. Yet.

Curious about other Crossroad Press books?
Stop by our site:
http://store.crossroadpress.com
We offer quality writing
in digital, audio, and print formats.

Enter the code FIRSTBOOK
to get 20% off your first order from our store!
Stop by today!

Printed in Dunstable, United Kingdom